£3.50

PENGU

SETHJI

Shobhaa Dé's seventeen books include the bestsellers *Socialite Evenings*, *Starry Nights*, *Spouse* and *Superstar India*. A widely read columnist in leading publications, she is known for her outspoken views, making her one of India's most respected opinion shapers. Dé lives in Mumbai with her family.

Also by the author

Fiction
Socialite Evenings
Sisters
Starry Nights
Strange Obsession
Sultry Days
Snapshots
Second Thoughts

Non-fiction
Speedpost
Surviving Men
Selective Memory
Spouse
Superstar India

SETHJI

SHOBHAA DÉ

PENGUIN BOOKS

PENGUIN BOOKS
Published by the Penguin Group
Penguin Books India Pvt. Ltd, 11 Community Centre, Panchsheel Park,
New Delhi 110 017, India
Penguin Group (USA) Inc., 375 Hudson Street, New York, New York 10014, USA
Penguin Group (Canada), 90 Eglinton Avenue East, Suite 700, Toronto, Ontario,
M4P 2Y3, Canada (a division of Pearson Penguin Canada Inc.)
Penguin Books Ltd, 80 Strand, London WC2R 0RL, England
Penguin Ireland, 25 St Stephen's Green, Dublin 2, Ireland (a division of Penguin
Books Ltd)
Penguin Group (Australia), 707 Collins Street, Melbourne, Victoria 3008, Australia
(a division of Pearson Australia Group Pty Ltd)
Penguin Group (NZ), 67 Apollo Drive, Rosedale, Auckland 0632, New Zealand
(a division of Pearson New Zealand Ltd)
Penguin Group (South Africa) (Pty) Ltd, 24 Sturdee Avenue, Rosebank, Johannesburg
2196, South Africa

Penguin Books Ltd, Registered Offices: 80 Strand, London WC2R 0RL, England

First published by Penguin Books India 2012

Copyright © Shobhaa Dé 2012

All rights reserved

10 9 8 7 6 5 4 3 2 1

ISBN 9780143102595

Typeset in Sabon by R. Ajith Kumar, New Delhi
Printed at Manipal Technologies Ltd, Manipal

ALWAYS LEARNING   **PEARSON**

To
Our beloved politicians.
May their tribe decrease.

'The arrow shot by the archer may or may not kill a single person. But stratagems devised by wise men can kill even babes in the womb.'—Kautilya

Part 1

'Do not be very upright in your dealings for you would see by going to the forest that straight trees are cut down while crooked ones are left standing.'

—Kautilya

CHAPTER 1

'Babuji, Babuji. Open the door. It's urgent, very urgent.' Sethji opened his eyes, the masseur's fingers ceased momentarily. Sethji shut his eyes, turned his neck to face the wall and gestured to the waiting man with an impatient flick of his wrist. 'Don't stop,' he said, his voice a low growl. The masseur resumed kneading the fleshy folds below Sethji's thick neck. The knock on the door was louder, the voice more insistent. 'Babuji, emergency hai, please, please open the door immediately.' Sethji sighed deeply and kept his eyes resolutely shut. Today was going to be a long day. He needed his uninterrupted sakat haath ki maalish to prepare himself. The masseur slowed down the dance of his nimble fingers. His wrists were tense as he awaited further instructions. The knocking persisted. This time the first voice was joined by three more. 'Sethji, Sethji.' It was impossible to ignore.

Sethji pushed the masseur's hands away and turned his oiled body around heavily. The exertion involved in that simple act seemed to tire him. He clutched his temples and exclaimed, 'Haramzaadey, don't they know I am not to be disturbed while the maalish is on? These dogs. They never learn, never.' His bulging, dark eyes regarded the masseur closely. 'Come tomorrow,' he said wearily. The masseur began wiping the sesame oil off his hands on the hand towel secured around his waist. Sethji changed his mind. 'No, wait, my ankles are sore and swollen. Massage them carefully – without hurting me. Let those dogs wait. Nothing in the world can be that important.' With that he swung his legs over the edge of the sturdy massage table, resting his weight on his arms as he spoke.

The masseur noted the familiar malicious gleam in Sethji's eyes and dutifully bent down to relieve the discomfort in his master's left ankle, easing the stiff muscles expertly. Sethji closed his eyes and began to make a gurgling sound at the base of his throat – the same sort of sound a well-fed infant makes after a good burp. The masseur suppressed a smile. If he performed his daily task of relaxing Sethji better than usual, he'd receive a generous tip. And who knows, if Sethji seemed pleased enough, he would ask him for that special favour, too. It wasn't a very big one. A job for his wife's younger brother – any job. Himmatram, the masseur, had been pressing Sethji's spongy flesh for close to two decades. He knew his client and his corpulent body well, perhaps better than Leelaji, his dead wife, had ever known it.

Himmatram closed his eyes for a moment and brought Leelaji's image into focus. He'd liked the small, spry woman who rarely spoke, even to her husband. He recalled the day she'd died. In fact he'd been massaging Sethji at that very instant. And the urgency of the knocks on this very door had been similar to that of today. Maybe something was wrong this time as well. Normally, Himmatram would have kept these thoughts to himself. He'd learned early enough that none of this was his business. The reason Sethji preferred him to other maalishwallas was that Himmatram had trained himself to act deaf, blind and dumb. He'd seen a great deal and heard much but his lips remained sealed. Not even his curious, talkative wife, Lajwanti, could get anything out of him, much as she tried.

Sethji and Himmatram shared a strange understanding. In all honesty, the masseur couldn't exactly call it a pact, since nothing had ever been discussed openly between them. But he knew that Sethji knew that all his secrets were entirely safe with the man who was familiar with every inch of him – every wart, mole, discoloured patch of skin, infected hair root, summer boils – and Sethji's best-kept secret, the pinkish leucoderma stain on his groin that was steadily growing. That was the only subject Sethji had spoken to him about discreetly. 'Dekho,' he'd muttered, 'this little skin problem, you know what I'm talking about? Nobody should hear about it. Do you understand? It is nothing. It will disappear. But I don't want people – those fools outside – to start a discussion about this matter. It is between you and me.' Himmatram had nodded and asked Sethji to turn over and lie on his stomach. This way, both could pretend they'd seen nothing. A few days after this conversation Sethji had asked him softly if he knew of any vaids – medicine men who specialized in traditional herbal cures. Himmatram had solemnly sworn to get the best man from his village and put him on the job, knowing all along that there was no known way to halt the progress of the mottled pink stains across Sethji's groin.

There was another knock. This time a female voice entreated Sethji to kindly open the door. Himmatram stiffened. It was Bhabhiji, the woman who ruled Shanti Kutir, Sethji's sprawling colonial bungalow located in the heart of New Delhi. Bhabhiji – the daughter-in-law of Sethji's parivaar, good-looking, imperious and ruthless. This time Himmatram wiped his hands for the day and put away the bowl of oil in its designated place. Sethji was bound to get up, get dressed and let Amrita in. How could he refuse the woman who controlled every aspect of his life – from the food on his thali to the favours he doled out. Amrita was well aware of the power she had over her father-in-law and she made sure everybody was aware of this fact, too. Amrita belonged to a different class from the family she'd married into. She never let anyone forget that.

CHAPTER 2

With a long and guttural groan Sethji rolled his eyes heavenwards and reached for his dhoti. This signalled the end of Himmatram's ministrations for the day. He rushed to wipe Sethji's sweaty, hairless back as the old man tied his dhoti tiredly after mumbling, 'One minute, one minute,' in the direction of the door. The room was large and airy with the smell of lime still fresh after the recent whitewash. Sethji's heavy copy of the Mahabharata lay on a reed mat in one corner of the otherwise starkly bare room. Two or three white kurtas hung from a peg on the wall along with the loosely woven, thin red-chequered gamchas Sethji preferred over the fluffy Turkish hand towels that were used in all the wealthy homes of Delhi.

His earthen pot filled with boiled water was on the floor near the mat with a copper drinking glass placed over it. Sethji had been told water drunk out of a copper container kept joint pains at bay. It was for this reason that he wore a crudely crafted copper bracelet on his left wrist and kept magnets under the mattress. On the other side of the room was Sethji's bed – a rustic rope cot from his village with a lumpy cotton mattress spread over it. Not many people knew that Sethji often left the enormous white and gold leaf embellished double bed in his 'official' bedroom to come and get a good night's rest on the same cot on which he'd spent his adolescence in Mirpur, his village in Uttar Pradesh. This cot held several memories for him. It was the one he'd lain on at the age of twelve, burning with fever while his mother placed muslin strips soaked in tepid water over his hot forehead. 'Diphtheria' he'd heard the dreaded word – 'Are there any cats in the house?' and Sethji had held his breath even in his weakened state.

That cat, the black-and-white tabby belonging to the neighbouring farmer. It had to be that monster that was responsible for his condition. If only he hadn't provoked it by trying to push a twig up its anus. Could the others have found out? Was he being punished for doing that? Had God seen him while he held the cat's neck with one hand and tried unsuccessfully to force the smooth twig up the protesting cat's constricted rectum with the other? For twelve days Sethji had hovered precariously between life and death on this very cot. The episode had taught him, even at that tender age, that if you kept your mouth shut and prayed very hard, you could get away with anything – even a crime against a defenceless animal. While his fever had raged and his mother's sobs had turned to moans of resignation, Sethji had resolved to keep his secret about the cat's abuse to himself, confident that he would emerge triumphant even in his duel with death. It would be the cat that would have to die. And sure enough, it did. Poisoned by an unknown cat hater. Someone had to pay the price. Law of the universe, Sethji had reasoned.

CHAPTER 3

Himmatram held a hand mirror in front of Sethji's face. This was his final duty before touching Sethji's feet, seeking his blessings and leaving Shanti Kutir for the day. He'd decided the time was not right to ask for any favours. With the daily massage half done, Sethji would be in a foul mood, his temper high. It was best to leave in silence. The favour could wait; even if his wife would sulk through dinner and serve him cold chapattis for not bringing up the subject of a job in the railways or any other 'good' government job for her wayward brother.

Sethji was dressed now – a fresh dhoti, kurta, gamcha and white rexine sandals with a heavily padded sole. He thought of something suddenly and kicked off his standard chappals before slipping his rough, calloused feet into a pair of sturdy embroidered mojris crafted out of untreated camel skin. Himmatram saw him adjusting his khadi cap to the preferred angle and taking a quick look inside his nostrils to check for untrimmed hairs. Sethji was a fastidious man who liked Bholanath his barber to keep his nostrils and earlobes hair free. Today he spotted two hairs that had escaped the barber's sharp eyes and cursed him and the next seven generations aloud.

Himmatram suppressed a smile. He hated Bholanath the barber, always had. They were from the same village –

Sethji's village, Mirpur – and Bholanath's family had once insulted his father near the village well. Himmatram was still smarting after all these years and waiting for an opportunity to settle old scores. Sethji liked his barber and shared a far more relaxed relationship with that rascal. It was something that annoyed Himmatram and amazed him. Sethji certainly never cracked those kinds of jokes with him. Neither did he ask him about his 'gharwaali' or pass comments on the scraps of village gossip that made the long journey to Delhi via a complicated network of people for whom Sethji was the undisputed leader – the first man from their community to emerge as a 'national' figure.

Himmatram smirked at that thought – why, even he, Himmatram, enjoyed a superior standing in their village thanks to his proximity to Sethji. But Himmatram always believed he was one up on his patron. No doubt the maalishwalla was poor, but compared to Sethji, he was highborn. His forefathers were landowners who had ended up as paupers. Back in the village, Himmatram's superior caste gave him confidence, status. In Delhi, nobody cared. All they thought about was money and position. Himmatram sneered at the closeness Sethji shared with his barber, Bholanath. No wonder the two of them got along so well – it was because they belonged to the same subcaste. What an equalizer caste was! As Himmatram prepared to leave, he straightened his back and thrust his chin out. Whatever Sethji may have become in Delhi, back in their village, to this day, the elders still regarded Sethji as the son of the efficient but lowly barber who trimmed their whiskers, carefully cut nostril hairs and shaved them, just as his father had before him and his father before that. In a way, Himmatram told himself as Sethji and he approached the locked door, there was no real difference between his master and Bholanath. Sethji had power and money – unlimited power, incalculable wealth, no doubt – but he, Himmatram, had the one thing Sethji would have given anything for – a higher caste and better status in the eyes of the village elders. And thus more respect, real respect. He was superior by birth. His wife wasn't shunned by the high-caste women at the village well, but Sethji's dead wife most certainly had been. Even after Sethji had begun to establish his fledgling political career in Uttar Pradesh, even after he had left for Delhi and climbed the ranks of the newly formed Azaad Bharat Socialist Party (ABSP).

The way Himmatram looked at it, netagiri was all very well – a business, a dhanda, like any other. But caste was god-given. For all his money Sethji could never buy a higher caste. He, like the damned Bholanath, was cursed for life from the day he was born into one of the lowest rungs of the complex caste system. A nhaai he was at birth and a nhaai he would die, just like his forefathers and far-flung cousins still struggling in the village without status or land to call their own.

CHAPTER 4

One look at Amrita's eyes and Sethji knew something was wrong. Something serious enough for her to have interrupted his massage. He didn't have to ask. 'Suraj?' Amrita nodded her head. 'Dead?' She shook her head. A no. Sethji let out the breath he'd been holding within him. If his younger son was still alive, whatever it was that had taken place could be handled – *would* be handled. It was only his impetuous, headstrong son's death that Sethji feared.

Suraj had got into trouble before, the worst kind of trouble. But Sethji had always been there to take care of it – after all, that was a father's obligation. Young men the world over behaved no better. Just because his own youth had been different and deprived didn't mean that he'd display a lack of understanding when it came to his own beloved son. So what if Suraj occasionally flew off the handle and showed the sort of recklessness that his enemies described as lunacy? What did they know about the hot-bloodedness of a virile, handsome twenty-five-year-old, when they'd led such dull, sterile lives themselves?

An image of Suraj, wild, mercurial, devilish Suraj, rose before him. Sethji continued to marvel at his younger son's good looks. Where had they come from? Srichand, his elder brother, was every bit his parents' child. He resembled his father closely, although one could also clearly see something of his dead mother in the distant, distracted look in his large eyes. But Suraj seemed to have come from somewhere else altogether, with his fair complexion, pale brown eyes and thick, wavy hair. As Sethji never failed to note, Suraj alone belied his lowly origins – he looked and behaved like a high-caste young man, light of skin with fine features and the manner of an arrogant prince.

Amrita swiftly shut the door behind her after making sure the room was empty. Sethji looked at his beautiful daughter-in-law and touched her upper arm lightly. She reminded him of the lotus blossoms that she daily offered to the marble goddesses in the family temple in the courtyard. Amrita had obviously left her puja halfway this morning. Sethji inhaled deeply. Amrita exuded such a special fragrance, he could recognize it anywhere. He shut his eyes briefly and the image of her naked body flashed before him. He didn't want her to break the spell. Sethji reached out in an attempt to enfold her in his arms. The heady aroma of sandalwood paste, rose petals, joss sticks, pure ghee, incense and kumkum filled the room. Amrita looked like the goddesses she worshipped so faithfully at dawn each day.

She was clad in a freshly starched white sari with tiny embroidered rosebuds scattered over it. As always, the neckline of her choli was low and deep. The cut so impeccable she didn't require a bra to hold her shapely breasts in position. Sethji yearned to pull her on to the bed in the corner of the room. She appeared so chaste with her long and lustrous hair covering half her back, the parting in her hair filled with sindoor, the keys to various cupboards and the heavy iron tijori of the house anchored at her narrow waist in a heavy silver bunch.

Sethji imagined Amrita's ankles which were always hidden from his view. The soft tinkle of the gold anklets she wore always alerted him that she was approaching. He loved the way the ankle bone jutted out provocatively. He loved the arrangement of her toes – especially the way the smallest one looked all twisted up and out of alignment.

Amrita's urgent whisper pulled him out of his reverie. 'Babuji, Babuji. Aapne suna nahin? Suraj has done something terrible.' Babuji held her at arm's length. 'He has done something to himself, right? That's okay. If somebody had done something to him – then I would have been worried.' Sethji tried to embrace Amrita. He wasn't looking for sexual satisfaction at that moment, just the indescribable comfort that proximity to her warm, supple body provided. Amrita pushed him away impatiently. 'Babuji, please pay attention to what I'm saying, it's serious. Suraj has raped someone. The girl could die, we have to do something.' Sethji stepped back, looked skywards and chuckled. 'Bas? That's all? Just a rape? Then why all this tamasha? Couldn't this big news have waited till I finished my massage? You people are impossible. How many times do I have to remind you not to interrupt my maalish? That is the most important part of the day for me. What is all this rape nonsense?'

Amrita's eyes were cold and expressionless as she led her father-in-law to the narrow cot. The same one she had often slept on, bearing his weight over her own strong muscled body. 'Babuji, rape is a serious crime these days. Forget your own years in the village when a man could pick any woman from the field and force himself on her. Times have changed. If even a single word about this gets out, Suraj could land in jail, and if the girl dies, then he has had it. Plus, you have had it too, Babuji. Rape is seen in a very poor light now. A criminal light. There are strong mahila samaj groups. You know that if Kavitaji hears about this incident, you will have to face hell. It's such a critical day for you – think, Babuji, think carefully. Kavitaji will blow it all up at the meeting to disgrace you. Babuji, this incident could cost you the confidence vote. This is just what Kavitaji has been waiting for. If it is not handled immediately, Kavitaji wins, you lose!'

Sethji may have appeared indifferent to his daughter-in-law's words but his brain had begun to tick. Amrita knew his mind only too well. He couldn't fool her at all, even if he tried. If there was one individual in the world who knew him, it was his daughter-in-law. He turned to her, his voice deliberately careless, as if he were trying out the arguments he could use later. 'Arrey baba. The rundi must have invited it. How do you know she didn't seduce him? It could've been a trap. You know how women are – all women, no exceptions, not even you. They see a powerful, good-looking man and they have only one thought in their heads – how to phasao him. Suraj doesn't need to rape anybody. He can get whichever woman he wants in the world – kyon?'

Amrita snapped. 'Babuji, you may think of your precious beta as a maha hero, but the whole world does not think like you. Besides, the girl is a minor, just sixteen, and a virgin. I have the full medical report.' Sethji began to stroke his left thigh. Amrita watched his pudgy hand as it moved up and down the length of his exposed leg. It was a sign her father-in-law was thinking rapidly and shrewdly. When Sethji was required to assess a tricky situation he had the ability to focus on it with the sharp edge of a laser beam. 'Who is the girl?' he asked Amrita, his voice low, his eyes staring fixedly at the framed, garlanded portraits of his dead parents and late wife on the opposite wall. Amrita replied shortly, 'A student, from Meghalaya, staying in a hostel. We are trying to trace her parents.'

Sethji looked up sharply. 'Don't! Are you stupid? If she is some unknown student in Delhi, let her remain unknown. Why do you want to attract trouble and attention by finding out who brought her into the world? If she dies it will be easier to hush it all up – if we use discretion. I know these Pahadi girls. They have no morals at all. No upbringing either. They are raised like animals in the wild. Probably her parents don't even know where she is or with whom. They must be poor and illiterate. Even if they get to know about this later, we can always offer them money to keep their mouths shut. I have contacts in the North-East – don't worry. Buy them some land, give them cash and finish the matter off. Listen, let's keep this quiet. Don't even tell that husband of yours, he doesn't have to know. Tell me, how many people are aware of what has happened?'

Amrita started pacing the room. 'Suraj's driver told me – so he knows. Maybe he has told the other servants by now. But Ramji is generally very reliable and loyal. He loves both the boys, especially Suraj. He used to drive Suraj to school, taught him how to drive. But, Babuji, don't you understand? We can't contain this. The girl has been taken to hospital. The police will be involved. We can't bury this. And then the problems within the party . . .' Sethji got up abruptly. 'You go back to your puja, let me handle this personally. Send Ramji to me. Speak to Suraj immediately and tell him I want him to leave Delhi for a few days – immediately. Let him go to Mumbai and from there he can take a plane to London or

wherever he wants to go. Do not involve the PA or our travel
agent. Call Arun as soon as possible. He will sort it out. You
and he should take care of those arrangements. Now go, ask
Ramji to see me.'

Amrita hesitated. 'Babuji, Suraj came home very drunk.
Ramji had to carry him inside the kothi. He is in his bedroom,
dead to the world.' Babuji sighed and nodded. 'I'll see him
later. Suraj has been under too much pressure lately, poor
fellow. He misses his dead mother. I know that even if he
doesn't say so. He has never stopped missing her – the poor
motherless boy.' Amrita was tempted to say something but
held back her words. Suraj – the corners of her mouth twisted
at the very thought of his name. Sethji always referred to his
younger son as 'that poor motherless boy' but what about
Srichand, her husband? Wasn't he motherless too? Why
were no concessions ever made for him? Why didn't Babuji
think he needed sympathy and understanding? What special
power did Suraj have over his father – a man so astute in his
assessment of people that nobody had been able to get the
better of him, not even his toughest adversaries?

Amrita turned to leave the room. At the door, she whirled
around to face Babuji. 'All right,' she said softly, 'I'll do what
you want me to. But . . . but . . . Babuji, this time I'm afraid
Suraj may have gone too far. It might be the perfect set-up
Kavitaji needs to defeat you today.' Someone or the other was
always after Sethji, and Amrita had given up keeping track.
There was no way of monitoring his many messes. Sethji, for
all his cunning, never bothered to cover his tracks. 'Dekha
jayega,' he'd say arrogantly if she ever pointed it out to him.
He'd boast at unlikely moments, chuckling, 'I am as good
as a desi rubber ball. Throw me, squeeze me, do anything

you want – but I always bounce back.' So far, Sethji had lived up to his rubber ball self-image. But Amrita knew all the braggadocio in the world might not save him this time.

Sethji's face was expressionless. His problems, he would handle as he had always done. It was Suraj who was now the priority. He summoned Amrita towards him. 'It is no longer your worry, you have done the right thing by telling me. Your duty is over. Leave everything to me – everything. I have faith in the Almighty. He will look after the problem.' Sethji joined his hands and said a short prayer. 'Hey prabhu, daya karo,' he concluded as he always did. Amrita waited for the signal that would end this meeting. Sethji held her close and placed one hand over her head. He spoke to her in a low, cooing voice, the sort of voice fond grandfathers adopt while comforting very young children. 'Sab theek ho jayega,' he repeated while she leaned her head against his chest. Sethji could feel her firm breasts as her breath came in short, sharp bursts.

'Relax,' he advised Amrita, 'or else your blood pressure will go up. Calm down. I am here. Trust me, I understand how all this nonsense can be handled. Rape! Rubbish! These days it is easy for you women to scream "rape" if a man looks at you! What is our society coming to! Women have become so shameless. In my time even if a woman was raped a hundred times, she kept her bloody mouth shut! How you women have changed! Anyway. You don't worry about Suraj. Worry about yourself, and remember I'll always be there by your side. Go now. You can't keep the gods waiting for the puja and prasad or else they'll get angry with you and sulk.' Amrita smiled. She knew Sethji would do it yet again. Save his errant, reckless son. Nothing would happen to Suraj, nothing at all.

CHAPTER 5

Suraj had just woken up when he heard Sethji's heavy, measured footsteps as they echoed along the long, narrow corridor leading to his room. He pulled the covers of his satin quilt over his eyes and lay very still. Without knocking on his son's bedroom door, Sethji strode in and waited in silence. Suraj had stopped breathing underneath the covers. The room smelt strongly of Blue Label, his favourite whisky.

Combined with alcohol fumes, Sethji's sensitive nose detected the sharp, unmistakable stench of urine. So, he concluded, Suraj hadn't been able to make it to the bathroom – yet again. Sethji walked up to the servant cowering on the carpet near Suraj's enormous, canopied bed and kicked him sharply. 'Get up, dog, and get out.' The man whimpered, rolled over and lay on his side, hands folded, his voice a low whine. 'Sethji, I didn't do anything, I swear on all the gods. I didn't see anything either. I wasn't there, don't beat me – please – don't beat me.' Sethji glared at him, his eyes bulging dangerously. 'Out!' he bellowed. 'Before I kill you. Dog!' The terrorized man picked up the ends of his threadbare dhoti and scampered off, still whining and crying aloud.

The figure underneath the satin bedcover remained still, as if asleep. Sethji crossed the large, windowless room and sat down on a throne-like chair at the far end. He was prepared to wait. He knew Suraj far too well. He was awake and pretending, hoping his father would get impatient and leave. This little performance wouldn't last very long. Sethji was in no hurry. He put his head back, crossed his legs and began thinking of Amrita.

The first time he had seen her was at her father's sprawling home. She'd been a slip of a girl then, no more than thirteen or fourteen years old. But as she'd danced into the room to retrieve a book and glanced in Sethji's direction he had been struck by her – what was it? Not beauty. Amrita was not conventionally beautiful. Sexuality? Yes – that, but something more as well. It was a subtle wantonness. Amrita was unambiguously sexual even at that age. It showed in the way her body moved, the language of her broad hips, the tilt of her head, the challenging expression in her eyes, the manner in which her torso shifted as she bent to pick up the tea tray. She gave the impression of an unharnessed filly waiting for someone to break her in. Amrita's defiant nature had stayed. It was her most attractive quality. No man could ever hope to possess this woman. Sethji smiled at the memory. Nothing would stop him from trying either.

He'd noted her parted lips, smooth, dusky complexion and dark eyes that invited men to drown in them. Amrita had dutifully bent even lower to touch Sethji's feet after her father had introduced his daughter as the 'lal mirchi' in the family. Hearing those words, Amrita had bitten her lower lip and pretended to blush. Sethji had not failed to notice the little pantomime and it amused him that Amrita's old habit still endured whenever she felt self-conscious or was caught out.

Amrita's father, Seth Jamanlal, would die soon after that meeting. He was a wealthy landowner who behaved in exactly the same manner as his forefathers had for centuries. Acres of wheat fields surrounded his ancestral home in Ujwal, a prosperous village where he lived in a sixty-year-old haveli with his younger brothers and their families. There were well-fed cows and buffaloes in the shed behind the house, and enough milk and butter at all times in his vast estate, enough even for servants and stable hands. It was Amrita's mother's duty to ensure that visitors were looked after lavishly, with heavy silver glasses filled with sweetened warm milk flavoured with cardamom and saffron offered to all on arrival.

Seth Jamanlal was not a politician himself but he wielded sufficient power in his district to attract the 'sarkar' (as he called local bigwigs) to his durbar on a regular basis. After all he owned three hundred and seventy-five acres of land – inherited from father and grandfather in front of whose garishly painted portraits he folded his hands in gratitude five times a day. Seth Jamanlal's green and verdant lands, growing sugar cane and wheat, produced a large enough revenue for him to employ over four hundred workers and own five tractors. People feared and respected him, there was no doubt about that. Just as they'd feared his forefathers who had tilled the rich soil of Uttar Pradesh themselves and left an attractive legacy for their heirs. Local politicians had thus always been at pains to remain on the right side of him. The need was mutual. They required Seth Jamanlal's money power just as badly as he required their muscle power.

Sethji and Seth Jamanlal's association went back a long way. Their first meeting had been a dramatic one. Sethji, then all of twenty-five, had burst into Seth Jamanlal's home demanding protection and money. 'Who are you?' Seth Jamanlal had thundered. Sethji held himself tall before replying, 'I am a neta . . . a leader.' Seth Jamanlal burst into derisive laughter hearing that cocky statement. 'Oh, a neta! Really? So happy to meet you, netaji! I see we are all netas here – some big, some small. In which category do you fall?' Sethji, his eyes burning, replied, 'Today, I may be a small man, but tomorrow I'll be more powerful than the pradhan mantri or anybody else. I have fire in my belly, a good brain, strength in my limbs and enough courage to vanquish all those who stand in my path.'

Seth Jamanlal stared at the dark, squat, ugly man in front him, unsure of how to tackle his foolish claims – with scorn or tolerance. 'Then why have you come to me?' he asked, scratching his fleshy ear. 'Because at this particular moment I need your help,' Sethji said, 'but I shall repay it many times over, that's my promise to you.' Something about Sethji's passionate and confident manner interested Seth Jamanlal. He'd helped several worthless fellows in the past and forgotten them soon after. So why not this wild-eyed man with his uncouth manners and rustic ways? 'What kind of help?' Seth Jamanlal asked deliberately.

'Money,' Sethji answered boldly. 'I need money to settle a loan that I have to repay immediately.' Seth Jamanlal looked at him steadily. 'Everybody needs money. I need it too. Who should I go to for it – tell me? My neighbour? Will he give it to me? My relatives? My enemy? Or a complete stranger? Who are you to me? I don't know you – you don't know me. What gives you the right to come begging at my doorstep?' 'I don't need speeches. I require money,' Sethji responded, and strode off, his stocky frame swaying, his dhoti flying in the evening breeze.

Seth Jamanlal was in a good mood and he was struck by

the stranger's daring. 'Hey, you – come back, let's come to an agreement,' he called after the retreating figure of Sethji. 'How much and what for?' Over his shoulder, barely glancing back, Sethji inquired, 'With interest or without?' Seth Jamanlal roared with laughter. 'Arrey behenchod saala – you sound more like a bloodsucker. Am I doing you a favour or are you doing me one, hah? Aa jao, come here – sit down,' he said, indicating to the baked mud floor at his feet. Sethji took his time to stroll back, he didn't want to seem to be in a hurry or appear too desperate. 'Get the man some water,' Seth Jamanlal ordered a servant. Sethji remained standing, feet apart, his thick bull neck prominent above his collarless, threadbare kurta. 'Sit,' ordered Seth Jamanlal impatiently, once again pointing to the floor.

Sethji shook his head. 'I do not sit at anybody's feet. I'd prefer to stand.' Seth Jamanlal looked up, his eyes registering surprise. 'Saaley, you come to me for help, for money and you're showing so much ghamand. Such arrogance. Trying to act funny, throwing your weight around. Be thankful I haven't asked my men to throw you out. When a Thakur orders you to sit, you sit. Understand?' Sethji shook his head and said in a firm voice, 'I need your money – that much is right. But for that I don't need to sell myself. I told you – I'll pay you back. It's a deal. Dhanda. I want a loan, not alms.'

For a moment Seth Jamanlal looked stumped, as if unsure how to react to such an unexpected attitude. He pretended to flick non-existent flies from his arm as he calculated his next move. 'All right. Speak up. I have no time to waste.' Sethji's words came rushing out, 'I am looking for five lakh rupees. I am willing to pay a reasonable interest. In return for which I'm prepared to work tirelessly and long on your farm or serve you in the house while I reorganize myself and plan for the future. Are you willing to finance me on these terms?' Seth Jamanlal took his time to drink a large brass glass full of fresh milk before replying slowly, 'How do I know you won't run away with my money? Don't answer. Just listen. You won't dare do something so foolish because wherever you might be my army of able-bodied men will hunt you down and kill you. Previous debtors have tried that trick. They haven't got further than the next village.'

Sethji maintained a steady gaze as he said in a strong voice, 'If you give me the money now, it will be the one decision you will not regret. I shall pay you back and I shall remember what I owe you. You too will not forget that there was a man – a stranger – who had come to your door asking for help – and who not only honoured his debt but repaid the original loan, many times over.' That said, Sethji turned around and walked away, leaving Seth Jamanlal to stare at his retreating back.

With the money he took from Seth Jamanlal, Sethji began his political career, travelling around the area, garnering the support of the villagers with small gifts of wheat bags, sugar, soap, oil, etc., making speeches, greasing palms. Part of the money was sent back to his own village where the moneylender had been harassing his old father for the return of a small loan while threatening him with dire consequences if the money wasn't repaid with crippling interest. But Sethji made sure to keep his side of the bargain. He'd go to Seth Jamanlal's house at dawn each day and ask for work from the sadistic headman who terrorized the labourers and assaulted their women. He'd give Sethji the most menial of tasks. 'Go pick up all the cow dung and buffalo shit lying around and bring it back. After that I will decide whether to make you eat it or order you to dry the shit, make cakes for fuel – and then eat them.' Sethji would do as he was told. This was not the time to pick fights with local people. He needed them for the bigger fight ahead.

Occasionally, he would spot Seth Jamanlal as he climbed into his private tonga and rode out in style. If Seth Jamanlal noticed him he didn't reveal it. Every week, the miserably thin accountant would send for Sethji and hold out his open palm. Sethji would place five hundred, one thousand, two thousand, sometimes five thousand rupees on it and wait for him to enter the repaid amount into his red, cloth-covered register. The conversation never varied: 'Still a long, long way to go. Who knows, you might die repaying this loan. Five lakh rupees. I wonder what made Seth Jamanlal give the money to you. Did you cast a spell on him – confess! Our boss is the sort of man who wouldn't give five lakh to his own grandfather without first taking something as security. But for you – he gave the whole amount on a platter. Why? Let me hear the truth. Have you given him your beautiful wife to sleep with? Come on – you can tell me or are you getting him virgins from your village? Maybe a little ganja too?' Sethji would remain absolutely still, his eyes giving nothing away. He knew it was only a matter of time before this very man would be at his feet begging for mercy.

CHAPTER 6

Unnerved by the silence in the room, Suraj cautiously pulled down the covers to see if his father had left. Sethji got out of his chair and crossed the floor in quick strides. He caught his son by the scruff of his neck and hauled him off the bed. Suraj fell clumsily at his father's feet, hands folded, eyes shut. Sethji could hear him whimpering. 'Stand up,' he commanded, while Suraj grovelled and groaned. Sethji noticed a small damp patch growing on the carpet and he knew Suraj had urinated into his pyjamas – just as he used to when he was much younger. Sethji poked his well-muscled buttocks with the toe of his rough leather mojris. 'Be a man. Stop your nonsense before I peel the skin off your back with my hunter. I've done it before and I'll do it again. Peshaab ke bachchey!'

Suraj covered his head and face with his arms and curled his strong, well-built body into a ball. Sethji bent towards his cowering body. 'Behaving like a virgin bride, are you? I'll show you what some men do to such delicate women. They teach them a lesson or two about life, a lesson they remember forever,' he thundered. With that, he cracked the side of his hand across his son's unprotected ear – a slap so stinging, it made Suraj howl in pain. Sethji ignored the urgent knocking on the door as he brought his hand down over and over again, pounding Suraj's face and head, while kicking him viciously

26

in the small of his back. Dazed by the pain, still full of the excesses of the night before, Suraj vomited as a sharp kick landed in his gut. The bedroom was filled with the sour, rancid stench of fermented food combined with regurgitated whisky. Sethji placed his foot on Suraj's neck and rubbed his face in the puke. Suraj's cries stopped momentarily as he tried not to gag and choke on his own waste.

Sethji flipped him over with an expert flick of his mojri and stood towering over his son's prone form. 'I am tempted to shove a bamboo up your arse – not just an ordinary bamboo, but one dipped in freshly ground chilli powder. That would give you an impressive erection I'm sure – one big enough to make all those whores you patronize take a second look at your miserable cock.' Suraj looked like he had stopped breathing. Sethji pressed down on his genitals with his mojri. 'You still have something left there I see. Maybe I should crush your balls right now – they seem to get you into a great deal of trouble.' Suraj's entire body seemed to shrink as he contracted all his muscles and waited for the next blow. Sethji stood still, watching his favourite son lying in his own urine and vomit. The sight revolted him more than anything he'd ever seen. He considered his next move, while Suraj attempted to cross his legs as unobtrusively as possible. Sethji caught the slight motion and barked, 'It's too late to save your balls now. Let me take care of them for you since you obviously don't know how to take care of them yourself.' With that he brought down the heel of his rough footwear heavily on to Suraj's groin and rotated his foot over his son's swollen testicles while Suraj let out a high-pitched yelp that emanated from the very core of his being. Sethji spat contemptuously on his son as he writhed around clutching his groin, doubled up with a pain he could not have imagined existed in the world.

Without another word Sethji left the room swiftly and strode towards a waiting car. Amrita ran behind her father-in-law, not daring to ask a single question. Without meeting her eyes, Sethji instructed, 'Send some ice cubes to that scoundrel, and get his room disinfected. Tell him to stay home and out of sight. And make those travel plans jaldi se. We need him out of the country tonight if possible. I will handle the police. Have you been in touch with Arun?'

'Yes. He is making arrangements for Suraj. It might be a problem for you though. Be careful at the party meeting today.' Sethji looked at Amrita in admiration. An hour ago she had seemed full of fear, but now she was composed, collected, completely in charge.

Seeing the party workers who had arrived to escort her father-in-law, Amrita hastily covered her head with the edge of her starched sari pallu. She knew it was going to be a particularly rough meeting. She hoped Sethji would calm down sufficiently en route to the distant venue. He needed to remain cool while the party leadership decided his political future.

A major news channel had done a report on Sethji's 'extremely' close ties with industrialists and how he had compromised his position as Minister of Road Transport. Ten years ago, news like this barely mattered and Sethji could have brushed away his party's concerns like swatting off flies. But not now. Cleaning up politics was the flavour of the month, championed in the party inevitably by Kavita Saxena who had been gunning for his position for years and who (he knew) had been responsible for delivering the anonymous file to the media house that made the links between him and his industrialist friends.

Kavitaji was known for the prominent ribbon of bright red sindoor she plastered into the parting of her jet-black hair. Critics referred to it as 'Kavitaji's airstrip'. Her admirers liked her tenacious personality. 'Kavitaji ke saath takkar mat lo, bhaiyya,' they'd half-joke. She was a seasoned political creature who had inherited her father's passion for netagiri. When he died, she took over, bullying her way into local politics, supported by her meek husband and a daughter who wore a permanently distraught expression, especially in her loud, domineering mother's presence.

Kavitaji projected the picture of the perfect 'Bharatiya naari' – the idealized Indian woman, modestly attired, a loyal wife and caring mother. But those who knew her well insisted there was another side to her – a demanding, aggressive sexual side that was carefully kept under wraps. Her affairs were conducted during her constant travels. 'I am the party's most energetic campaigner,' she would boast, setting off for yet another rally in the badlands, accompanied by a muscular party flunky. Nobody minded. Kavitaji had her uses. She was the only one who could occasionally checkmate Sethji and counter his autocratic diktats with her chutzpah and sliminess. Despite such skills, Kavitaji remained a political lightweight, sometimes used by Sethji's enemies but rarely taken seriously, much to her frustration and rage.

Kavitaji and her faction were planning to withdraw their support to the shaky government coalition that ABSP was a part of. It was an alliance that Babuji had pushed hard for, cajoling his reluctant party along with him. He had argued that by joining the government, their regional, UP-based organization would finally gain national importance, and this was crucial. Sethji had anticipated of course that the ministerial position he would be given as part of the deal would be very lucrative. And it had been. Extremely. This era of coalition politics, where the ruling party was heavily dependent on its partners, was a godsend for wheeler-dealers like Sethji. People like him held all the important cards in their hands, and exploited the insecurity of those in power. Threats to withdraw support received instant conciliatory responses from the ruling party. Sethji loved it! He felt important, even invaluable as he cut deal after deal, always making sure the sword of Damocles hovered over a few VVIP heads. But now with the instability in the government and the corruption charges on him, his position had weakened. The party's old doubts about the coalition had resurfaced. Kavita Saxena claimed Sethji had become a liability. If the party were to survive, it was time for a change in leadership.

Sethji had never taken that chattering fool seriously and found her machinations too simple to be dangerous. But this time there was a powerful faction bolstering her – including the four key deputies in the party. So there was to be an internal party debate followed by a vote by the central committee. Where he would have to perform at the top of his game. And on this day of all days, this news of Suraj. It felt like a bad sign. But this was not the time to worry about such matters. Suraj had been dealt with. It was time to focus on the battle ahead.

Amrita watched as he got into the white Ambassador car with its dark, tinted windows. Pandey, his bodyguard, slid into the front seat with Sethji's regular driver, Raju. Sethji's face, grim with worry, softened as he looked at her. 'We may not be able to talk all day,' he said gently. She nodded silently and watched the car drive away.

CHAPTER 7

As Sethji's car sped away, Amrita shuddered involuntarily and wiped away the sweat beads from her upper lip. A slow feeling of dread was uncoiling in the pit of her stomach, as if something terrible were about to happen. She remembered feeling the same way when she had lost her father. After his death, Amrita's life had undergone a cataclysmic change. She'd watched her mother struggle in a way that had made her determined never to be in such a pitiable position herself. Money became a sickness and an obsession. There was never enough of it. With Seth Jamanlal dead, large portions of his land had been grabbed by his cousins, leaving his helpless widow with only a few, comparatively less fertile, acres. Her mother's poor management of the estate just about generated enough income to pay for Amrita's school fees and their meagre daily needs. Her mother's orphaned nephew Sonu was inducted to help them with the running of the farm.

But Sonu spent his days loitering around the village and playing cricket with other dropouts. Amrita's mother was far too exhausted to chase the young man. She preferred to pretend Sonu was meant for other things in life. 'One day he will play for India – you will see,' she'd tell Amrita each time Sonu sauntered out of the house practising his latest bowling action. It was left to Amrita to take on the role of the head of the family and deal with men who'd show up claiming Seth Jamanlal owed them money. The land had to be sold, parcel by parcel, till Amrita and her mother were left with just the small outhouse where the staff used to live earlier. Before she knew it, Amrita had started giving tuitions to girls in the neighbourhood. Hindi and arithmetic – the two subjects she excelled at. But there was one condition her mother insisted on – Amrita's 'students' would have to come home. Amrita could never step into theirs. 'Young girls are like delicate flowers. Their petals get crushed just once. After their fragrance is destroyed, what remains for anybody to enjoy? A crushed flower has zero value in a bouquet. No vendor will touch it.' It took Amrita many years to discover what exactly her mother had meant.

A few more years of struggling to keep up appearances and Amrita's mother was ready to accept the rather unusual marriage proposal of a wealthy Delhi businessman, Raghubir Prasad, who belonged to a neighbouring zamindar family. Raghubir Prasad behaved impeccably, approaching the village elders to broker the match with the hard-working widow. Impressed by his delicacy and utterly vulnerable, she quickly accepted.

Amrita's life took yet another turn. After her mother remarried, the family moved to Delhi. Her stepfather was a good man. Good to her mother, good to her. It was only years later that Amrita stumbled upon the secret of Mr Prasad's 'goodness'. He suffered from epilepsy and felt guilty about having concealed this from Amrita's trusting mother before the hastily arranged marriage.

By the time Amrita found the courage to ask her mother about it, close to a decade had passed as if in a flash, and

Raghubir Prasad had passed away, leaving their small family all that he possessed. This inheritance wasn't inconsiderable even by Delhi's exaggerated and often vulgar standards. Unfortunately for the family, being widowed twice over didn't do much for Amrita's mother's reputation, who was branded an 'unlucky' woman or rather a woman who invited death into her own home. A husband killer. A black widow. Toughened by all the taunts the family was made to endure after Raghubir Prasad's rather dramatic exit from the world (he was about to break a coconut on the bonnet of the latest flatbed truck to join his fleet, when he suffered a cardiac arrest and dropped dead, the coconut gripped in his right hand), Amrita had to regain lost ground all over again.

Raghubir Prasad's funeral was as well attended as her father's. It was at her stepfather's funeral that Amrita caught sight of the man who was to become her future husband. Srichand had accompanied Sethji, who had remained in touch with Amrita's mother and given her money after Seth Jamanlal's death. Amrita noticed Srichand's forlorn expression, slouchy shoulders, the round-framed granny glasses perched over the prominent bridge of his nose and dismissed him. Srichand, on the other hand, was instantly drawn to her as she stood consoling her mother in a distant corner, away from the men. Something about the way her long hair blew across her face as the gentle wind swept across the banks of the Yamuna made his heart melt. He had not really noticed women in the past. Never had a girlfriend. Nor 'fallen' for any woman. But, later he would tell Amrita, that the sight of her outlined against the leaping flames of her stepfather's funeral pyre stirred an emotion within him that he didn't quite recognize. Too shy to tell anyone, he kept his fantasy to himself, little knowing that his father was already plotting an alliance in the background.

Six months after the funeral, Sethji dropped into Amrita's home with a formal proposal. 'You know I have always been in Seth Jamanlal's debt since he lent me money all those years ago, bhabhi,' he said to Amrita's mother as the young woman eavesdropped from the kitchen. 'I have tried to look after you during your troubles but now it is time to repay my debts completely. Let Amrita become my bahu and marry my son Srichand. I promise she will be well looked after all her life. With me by her side, she will have nothing and no one to fear.'

Amrita couldn't bear to look at the man who would soon become her father-in-law. In any case, it would have been deemed 'inappropriate' for a potential daughter-in-law to make eye contact with him or speak before being spoken to. 'In this bloody day and age,' Amrita had spluttered to her mother who shushed her with a soothing sound before adding, 'Sethji is the best man for you. He has been very kind to us. Remember, getting a good alliance in your case is not easy.' Amrita shot back, 'Why? What's wrong with me? Tell me – what the hell is wrong with me, Ma?' Her mother answered slowly, softly, 'Your real father left us years ago, with absolutely nothing. It is our time to pay back Sethji for saving us. We owe it to him. You have seen how society has shunned us after Raghubirji's death. Who will marry a girl whose mother's reputation is so tainted? You are aware of what those bridge playing bitches at the club call me, right? Praying mantis! Black widow! Do you think they'd allow their sons to marry you? This is your chance – take it! You may not get another one.'

Amrita snapped back, 'No, Ma, "we" don't owe anything

to Sethji – you owe it to him. Both of you are using me for your own gains. Why am I being sacrificed?' Her mother answered patiently, 'In our society, we don't call this sacrifice. It is a daughter's duty to obey her elders. Your stepfather always had your interests at heart. He was a wise man and knew what he was doing when he lovingly groomed you, sent you to a good college. Bought you fancy clothes. Gave you foreign holidays. He spared no expense, God bless his soul. Besides, you are not marrying Sethji. You'll be marrying his son Srichand. And he is quite handsome.' Amrita snorted. 'You call that man handsome? He may not be as revolting as that Sethji. But handsome?' Amrita's mother pretended to fluff up cushions as she tried to change the subject. 'Sethji has really helped our family. He will help us even more in case this alliance works out. Mind you, they've seen a lot of girls, even some good-looking, rich NRI ones. But somehow Sethji has taken a fancy to you.' Amrita shuddered involuntarily, and said under her breath, 'And that's exactly what I fear.'

* * *

The rest now seemed a blur to Amrita. She had protested, cried, shut herself in her room, refused to eat or bathe. She had just finished college, she dreamed of love (a love that at the time seemed to be in the palm of her hand, but that was another story altogether). This was not how she had imagined her future. But her gentle mother who had always let her have her way remained, for the first time, unmoved. She had watched Sethji climb up the ladder of power, leave their dusty village behind and settle himself as one of the new kings of the capital – even as her own family's fortunes declined. There were whispers about him, but there were whispers about everyone. He had always been good to her. He was strong. She knew he would take care of Amrita.

As for Srichand, Amrita would have to tolerate him since loving him was not an option. Shrewdly, her mother had concluded that it would be Amrita's womanly skill at keeping Sethji's interest in her alive that would make the alliance work. Srichand was only a minor player here. If Amrita could set her revulsion for Sethji aside and accept him, it would be good for both – they were alike in so many ways. Tough, full of fight, stubborn and proud. They would make a good team.

Amrita's resistance finally broke down late one evening when Srichand paid her an unexpected visit. He saw the undisguised hostility and loathing in Amrita's eyes and asked just one question: 'Are you in love with someone else?' Amrita snapped, 'Yes.' Srichand was silent for a while before saying, 'What stops you from marrying him? Please be honest with me.' Amrita paused before replying softly, 'He is already engaged.' Srichand rose to his feet abruptly. He was beaming. 'Wonderful, wonderful. So you have no future with the fellow. Marry me! I will give you the best future. The best life. You will be treated like a queen in our home. And you will always be the empress of my heart, Amritaji. I love you!' It was a declaration she had no defence against. Before she realized it, she'd said yes. Her heart was heavy with regret, full of longing for a man who seemed far, far away. It was a sign. That chapter would have to be permanently closed now.

Phoolrani, Amrita's maid, remembered that fateful day too, but for other reasons. She was perhaps closest to Amrita, the two having grown up together. Even if they rarely exchanged more than the customary greeting, she knew her mistress's every mood. The maid was much younger than Amrita. She used to sleep on the carpeted floor next to Amrita's bed and her duties were clearly defined. She was in charge of young Amrita's well-being and physical comforts, which meant that the maid ranked somewhere in between a nanny, a lady-in-waiting and a sister. When her marriage negotiations were going on, Amrita had asked to take Phoolrani to Sethji's house, as a part of her dowry. She had told her mother, 'I don't really care whether or not you give me that pearl set or those jadau bangles. Just let me take Phoolrani with me.' Her mother had smiled indulgently. 'Take her, but where is she going to sleep? Surely not on the floor next to your marital bed?'

Phoolrani made sure Amrita's room was kept meticulously clean and tidy, the curtains drawn, the perfume bottles on the dresser placed exactly where Amrita wanted them, her wardrobe arranged neatly in colour-coordinated piles, with accessories like bangles and bindis organized so they were within easy reach, her countless pairs of shoes, sandals, jooties and slippers tucked away in low drawers, handbags stored with the original stuffing on a deep shelf, saris and petticoats placed in neatly folded piles, sari blouses kept in a drawer right above the lingerie cabinet. Not a pin got lost with Phoolrani around to guard her mistress's belongings with hawklike alertness.

Till that memorable day when Srichand made his final bid – and Amrita's solitaires went missing. Amrita always placed them on her bedside table before retiring for the night. It was Phoolrani's job to transfer them to Amrita's locked jewellery box inside the almirah. Srichand was to arrive in just twenty minutes. Twenty minutes during which Amrita had to make sure she looked her prettiest. 'Wear pink, my dear,' her mother had suggested. 'It suits your complexion.' Amrita had decided on yellow. Her mother, sensing Amrita's quiet anger, said in a placating tone, 'It's okay – wear whichever colour you want to . . . but please remember to smile.' Amrita pulled a face. 'Smile at that stick of a man? You know what I feel about him. He is neither handsome nor charming nor—' Her mother stopped arranging rich malai burfees with varq on the large monogrammed silver salver and interrupted her. 'Don't say that about your future husband,' she reprimanded Amrita, who remained silent, her eyes full of tears.

Phoolrani had overheard this exchange just like she overheard most conversations in the house. But she was well aware of her place in life. She knew good servants are trained to pretend they are deaf, dumb and blind, if not entirely invisible. Phoolrani had become an expert. Nobody ever realized she was present in the room, even during the stormiest of arguments. She'd go about her chores silently, moving from room to room with her head lowered and her shoulders exaggeratedly hunched. It was the posture of surrender and servility that she'd been taught by her mother and grandmother. 'Keep you eyes lowered, girl, head down, and shoulders stooped at all times, but especially when you are in the presence of your masters.' Phoolrani was the third-generation maid in Raghubir Prasad's home and proud of it.

As an earnest teenager, Amrita had tried hard to get her out of this 'trap' (as she called it) and into a school. 'I'll pay for everything. Come on. Just go to a school and study. I'll help you. Promise.' But Phoolrani had pulled the corner of her dupatta over half her face and shaken her head stubbornly. 'My place is here,' she'd stated in a flat, emotionless voice.

'What will happen to you once I get married?' Amrita had asked laughingly. 'I'll come to your new home and wait for you to have babies. Then I will look after them,' Phoolrani had replied serenely before going off to iron Amrita's kurtis. 'Don't you want your own babies?' Amrita had called after her. 'No. Never. I will think of your babies as my own . . . God's will,' Phoolrani had answered.

But the gods in the gigantic residence were obviously not in the mood to look after Phoolrani when Amrita's solitaires went missing. Amrita's mother summoned Hariji – the senior-most servant who supervised the others. 'We must search Phoolrani's trunk,' Hariji announced. 'If the diamonds are found there, we will punish her accordingly. But before we do that, let us call her and ask.' Phoolrani was quaking as she stood in the centre of the large kitchen with an adjoining pantry that opened into the back garden. All eleven servants had abandoned their routines to witness the questioning. Hariji told Phoolrani in a firm, steady voice, 'This is your only chance to confess and tell the truth. I'm asking you one last time – have you taken Babyji's diamonds?' Phoolrani shook her head, tears rolling down her face. She pinched her throat to indicate she was ready to swear on the gods, her own mother, that she hadn't stolen from her young mistress.

Hariji walked up dramatically to the small shrine in the kitchen that was referred to as the 'servants' temple' by the family. The deities were the same – Hanumanji in a frame, Ram-Sita-Lakshman in another, a clay image of Ganeshji, another one of Saraswati. The family's gods were housed in a grand marble temple near the entrance of Raghubir Prasad's bungalow that overlooked the lush Lodhi Gardens. Those were the 'saab log's' gods, dressed in silk and velvet, bathed daily in cow's milk and fed a variety of mithai after the morning puja conducted by the bare-chested, overweight family priest. Phoolrani's job was to make sure there were enough fresh flowers plucked from the garden for the elaborate rituals that were compulsory for all family members. But that particular morning it was noticed by all that Phoolrani had forgotten to place the flower basket in its customary place at the foot of the mandir, within easy reach of the pujari. The gods must have been furious with her.

Hariji plucked out Hanumanji's framed picture from the altar and brought it towards Phoolrani. 'Place your right hand on this and swear you are innocent,' he commanded. Phoolrani's hand was trembling as she placed it over the monkey god's image. At that precise moment, there was a loud and long shriek from down the corridor. Everybody froze. Phoolrani's hand remained where it was, over Hanumanji's head, as Amrita rushed into the kitchen holding aloft the glittering stones. 'Found them! I had forgotten them near the washbasin in the bathroom last night,' she exclaimed triumphantly as Phoolrani's hand fell limply to her side, and her tears continued to flow. Perhaps, the rich gods had told the servants' gods to spare the poor girl. Perhaps rich gods understood the tragic plight of maids. Perhaps Phoolrani was forgiven. But what nobody knew was that Phoolrani had neither forgotten to pluck the flowers for worship nor misplaced the diamonds. It was the first time Phoolrani had menstruated and she'd remembered her mother's words which had instructed her to stay away from anything auspicious, especially the sacred abode of gods on earth – the many temples in which they resided in countless forms. 'Don't make the temple impure during those five dirty days when you bleed,' she'd told her young daughter. 'For if you touch anything during this period, it becomes sullied. Remember to stay away and keep to yourself till you are clean again.'

In her confusion and anxiety, Phoolrani had forgotten to retrieve the solitaires from the glass shelf above the washbasin and keep her young mistress's diamonds in the locked jewellery box that nestled within the soft, silken folds of Amrita's precious saris.

There were exactly eighteen minutes left before Srichand arrived, before Amrita had to give her final yes or no. And Phoolrani's life would change as irrevocably as that of her mistress.

CHAPTER 8

Amrita snapped herself back to the present. She had work to do. She made her way back into Suraj's room. She crossed it swiftly and made for the heavy steel locker that stood on a pile of old trunks with gaudy pink lotuses painted on them. She could hear Suraj moaning as he lay doubled up on the floor. 'The keys,' she commanded her brother-in-law. 'Where have you kept them? Quick! We don't have time to waste. Wash up, get dressed. I'll help you pack your things. But first – the keys.' Suraj continued to groan and refused to respond. In five long strides Amrita was by his side, shaking him roughly. He lunged at her and clung to her knees whimpering, 'Bhabhiji . . . I am sorry . . . I didn't mean it . . . God knows what happened . . . please tell Babuji to forgive me . . . it was an accident.'

Amrita shook herself free and extended her hand. 'Keys. Just give me the keys.' Suraj gestured to the side table next to the big armchair. Amrita walked towards it, barking orders at Suraj all the time. 'Where do you keep your passport? You have to get out of the country immediately. Take just a small suitcase with a change of clothes. I'll arrange for a new cell phone and SIM card. Remember just one thing in case you are caught – you are innocent until proven guilty. Keep mum. Say nothing. Leave it to me. But for now, just get up and get out. Do it before Babuji gets back from the meeting and kills you. One more thing – hand me your gun.'

Suraj whined, 'But why? I need my gun. What if someone harms me? How will I defend myself? I can't give you the gun. Please, take everything but not my gun.' Amrita looked at her brother-in-law and narrowed her eyes before saying contemptuously, 'The gun won't protect you from your fate, Surajji. Now hurry up. Your pick-up will be here soon. Go take a shower quickly. I'll be back to help you pack.' With this she locked away Suraj's gun in his safe, keeping the keys with her.

Amrita briskly crossed the dimly lit corridor that led to her part of the sprawling bungalow. She heard the mocking cry of a fat, pregnant lizard that lived behind the heavy reed curtains lining the corridor. It was an ominous sign. She remembered her mother's words. When a lizard calls thrice, it is warning you: 'Satya hai, satya hai, satya hai.' What was the horrible truth waiting to confront Sethji's family now? Amrita also noticed a pale owl swooping down noiselessly to grab a garden toad calling out to its mate. Another ominous sign! An albino owl spotted during daylight hours? As she entered her spacious, fragrant bedroom, Amrita felt irrationally calm. Amrita had a weakness for fragrances of all kinds. Traditional dhoop was lit at dusk every evening, and the household help had been instructed to light aromatic candles right before her afternoon siesta. Amrita hoarded her precious collection of exotic vials of concentrated oils from across the world. She frowned at the sight of Srichand, her husband, snoring unconcernedly on their carved four-poster bed. For just a brief second or two, she felt protective towards the man who seemed to have not a care in the world. He ate well, slept well and lived well. Srichand was the baby they could never have.

Poor Srichand. The one thing he invariably failed at was to fulfil his haughty wife's sexual desires. His clumsy attempts to pleasure her always ended with a sharp slap across his straying wrist – a signal for him to stop and leave her alone. But even those frequent rebuffs did not upset sweet, docile Srichand. He was too good-natured to protest or demand his conjugal rights. Just once he'd shown her a newspaper report which said the Supreme Court of India had deemed it 'cruelty' if a spouse refused sex. Amrita had scanned the newspaper and retorted sharply, 'Rubbish! It's the other way around. If a woman doesn't want it, she doesn't want it!' Srichand had promptly retired to his favourite divan and switched on the huge flat-screen television mounted on the wall opposite their bed – a gift from one of Babuji's supporters who had the dealership of the latest TV sets imported from Korea. 'Come on, India!' Srichand had cheered the losing cricket team, oblivious of Amrita's contempt for his own uninspiring performance.

CHAPTER 9

Amrita sniffed the air. Wrong fragrance! It should have been khus – wasn't it Thursday today? She'd definitely pull up her maid tomorrow morning. Phoolrani had become moody and dreamy ever since she had begun an affair with Srichand's sturdy, swarthy driver-cum-bodyguard. Amrita wondered if Phoolrani occasionally dabbed herself with her mistress's all-time favourite perfume, the heady, clingy Joy that was given a place of honour on her overcrammed dressing table. It was the one Srichand had said he couldn't bear to smell on any other woman! Amrita had suppressed a smile, coiled her hair, glanced sideways at him and pottered around the room, trailing Joy as she moved around restlessly.

That evening her own joylessness had struck her as she'd presided over Sethji's midnight bhojan, during which he plotted his rival's downfall. While serving the men oily parathas, Amrita had been struck by the absurdity of her own position in this strange household. Take the guard dogs. Despite the best imported dog food, and a vet on call, those dogs remained just that – guard dogs. They were trained to know their place and stay there. Their 'job' was to guard the family. Love and feelings didn't come into the picture. They adored Suraj and Srichand and the brothers were affectionate towards them but regarded them as part of the furniture, occasionally taking them for a walk or spending time with them or worrying about their health. Rocky 1 and Rocky 2, Suraj had grandly christened them when they'd arrived after a tiring smuggling operation that involved slippery agents in Bangkok. She often felt her place in this house was like that of those two dogs. She had everything she could possibly desire – but did she have the things she most wanted?

＊

As Amrita reorganized the contents of her handbag and made sure her credit cards were secure in the familiar ostrich skin holder, she thought about the strange relationship she shared with Sethji, and how it had started soon after she moved into his home as a reluctant bride. He'd found her crying in her bedroom one Sunday afternoon, when Srichand was out playing golf. She had hastily wiped her tears and pretended to cough in order to cover up her sobs. Sethji had walked up to her wordlessly and held her in his arms. Amrita had felt immensely comforted, despite herself. Here she was being intimately embraced by a man she loathed on every level. And yet, she was reluctant to get out of his grasp.

In her confusion, she hadn't realized that Sethji's hands had strayed and moved slowly down to caress her hips, while the other hand cupped her right breast. She tried to push him away but he held her too firmly. He lay down next to her and raised her sari above her knees while he pinned her down with his other hand. Amrita tried to bite him, kick him, but he was too strong for her. Soon she felt as if she was in a trance and gave up struggling. It felt too inevitable. She'd closed her eyes, clenched her fists.

Sethji did not attempt to kiss her mouth, restricting his kisses to her thighs, while his hands remained on her breasts, playing surprisingly gently with her nipples. Soon he'd entered her, after expertly removing her panties with a single tug. She didn't realize she was aroused until he was inside her. She should have been hurt, but instead she was wet, ready for him. He repeated her name over and over again as he groaned and moaned, and accelerated the pace of his thrusts. Amrita tried to stop herself, but wave after wave of sensation entered her. She couldn't control herself and came in a shudder alongside him. Amrita was numb when her father-in-law left the room. She should have felt violated and sullied, she told herself. But that was not the truth. In an inexplicable way, Amrita felt complete. What had just happened? She had no answer. The self-hate came later.

But today was no day for such thoughts, she told herself tiredly. Srichand remained asleep, undisturbed by the storms outside, or the ones inside her head. Watching him, Amrita let out a sigh of relief. The less her husband knew about 'this' – or anything else, for that matter – the better. Amrita picked up the cell phone from her dressing table and tiptoed out of the room to make another call to Arun Mehta.

CHAPTER 10

Rocky 1 and Rocky 2 came charging into Suraj's room. Suraj's mouth twisted into a wry smile at the sight of the dogs. Both were staring balefully at their young master. He lifted one of Rocky 2's hind legs and laughed. 'No balls! What kind of a bloody guard dog are you, yaar? Teri goti bhi nahin hai.' It was a sensitive topic for Babuji – he had paid a premium to smuggle two pedigreed dogs for the household, without checking that they came with all their body parts intact. Poor little Rocky 2 had a problem – his testicles had not descended. By the time Sethji discovered the unfortunate abnormality, it was too late to 'return to sender'. So there he was, a 'hijra of a dog', as the others dubbed him. Playful and cute, but minus balls. Suraj touched his own. 'Mine are still there – ouch,' he grimaced as his sister-in-law packed his shaving kit. 'Bhabhiji, don't forget my Armani.' She cursed Suraj under her breath as she threw in his favourite cologne into the LVMH toilet case she'd bought for his last birthday. She added, 'Take an extra one – you may need it to cover up the stink.' Suraj glared at her and snarled, 'Always sarcastic with me – always! Why? Why do you hate me so much, huh? That bloody Pahadi bitch asked for it. She wanted it – she begged me – BEGGED! Ask Shakeel and the others.' Amrita placed her delicate, long-fingered

hands over her ears. 'Please. I really don't want to know. Just
pack and leave – fast. The car will be here in fifteen minutes.
Babuji will be phoning to ask about the arrangements any
time now. So . . .'

Soon an SUV with tinted glass raced up the gravelly
driveway. No headlights. But enough noise to disturb the
owls, bats and the two Rockys, who started to bark. A couple
of servants emerged from their quarters at the back of the
bungalow to see what was going on. The watchman who'd
opened the gate to let the SUV in was standing to attention
– Amrita had instructed him earlier not to stop the driver or
check the car.

Suraj slung a trendy Diesel backpack over his broad
shoulders and tried to dive for Amrita's feet in a half-serious
gesture of 'showing respect'. She stopped him sternly and
said, 'Just go! Don't ask where. You'll know when you get
there.' The pale owl hooted and the pregnant lizard heckled
thrice as Suraj swept out of the bungalow. Rocky 2 wagged
his tail and licked Rocky 1's balls.

Amrita's cell phone rang insistently. She looked at it. It
flashed a private number. 'Is he all right?' a man's voice asked
softly. 'Yes, he's in the car. Thank you for handling this so
promptly, Arun. Babuji had said you would take care of
everything.' 'Of course, you are family, Amrita. But now we
need to meet in person to settle the details. You never know
with phones these days,' he said with a low laugh. 'So come
soon, I am expecting you.'

Amrita didn't know too much about Arun Mehta. She
doubted anybody did. In a way, it was better to be slightly
ignorant about people like Arun in Delhi. That Sethji had
asked her to seek his help indicated two things: Arun would

deliver. And Arun was the last resort. Or else Sethji would
have turned to his own trusted aides to bail out Suraj, as they
frequently had in the past. But this time was different. Arun
had been inducted to 'take care of things'. Undoubtedly for a
price. At that moment, Amrita did not know what that price
was going to be. Her job was to keep her mouth shut and
ensure Suraj made it without getting caught. Arun was the
man who could guarantee it.

As a high-profile industrialist of long standing, Arun
was one of the most well-connected men in the country.
Frequently featured on power lists published by leading
publications, Arun was a familiar figure in the corridors of
power, chummy with politicians of all hues. He often joked
his best friends were Commies! And yet, not too many people
called him a friend. Not that Arun cared. 'I don't want to be
popular,' he used to say, 'I want to be powerful.' Which Arun
certainly was. His Holi party at his farmhouse had become
an institution to which the high and the mighty flocked.
From the prime minister to the leader of the Opposition, and
practically the entire cabinet.

It was whispered many megadeals were cracked over bhang
pakodas and thandai, and that all the ambassadors he invited
made sure they were discreetly wired so as not to miss a single
word of the so-called drunken banter that when decoded
often provided vital secrets, even classified information.
Arun's Davos address each year was closely deconstructed
for clues to future government policies. Or even whether
the government in power then would stay or go. In an era
of tenuous coalition politics, such insider track information
was indeed invaluable. Behind Arun's affable exterior lurked
a master manipulator. To dismiss him as just another 'fixer'

or 'wheeler-dealer' was to underestimate Arun's formidable clout. Amrita told herself never to make such an expensive mistake with this man. And since she had been summoned by him, she better be on her way.

CHAPTER 11

Amrita decided to drive herself – the fastest car in the seven garages on the property was Suraj's laburnum yellow Lamborghini Murciélago. She'd never driven that beauty before. It was brand new. A 'virgin' as Suraj put it. Obviously, a 'gift', claimed from one of Babuji's 'admirers'. Amrita knew exactly what that meant – Babuji had 'helped' the person with a major deal. Amrita tried to guess – telecom? Gas? Realty? Mining? Ooof . . . forget it. It was between Suraj, his father and the colourful favour seekers they patronized. She looked for the car keys in a small Bastar tribal bowl resting on a rickety walnut wood Kashmiri table in the foyer. There they were – the Lamborghini keys, gleaming invitingly. As sleek as the car itself. She changed out of her sari into her comfortable Juicy tracks, grabbed her orange Birkin, slipped her feet into tan-coloured Tod's loafers, and half-ran towards the garage. The engine of the latest beast was sure to roar aggressively and attract attention – but she didn't care. After the stress of the morning, she wanted to do something reckless. She repeated the Gayatri mantra three times as she expertly reversed the car out of the garage and hit the road outside the long driveway.

Wow! Amrita had surpassed herself. It was as if she had been driving the Lamborghini for months. The car responded to her lightest touch! A wave of adrenalin rushed through her as the car hit top speeds. All day she had been hurtling from one crisis to another – and it hadn't ended – but she had to admit this felt good. Her thoughts went back to her stepfather. Raghubir Prasad was a car fiend. The day Amrita turned eighteen, he had insisted on giving her the first driving lesson in his old Mercedes. She had surprised him and herself by getting the hang of driving after just three lessons. Raghubir Prasad was proud of her and promised he'd get her a spiffy sports car for her twenty-first birthday. He died seven months short of it – the order for the car that had been booked from a 'source' was promptly cancelled. But Amrita had known that one day she'd possess not just that car but any car that caught her fancy. The faster the better. There was no sexier 'high' than being behind the wheel of a powerful machine that followed your every command at a feather touch on a tiny button. Which man on earth could provide a similar kick?

As Amrita sped through the broad tree-lined avenues of Delhi, screeching past gigantic roundabouts, she momentarily forgot about Babuji and Suraj. She lowered the hood of the sports car and felt the hot wind of the plains go through her hair which was undone and flowing around her face. Her skin felt baked, but her fingers played lightly on the leather-covered steering wheel as the car stereo blared Suraj's favourite house music. Strange, she loved Suraj's taste in music and movies. Stranger still, she loved far too many things about that rascal of a man. Rascal? That was too mild a word. He was a scoundrel, a villain. Dangerous and crazy. The opposite of her husband. Perhaps that's what she found attractive about Suraj . . . perhaps.

CHAPTER 12

Sethji was in a pensive mood as he and Raju drove in silence. It was touch and go today. What would happen? Sometimes Sethji laughed at the 'khela' fate played and wondered why the gods had smiled on him in the first place! So much wealth, so much dhan-daulat – my god! Even he couldn't believe his own good fortune. He had made enough money to look after the next two generations. Yes, even with a wastrel son like Suraj, and a lazy fellow like Srichand – two inheritors who were likely to fritter away these natural advantages. What bewakoofs! But at least there was Amrita. Aah that woman was a jewel – clever, beautiful, and uncompromising. Except when it came to power – yes, for that, Amrita was willing to do anything, even change his soiled adult diapers if need be, and . . . and . . . make his flaccid member dance inside her warm mouth.

Sometimes he wondered whether she was carved out of stone. So solid. So silent. Except when she wanted to make herself heard during a crisis. Perhaps she conserved her breath? She hardly ever spoke just for the sake of carrying forward a conversation. Or to be polite. He rarely saw her talking to her husband, except to ask with exaggerated politeness whether he was done with his meal, or needed something else . . . daal? Roti? Dahi? Pickle? She spoke to party workers only if they spoke to her first. And to the servants, of course. But only to communicate instructions that needed to be conveyed by the lady of the house: 'Why did the dhobi not starch the tablecloths this week? Make sure Babuji's second car goes for servicing to the old garage, not the new one where Surajji sends his cars. And suno, tell the maali to water the lawns twice a day . . . the grass is turning brown in the heat.'

About Amrita's feelings? Sethji could only guess. Even her 'obedience' carried a hint of defiance. Like she was mocking him, mocking his authority, mocking them all and yet mechanically doing what she'd been asked to do. Did she hate him? Sethji avoided looking for an answer. He wasn't even sure whether or not Amrita actually did do his sexual bidding. Often, he thought he had imagined it all: those fetid nights, with just Rocky 1 and Rocky 2 keeping a close watch on the door, as Amrita slipped in and out like a 'billi' – sure-footed, cold and always in a hurry to leap off and return to her own private world, where nobody could reach her, touch her. Nobody. She was like that. They happened so rarely, these nights, and during the day both acted as if it had never happened, like a dream. But after each such 'dream', Sethji would be left shuddering with unfulfilled longings, heart empty. Just the way Amrita planned it. Always the way Amrita planned it. Always.

Sethji often shook his head in disbelief when he thought about his daughter-in-law. He'd remind himself he was not a confused man. He had always known his own game plan and rarely wavered even while taking difficult decisions. But this woman always stumped him. It was as if she sapped him of all his power, his good sense, his reasoning, his sanity.

It couldn't have been just a sexual hold. Sethji had been a seasoned brothel-goer in the old days. Today, the brothel came to him. He had always enjoyed whoring and never made any bones about his 'buri aadat' as he referred to it. But after enjoying Amrita's body, Sethji had lost his desire for other women. Nobody aroused him any more. And that was most upsetting.

He had tried several times to 'test' his prowess, often with young girls far more beautiful than Amrita – virgins, at that! But . . . phut! Nothing happened. After struggling to get his unresponsive, uninterested member up, and pinching the tender nipples of the girls for a few minutes in a distracted way, Sethji would turn away in disgust, blaming the girl for not doing her job well. But in his heart of hearts, he knew it was Amrita and Amrita alone he wanted and longed for. That woman had cast a spell over him. A spell he wished never to break. Amrita was his sole whore now. And he hated himself for harbouring this obsession.

Sethji never felt any guilt about this. He was a fortunate man. No action of his was terrible enough to make him feel bad about himself. It was such an alien emotion; it actually puzzled him – what was the meaning of 'guilt', he'd idly asked Raju, during one of their endless drives to visit some factory and extract money from the cowering owner. Raju's yellow eyes ('Do you suffer from permanent jaundice?' Amrita had once asked) had looked blankly at the road ahead, as the driver deftly went past an overladen bullock cart stacked with gigantic watermelons. Sethji had roughly nudged him in the ribs and demanded an answer. Raju's brief reply had startled Sethji. Without taking his eyes off the road Raju had said, 'Ask Bhabhiji the meaning. She will know.' Sethji didn't pursue the subject after that. He instinctively knew it was time to shut up. But Raju's remark stayed with him forever.

Yet despite the occasional twinge of guilt he might feel, he also knew he had opened up Amrita's world and allowed her to grow in ways she would never have had she been a bahu in some ordinary house. Admiring her intelligence, quick wit and polish, he had increasingly relied on her, giving her the task of liaising with some of the wealthiest, most powerful men in the country. Deals that took her out of her home and gave her the adventures and kicks she secretly craved for. The first time Sethji asked Amrita to meet a 'contact' at a five-star hotel, he had said, 'You handle all these types of people. I don't like dealing with men who cannot curse in Hindi. What is conversation without gaalis? Dhanda and gaalis go together. But yeh saaley suit-boot-waley vilayati chootiye? Their voices come out of the arse! Kya accent! Unki zubaan gand mein atki rehti hai. No, no, no. They look different. Smell different. Talk different. They forget their chamdi is still brown – not white. They are as dark as I am. But their mind is safed. You will do a better job with such fellows. Your angrezi vaghera will impress them.' Amrita suppressed a small smile. She wondered what exactly 'vaghera' would involve. She found out soon enough . . .

***

Just the other day she'd had an encounter with a minor but influential maharaja from one of the smaller states of Rajasthan that she hadn't stopped laughing about. Munnu Sinh of Pipla was quite a character. Some said he had links with Mumbai's underworld. Others insisted he floated those rumours himself so as to pump up his importance, since the family money had long run out. Munnu had recently wrested control of a priceless piece of real estate after browbeating his cousins who had inherited it from their grandfather. This control had given Munnu enough clout to play hardball with three political parties simultaneously.

Munnu had decided to jump into the fray and contest the next election from his own pocket-sized state. But to pull that off, Munnu needed political and financial backing. He had made it known he was up for grabs and would go to the highest bidder. In return, he was willing to enter a deal that involved developing the hot property he now owned. There were millions to be made if everything fell into place. Winning the election would automatically lead to bigger and still more lucrative deals. While developing the property would take care of his immediate problem – settling his gambling dues and perhaps buying time with the 'bhais' who had taken to calling him directly these days – Munnu was in search of respectability as a bona fide realtor. Sethji was sure Amrita would be able to get Munnu Sinh on board once they met. He was right.

The meeting was at a new luxury mall. Amrita had noticed that it was pretty deserted as she walked briskly past the opulent stores selling handbags that cost more than an average working person's annual salary. She looked around the gleaming Italian marble lobby, taking in Delhi's socialites as they nibbled on strawberry macaroons in the coffee shop, but couldn't spot Munnu Sinh anywhere. He was hard to miss, clad in trademark jodhpurs, eyes lined with kohl, with two pea-sized solitaires glittering on both earlobes – even though his foppish appearance was not that uncommon a sight in

Delhi. Munnu Sinh also showed off an additional accessory – he invariably carried his grandfather's handsome walking cane with its gem-encrusted ivory handle and a solid gold tip.

Amrita decided to settle herself on one of the plush suede sofas. She hated it when people were late – it displayed atrocious manners and scant regard for the other person's time. She caught sight of herself in one of the large etched mirrors that formed the entire facade of a high-end jewellery store. She'd stuck to her standard attire – a shaded chiffon sari, boring but safe. Especially when she hadn't met the person. She could have worked on getting other details in place a little better – the same old string of pearls, the whopping six-carat diamond ring, the discreet ear clips. But that was precisely the objective. After years and years of experimenting with different looks, Amrita had zeroed in on this one – classy yet sexy – depending on the cut of her choli, and her mood, of course.

She heard the sharp tap-tap of the cane before she saw Munnu Sinh. Well . . . they had met casually at Delhi's unending social events to which Sethji often requested her to go on his behalf. Munnu Sinh walked up to her and said in a strange, girlish voice, 'Please, please, don't get up. You look like a painting, a maharani.' Amrita found herself blushing, and it annoyed her a little to be caught off guard by a squeaky-voiced man. 'May I?' he said, pulling up a chair and carefully balancing the cane along its ornately carved arm. Amrita had regained her composure by now. She said in her best businesslike voice, 'We have a lot to talk about. Shall we do it here . . . or . . .?'

He smiled. 'Treat this place like home, please. I own half of it.' Amrita smiled at the obvious lie. 'Sethji wanted me to find out just how serious you are about politics and how much you know about our party.' Munnu Sinh raised his hand (buffed nails, French manicure, Amrita noted). 'Please, let's get to know each other first. You are too formal, my dear. A general knowledge test already? Let's chat first. Love your ear clips! Harry Winston? My grandmother had a similar pair. Ooh, love your bag. So 1990s. My sister is very big on the nineties. Even though, if you ask me, it was the sixties and seventies that influenced fashion the most. Are you coming to Mallu's finale tonight? Gothic is so passé, but our designers are totally stuck in that same old rut – who's to tell them? Black nail polish! Ugh! So yesterday!'

Amrita smiled, making sure not to allow her eyes to betray any emotion. It was a trick she'd practised in front of the mirror for two months as a teenager, frequently forced to be 'nice' to strangers who'd come home to meet her stepfather and then taken an extra interest in the young girl fidgeting with her dupatta. 'Say hello to uncleji, beta,' her mother would urge her, 'Namaste karo,' and Amrita would switch on the fake smile that never reached those watchful eyes. Today that smile wasn't going to leave her face and her eyes would remain hard and stone cold as ever.

Munnu seemed restless and distracted, as he delicately removed a pouch of smelly paan masala from his jacket pocket, threw back his head, making the prominent Adam's apple dance, and tossed the contents far back into his wide-open mouth. Amrita noted his horribly discoloured teeth and turned away. Amrita had an aversion to anything unclean about a person's appearance. Since Munnu Sinh's nails were perfectly well kept, it came as a shock to her to see that mouth. He caught her staring and said swiftly, his voice squeaking some more, 'Terrible habit, na? I've really tried to kick it. But you know how difficult that is! In any case better this nasha than what the rest of Delhi is on. You know – it's crazy – every second person is doing the white stuff. Even the minister's peons! I tell you, things really do go better with coke! Hey Bhagwan . . . it's hard to find anyone who is not coked out.'

Amrita continued smiling, till Munnu Sinh caught her off guard by asking, 'Have you had a job done? Botox? Your smile is so fixed! Sorry if I sound rude, darling. But you haven't stopped smiling for even one second!' Temporarily thrown by the directness of the remark, Amrita's studied expression changed instantly. 'Aaah. So much better!' Munnu Sinh clapped his hands like a child who'd witnessed something out of the ordinary. 'Now we can talk – like friends. Good friends. I'm very intuitive, na? I know we'll get along, you must be a number seven. I'm also a number seven. I'm December born. Typical Sagi. Naughty and flirtatious! And you? Are you a Scorpio? Must be! With those eyes and so secretive. Oh God! This is too much!'

Amrita didn't respond immediately. There was little she could say. And then she suddenly found herself giggling like a schoolgirl. Munnu Sinh picked up his cane and with great ceremony extended his arm towards Amrita. 'Shall we . . .?' he chirped, as they walked through the brightly lit lobby, past the luxury brand stores and into the even brighter light outside. And Amrita knew she had nothing but good news for Sethji.

'Woh saala hijra. How did he agree so fast? Did you discuss money, his land, other details?' Sethji grilled Amrita when she met him late at night as she gleefully recounted her story. He was in the middle of his massage, this time with pure ghee. She was expected to sit in a corner of the darkened room with her eyes averted, so as to maintain some decorum in the presence of the masseur. 'We just got along really well. And no, the details have still to be worked out. But basically Munnu Sinh gave me his word. He is with us. He will not go to anyone else. And he is keen for me to work with him on his hotel project – he is in talks with two international hotel chains.' Sethji snorted derisively. 'Arrey, tell that eunuch those things will come later. How much did he ask for? Bas, we need to stick to that for now. Five? Ten? Fifty?' Amrita smiled. 'Nothing.'

Thinking of Amrita's smooth and efficient dealing of the kadka maharaja and her obvious relish of it, Sethji now smiled to himself. Whatever Raju may think, and whatever guilt he may feel, Sethji knew that he had done well by his bahu, just as he had promised her mother. Putting away thoughts of Amrita, he retrieved his cell phone and dialled Srivastava Saab – the senior cop who looked after his interests for a fat fee. He needed to make sure there was no police inquiry about the rape. 'Srivastava Saab, there has been a small problem in the family. I need your help,' he said on the phone. 'Of course, of course, Sethji, what are friends for, what can we do,' purred the voice on the other end.

A number flashed on his phone as he concluded the conversation. It was Arun Mehta. 'I have chatted with Bhabhi and am meeting her soon, it's all under control. You must not worry.' 'I knew you would manage it, Arun.' 'All set for the meeting today? Dimaag se kaam lena padega. Kaafi crucial hai. Kavitaji has been working hard . . . you know what I mean.' Sethji snorted. 'Kavitaji is a nobody. Who has faith in her? Without my backing she is nothing. And she knows it. I will manage her. Don't worry, mera master plan hai. She will run away after she hears it. I think Kavitaji will find that she made a mistake counting on certain people.' There was a note of amusement in Arun's voice. 'Ah, but who can one trust nowadays, Sethji?' 'Bilkul,' replied the old politician and the two men began to laugh.

'Do you remember the first time we met?' Arun asked. 'How can I ever forget? It was like a formal dulha-dulhan meeting!' said Sethji. Arun roared with laughter. 'That's what I like about you, Sethji. You are so deliciously direct and crude! But who was our marriage broker? Have you forgotten that?' Sethji shook his head. 'How can I ever forget that rogue? He managed to cheat both of us!' Arun chuckled. 'Correct! But we fixed him in the end. Saala!' Sethji said, 'Let's forget that haramzaada. He was a cheenti. You and I have finished off haathis. What is an ant's life to us when we have elephants to kill?'

CHAPTER 13

Srichand woke up to use the bathroom and discovered an empty, unslept-in bed next to his. Amrita was missing. Again. He was used to that, of course. He never asked, although over the years suspicion had eaten him away, made him even more uncertain of himself. But that was their special, unspoken pact. So long as he didn't pry, they didn't fight. He kept the guesswork to himself. He inhaled deeply – there was a lot of Joy in the airless room. She must have sprayed it on before leaving. Srichand drank water from a large copper glass – doctor's orders. And went back to sleep. He knew that it was an important day for Babuji today.

If Babuji were to lose the party elections, their lives would be utterly destroyed. Of course there were the Swiss accounts, but everything would change. The reverberations would enter even his own small life. He would no longer be given the premier VIP parking lot at his golf club. His caddy, the most sought after one in the club, would take on other players who were on his long wait list. These may have seemed like insignificant things, but even more than the money it was the tiny perks of power that he loved. How he hated politics. Well, not exactly hated. Most times, he was indifferent. But would Babuji leave him alone? No, Babuji prodded and prodded his older son to play a more active role and become the treasurer of the party. 'I need people I can trust,' he'd say over and over again. 'How can I leave so much money in the care of those bloody gaandus? Pimps, the lot of them. I just have to turn my back for them to pounce. Poor Amrita, how much can she do by herself?' Babuji never raised Suraj's name during these discussions. Perhaps, in Babuji's scheme of things, Suraj was meant for greater things, Srichand would conclude without bitterness. And go back to practising his swing.

Years and years ago – it seemed like a hazy scene from his previous life – Srichand remembered being caned mercilessly by his father in front of his mother, who was cowering in a corner of their small quarters, pleading with Sethji to spare the child. Srichand had forgotten what he'd done to deserve such a beating, a beating so savage and severe that the cane had broken. Before Sethji could demand a replacement, Srichand's mother had flung herself across Srichand's narrow, frail body, crying, 'For God's sake, do you want to kill the boy? Stop it . . . or . . . or . . .' Sethji stopped pacing the room and demanded, 'Or what, woman? What will you do? Kill yourself? Jump into the well? Do it. Your womb has produced two useless boys. One a weakling, the other a rogue. It is a curse, and I have to pay the price for it. Why, I ask you? Why is god punishing me?'

'Weakling!' Srichand never forgot that word. 'Kamzor.' This is what his father had decreed of him; 'Badmash' was the judgement reserved for his younger brother. Yes, it was true. He was weak – his mother's milk had run dry during the first month itself. And Sethji had made arrangements for a wet nurse. Later in life, doctors had confirmed what Sethji had secretly feared – Srichand had a defective heart valve. His lungs were too weak to pump enough oxygen too.

Sethji had scorned the boy and told the mother, 'These are diseases from your side of the family. Look at you – had I known you were a consumptive, would I have married you? When you coughed in your parents' home, your maternal uncle lied to my father saying it was the constant smoke from the wood fire in the kitchen that made you cough. Your family deceived me. And this is the price we have to pay for the deception – two sons who are a burden. A burden for life.'

Sethji's wife had dared to splutter between sobs, 'That may be true. But it did not stop your family from demanding gold coins, a hundred silver coins, two cows, two buffaloes, part of our land and a tractor. Where would you have been today without my dowry?' Sethji had roared loud enough to attract people from the small courtyard next door. They had rushed in and found Sethji towering over his wife and son with a heavy brass lota in his hand. 'Kill me! Kill my son! I don't care,' his wife was screaming, as Srichand clung on to her knees, stifling his own howls in the folds of her grimy sari which reeked of gobar, mustard oil, coal and kerosene. Sethji put down the brass vessel reluctantly before storming out of the house. Suraj, who was the adored toddler of the neighbourhood, was busy gobbling ghee-dripping, extra-sweet pedhas made for Diwali by the halwai's plump wife whom everybody called 'mausi'. Suraj's weakness for sticky sweetmeats stayed for life, while Srichand never outgrew his revulsion of mustard oil.

***

Nor did he ever grow out of his fear and feeling of emasculation while facing his father. One of his 'duties' had been to 'deal' with his father's mistresses after the end of a relationship. Srichand hated this but couldn't say no to his father. But every encounter diminished him even more. He remembered the bewitching Tania in particular, from whom he had to collect the BMW that Sethji had given her for her use. He could still recall standing outside Tania's house wondering what he'd say to her – that is, if she was home and ready to meet him. Her security staff had not stopped him after recognizing Sethji's car and noting down the number in a large ledger. Srichand idly wondered what happened to those hefty ledgers. Did anybody really bother to check them? Ever? If not, what was the point in hiring two men whose jobs involved nothing more strenuous than noting down the licence plate numbers of every car entering the compound?

Then there were the mandatory (and pointless) car checks by ill-trained personnel who didn't always know which direction to point the mirrors that were stuck under vehicles. Nor did they succeed in swiftly opening the bonnets and boots to look for concealed explosives. The joke used to be 'What about physically searching passengers? What if there are suicide bombers inside the car with dynamite sticks strapped under their clothes? What if those shopping bags next to the fancy memsaab reclining in the back seat of her fancy Merc were filled with RDX and not Dior?' All these stray thoughts were running through Srichand's head when a voice behind him said, 'You must be Srichand! As handsome as your father said you were!' Srichand whirled around to face a sweaty woman clad in a velvet tracksuit.

'I've been jogging. Missed gymming this morning. Oh god! Soooooo hung over! These Fashion Week after-parties, na? Killers! Got back at five this morning! Trainer turned up at six! I told him to bhago. Can't handle it, yaar. It's too much. But that Rao, na, he never gets tired! Up all night, partying-shartying, and back in the office at eight handling solid files. Sorry, sorry, sorry! I talk too much. Come, come, come, let's have chai. I'm hooked on green tea. I know why you're here. For the car, na? Take it, yaar! No big deal. Your father, na? He's a darling. But so jealous and so kanjoos! I told him, "It's only a car. What's the problem? You can have it back any time. I'll get another one." But he blew up! Anyways, chalo chalo, bearer . . . Tulsiiiiiii . . . where's my juice? My green tea? And pucca chai for saab. Jaldi, jaldi. Don't mind, na? I'm in a bit of a hurry – want to catch Bimbo's show. Have to look good, na? Page 3-wallas will be there. Oh, like my hair?'

That was it. Srichand was instantly smitten! He followed her as if in a trance, jealous of how his father always managed to acquire such women. Speechlessly, he sat down on a lavishly upholstered sofa as Tania ran around bossing servants with noisy instructions in Hindi, English and Punjabi. Srichand couldn't take his eyes off Tania as she bunched up her blond, wildly streaked hair into an untidy ponytail and screamed, 'Arrey Chhotu – woh BMW ki chaabi leke aao. Jaldi! Get the bloody car keys! These bloody buggers, I tell you . . . toba! Most frustrating. Tea? Coffee? Milk? Juice? Have something, na? Your father is too much. Sending his beta to reclaim the car. Poor you! But chill, yaar. We can be friends. You're cute! I like your butt!' Tania threw back her head and laughed, her hands on her waist, to better show off her impressive breasts clearly visible under the body-hugging tee she was sporting under the velvet track jacket. She intercepted his gaze and shook her finger, 'Tsk, tsk! Naughty boy! Like father, like son. See tits and go mad!'

Srichand shot to his feet as if he had been hit by a thunderbolt. He was flushed with embarrassment and stuttering stupidly, 'I have to . . . please . . . just give me the keys.' Tania came up to him and giggled. 'Don't get nervous, yaar. I won't kidnap you, though I am tempted! You are really, really cute! Love your Gandhi glasses! Hasn't anybody told you that? And by the way your dad's a sweetie-pie. So innocent! Just like you. About the Beemer – like I said – it's only a car. Usme kya hai? Cars come and go. But special men remain special. Your dad will always be special. Sachchi. He helped me a lot. I was in such deep shit when we met. He has a good heart. But what to do? I am like a chidiya – I can't stay in one nest for too long. I need to hop around, move. Now I'm with Rao. He's gorgeous, na? Light eyes and everything. Badiya accent, also. Brilliant dude. Oxford-woxford. Pata nahin what he sees in me! Ha ha! Probably what all men see!' Tania walked around the well-lit room, restlessly arranging flowers, occasionally bending down to kiss the petals. 'Flowers are so sweet, na? They bring colour and joy in our lives and ask for nothing in return.' Srichand kept staring fixedly at the door, waiting for Chhotu to fetch the car keys. All of a sudden, he felt a pair of arms grabbing his chest from the back and froze! Tania looked up from the long-stemmed liliums delicately balancing in a tall glass jar and laughed. 'Relax . . . he's my dog trainer and he's just protecting you from my mad dogs, that's all. Let go, sweetie. It's okay!' Srichand didn't dare breathe or turn around. He stood transfixed as Tania's pet Rottweilers (one with a muzzle, the other without) sauntered in from the garden. 'Give mummy a kiss,' she pouted, as the dogs bounded up to her and licked her full on the lips. 'Meet my best friends – Badmash and Bahadur,' said Tania, adding,

'I'm sure they smelt your dogs on your clothes. So cute, na? Your dad had their pictures on his phone – not your picture!'

Srichand shifted from one foot to the other and said sharply, 'Excuse me, but I'm in a hurry. Please hand over the keys immediately. My . . . my . . . wife is waiting.' Tania burst into loud laughter and mimicked Srichand, 'Oh oh . . . my wife is waiting . . . my wife is waiting . . . too touching, yaar. As if I don't know. As if the world doesn't know who she waits for! Come off it. Stop this dramabaazi. Take those bloody keys and leave. The door's to your left. Give the fucking car to your wife. I'm sure she knows just how hard she'll have to work for it – know what I mean? Your father doesn't give anything for free. But guess what? With Rao in my life, I don't need anything.'

'Bye-bye, sweetie. You really are hot, you know. In case things get boring for me with Rao – I'll know who to call. Come on, come here, give me a hug. Don't worry, your frigid wife won't know or care. Baap re baap. Must meet her some day, though. She seems to get her men without giving her pussy – that's real power, na?' Tania walked boldly up to Srichand, stood on tiptoe, placed her palms over his buttocks, pulled his crotch right up against her own, stuck the tip of her tongue out and ran it over his dry lips. 'Nervous, na? It happens. Most men can't handle me. But asli men have no such problems. Men like Sethji, your beloved Babuji.'

Srichand was shaking when he went home. 'Amrita . . . Amrita . . . why does Babuji send me to meet chudails like that woman? Tania is a she-devil!' He groaned, as Amrita raised her left eyebrow to indicate she'd heard her husband's remarks, but wasn't particularly interested in furthering the conversation. Without turning her head towards him or altering her body language, she asked in a bored voice, 'Do you want to sleep with her . . .' and, after a short pause, the stinger '. . . also?' Srichand bellowed, 'Why do you say such horrible things? Why? What is the sin I have committed that you treat me with more contempt than you display towards our servants? Even Ramu gets a smile out of you, but not your husband.' Amrita continued looking through a thick cardboard box file. 'Where are those bloody papers? The car papers? We'll need them now that the BMW is back with us. By the way, don't let your rash brother drive it ever.'

Srichand walked towards his wife, stood in front of her and demanded, 'Am I not good enough for you? Do you find me repulsive? Come, tell me . . . how repulsive? More repulsive than my father? Huh? Tell me. Am I more repulsive than Babuji?' Amrita continued rifling through the file. 'Papers,' she said shortly, without bothering to look up. 'Prasadji will chew my brains if I don't find those damn papers.' Srichand looked at the woman – his wife. She appeared almost inhuman at the moment. Srichand said in a voice heavy with defeat . . . resignation, 'Don't answer. But don't think I don't know. I know everything, Amrita. Everything.' Amrita looked up coldly and responded in a low voice, 'Good. Since you know everything, please leave me alone. And . . . go sleep with Tania. It will be good for you.'

CHAPTER 14

Arun liked to call himself a 'kingmaker', but those who knew him said he would have loved to be crowned the king himself – if only he didn't have to fight an election! Delhi recognized Arun's skills at 'managing' governments. With no known party affiliations, he was everybody's best friend. His tentacles were everywhere, and he had most of the country's best legal brains on his team. He'd boast after a few shots of aged Cuban Rum (he drank nothing else), 'My lawyers understand my functioning well. Every contract I sign is on the assumption that we will be litigating some day.' Despite his unseemly wealth, Arun always wanted more and never ever missed an opportunity to make a quick buck. He'd laugh about this trait, saying, 'I can't help it. I was fathered by a professional gambler. I am a professional gambler myself – at birth, by birth! It's in my DNA. Tell me, is it possible to fight that? Why bother? Life is like a poker game. You make the best of the cards that are dealt to you.'

Right now, he was chasing a major national highways contract. And for that to fall into his kitty, he needed Sethji's support. Provided Sethji could hang on to his position within the party and in the process not allow his party to withdraw from the shaky government coalition. If all went according to plan, Sethji would keep his ministerial berth. And Arun, the coveted contract. A win-win situation for all. Of course, Kavitaji had been to see him several times at the farmhouse, pledging support and indirectly asking him to help her topple Sethji. But somehow, Arun liked the bandit, as he called Sethji behind his back. Sethji with his crude, coarse and direct mannerisms was easier to do business with and made a better ally than that annoying chatterbox, Kavitaji. He couldn't bear her strident attitude, that awful voice. Besides, she was a lightweight, a very pushy one at that. Kavitaji spent all her energy trying desperately to climb up the party hierarchy. But Arun knew that Sethji's cunning would eventually defeat her amateurish manoeuvres. Till such time as that highways contract landed on his table, Arun was prepared to play ball with both – Sethji and Kavitaji. That's what politicians were there for – pit one against the other, and extract what you want from both. Keep them hanging. Keep them insecure. That had always been Arun's signature mantra.

Arun knew the one golden rule of politics and blackmail – information was strength. He made sure to keep himself well informed at all times. No politician was too small for him to keep tabs on. No journalist too nosy for him not to cultivate. Arun had created a special cell in his office to 'monitor' what was going on. Rivals called it ACIA – Arun's Central Intelligence Agency. They knew Arun's special cell tapped phone lines and recorded, even filmed, VVIP conversations and that nobody was safe from their all-pervasive snooping. Leaking stories to news channels was Arun's secret weapon. Which made him an invaluable source for influential news anchors in search of scoops. Arun realized he could use Suraj's latest misadventure to his advantage. Sethji was at his most vulnerable right now. The crucial party meeting would have to be screened carefully. Arun's spies had told him it was likely to be stormy.

And . . . aaha . . . there was the lovely Amrita to handle before that, of course! He was waiting for Amrita in the vast living room in his heavily guarded farmhouse. Amrita walked in, and took in Arun's impeccable appearance. He looked, as he always did, like he'd stepped out of a spa seconds earlier. He was freshly shaved, and dressed in a perfectly tailored ivory linen kurta pyjama set, his feet in Bally slippers. Amrita noticed his pedicure first, since her eyes were downcast – was that shell-pink polish on the nails of his plump, fair, hairless toes? Absurd thought, but she couldn't stop it.

Arun embraced her warmly and asked, 'He really has done it this time, hasn't he, the bloody fucker?' It was said with indulgence, even fondness. Amrita knew that Suraj and Arun were close and occasional party-mates. Shaking his head, Arun said, 'That brother-in-law of yours is impossible – can't keep it in his pants, which I understand. But why stick his dick into the wrong woman when he can get anybody he wants – anybody?' Amrita didn't respond but tapped her watch to indicate urgency. Arun took her hand and stared admiringly at the Cartier, glittering enticingly with tiny champagne-coloured diamonds. 'Pretty, verrry, verrry pretty. New?'

Amrita was filled with revulsion, like a wave of nausea, whenever she met Arun. Especially today. 'Let's talk about Suraj. What have you organized? I know you didn't want to discuss it over the phone.' Arun touched her tense shoulders and drawled, 'Relaxxxx, baby. Now you are in my domain. It's all arranged. I'm sending that fucker to Dubai. First we drive him to the Nepal border. Then he grabs a flight to Dubai from Kathmandu. Let him cool his heels there. Stay out of trouble. After that, we'll see. Leave him to me. Get back home and tell that husband of yours not to worry. That is, if he knows about the hullabaloo in the first place. But one piece of bad news. The media will be on the story. I am afraid we couldn't stop it from leaking out – there was the hotel where it happened and after that the hospital. Thank god that hill girl hasn't died, or maybe it would have been better if she had. Dead bodies are so convenient, don't you think? Bury them, burn them, vaporize them. Suraj should have finished the job he started.'

Amrita nodded a little dully. Suddenly, she felt exhausted by this man in front of her. Arun rang for his valet. 'Coffee for memsaab. Strong,' he ordered the slim, well-dressed man with blond streaks in his trendily styled hair, and delicate ruby earrings. 'Gorgeous, na?' Arun laughed, noticing Amrita's expression. 'I like them beautiful.' Amrita smiled at the remark, and recalled her first meeting with Arun, soon after her marriage.

'What lovely emeralds,' had been his opening remark. They were at a polo match and Arun's team had won the prestigious Ranipur Cup for the third year running. Amrita was dressed in lemon yellow chiffon, her long hair cascading down her narrow back, ending just above her full hips. Her eyes were hidden behind tortoiseshell Balenciaga shades. She said, 'Thank you,' and looked away. Arun bent low, and whispered into her ear, 'Very few women know how to show off their emeralds – they foolishly wear them against black or match them with green. You've got it right, madam.'

'Are you a jeweller?' Amrita asked.

'No, I am not a jeweller, I am just a connoisseur. I buy beautiful jewels, some I wear, most I give away to friends.'

'Generous! You must have a lot of friends!'

'I do. And I'd like to make you one.' Arun smiled while extending his right hand. 'Golconda?' Amrita asked, staring at the stupefyingly big diamond ring on Arun's finger.

'Yes. My father's. He was a good friend and supporter of your father-in-law, Sethji, and since his death, I have continued that friendship. I know your husband a little, we meet on the golf course. And who doesn't know Suraj? I am happy to finally meet the beautiful Bhabhi he can't stop talking about.' Amrita looked into the distance and answered briefly, 'I don't go out much. I really don't know too many people any more. Besides, I find Delhi society extremely incestuous, even boring.'

Arun laughed. 'That it most certainly is. But my set isn't boring at all. You should get to know us better. We aren't hard-core Delhi types. We like our fun. Oh, here's Gulu. You'll adore him. Beautiful women and Gulu go together. He has exquisite taste, is single, great sense of humour, fabulous cars, amazing lifestyle. And he knows everybody there is to know – not just in Delhi, but the whole world. Gulu, come here and meet the Emerald Lady. Gulu, this is Amrita, you know her father-in-law – Sethji – and her husband – Srichand. Plus, as I said earlier – who doesn't know Suraj? Gulu beta, didn't Suraj almost kill you recently? Something to do with a woman, of course? Well now, we have to convince Amrita – or should I call you Amritaji? – that we aren't such terrible chaps! Let's get a glass of champagne and raise a toast to beauty. To emeralds. To Amrita.'

In those days, Amrita was still a little naive and she had been intrigued by Arun. 'What business is Arunji in?' she asked curiously. Sethji tried to change the subject. 'Why do you want to waste time on them? I told you, na, they are my associates in some building projects, road development schemes, bridges vaghera. That's all. We do business together. I've helped Arun. Arun has helped me. Arun's family and I go back a long way. If there is a crisis, Arun will help you out. '

Amrita had been smart enough to understand the note of warning in Babuji's response. Arun was a friend but a dangerous one. 'Let me tell you something that my stupid sons don't understand. In our political world you don't have friends, only contacts. Arun Mehta is a contact. Nothing more. He needs me. I need him. No favours. Anyone can betray you. Family is the only thing to depend on,' he had once said to her and she always remembered those words in the businessman's company. Babuji was very clear about a few things – family matters remained family matters. No outsider was invited home. Even Suraj had to throw his parties at their Chhattarpur farmhouse, not the main residence. Business was conducted at different venues – mainly little-known three-star hotels, guest houses, farmhouses or homes of party workers of little importance. 'Trust no one, least of all your friends,' Sethji would tell her. And she had also come to feel this way. Amrita's trust was invested in just one person – herself.

CHAPTER 15

Today, Suraj's life depended on the help provided by this man, Arun Mehta. But there was no other option and Amrita, more than anybody else, knew as much. Fatigue was beginning to get her down. The strong coffee served in exquisite porcelain didn't help. She felt her heart racing impossibly. Black coffee on an empty stomach was a recipe for ulcers and splitting headaches. She asked to visit the washroom. A brisk splashing of cold water on her face would wake her up. Arun was talking softly into the cell phone, making arrangements. He waved and winked. 'Damage control,' he added after disconnecting. 'Hope you don't mind – but I've done something without checking with you. I phoned Akshay Tiwari – you know the guy who heads Bharat News. I have given him the "scoop", if we can call this horrible development that. It's better to break the news ourselves with an exclusive rather than let all those vultures descend on us and report whatever they feel like. I told Akshay you'd talk to his channel.'

Amrita took some time to absorb what Arun was telling her. She was annoyed by the presumptuousness Arun had displayed. But it was a fait accompli. He was obviously returning a favour he owed Akshay Tiwari, the powerful anchor whose job it was to make politicians squirm and wilt in his studio, while he conducted his aggressive interrogation at prime time. Loathed, feared and grudgingly admired by viewers, Akshay was the most courted mediaman in India. Amrita was cornered. She recoiled at Arun's suggestion but stuck her chin out and said in a firm voice, 'I'm ready. Tell me where we are doing the interview.'

Arun was caught off guard by her willingness, but hid it well. 'That's my girl! Studio, of course, Noida. Keep it official. Say only as much as you have to. Do not lose your cool. Stick to the script. Repeat yourself over and over again, so as to wear down the anchor. Don't incriminate yourself by getting flustered. Any and every sign of nerves is caught by the camera. You are not a criminal. You are not an accused in a complicated case. You are merely doing what any good Indian bahu would do – defending your in-laws. Remember, you are only on a TV show with a sharp interrogator, and not in a court of law. Do not compromise yourself. Say little. But say it well. My car will take you there. Leave the rest to me.

'My men are dealing with the Pahadi girl's family. I think we can work out a settlement with them. All you have to keep repeating like a parrot to Akshay on his show is that Suraj was very much at home the night of the alleged rape. That's it. Nothing more. You can make up the dinner menu that night if you want to sound more convincing. Say that Suraj left for a scheduled business trip after having dinner with you and Srichand. Stick to that, no matter what Akshay asks you. About Sethji, tell Akshay you have full faith in him and that you know he will win the party election. Even if Akshay names people – you know, Kavitaji and her chamchas in the party – ignore the provocation. Amnesia is the best strategy. Just ask for people's prayers and blessings. Good luck, my dear. You can do it! Don't forget to cover your head with

your pallu. Fold your hands in a namaste. And look suitably
worried. Remember – nautanki is everything on TV.'

Amrita heard him out patiently, without flinching. Sethji
at this very moment would be struggling to save his future,
his political ambitions, his ministerial kursi; Suraj racing
towards the border; and her dolt of a husband would be
asleep unconcernedly dreaming of a perfect birdie.

CHAPTER 16

The party headquarters was swarming with reporters. 'What are you going to do, Sethji?' said a loud-voiced girl as she thrust her microphone at his face. 'What happens to the ABSP today?' 'Where is Suraj? Is your son innocent? Rumour has it that he has disappeared.' 'The party will remain united,' said Sethji shortly and walked on briskly.

Santosh, his secretary, was waiting by the door. 'The debate is just about to begin, sir.' 'Will you organize some chai for me, Santosh, and put in an extra spoon of sugar, will you? I need all my strength today,' Sethji said with a smile. Santosh wondered, as he had so many times before, how this grizzled old man could remain so unruffled in any crisis. He had won every battle so far, but could he really win this time?

Sethji walked in into the middle of Kavita Saxena's high-pitched rant. 'And now this scandal with Suraj bhaiyya,' she was screaming. 'This is the final straw. For the good of this party, Sethji must step down. There have been too many controversies attached to him. The party's reputation is affected.' 'Kavitaji, I accept all your points but Sethji is the person who has driven the party forward. We have all grown with him, because of him. Today we are in a strong position at the centre and Sethji has a key cabinet position. They need our MPs. If we fight and break up, it will damage our reputation – affect our future. All of us will be finished. Future ke baarey mein socho, Kavitaji. Have faith in our leader. Sethji will manage something and get out of this problem quickly. He alone has zabardast contacts.'

It was Aggarwal, a loyalist. Sethji sat in a corner, barely absorbing the debate as the party members parried and thrust. His mind returned to the conversation the night before. Sethji had arranged a closed-door meeting with the four key party rebels at his home that evening. The tension in the room had been palpable. Sethji had kept the men waiting – a tactic he often found effective. His behaviour with them had been genial with a hint of a little hurt, like an ageing uncle slightly surprised that his younger relations were overtaking him. He had talked about the early days of the party, asked about their families, and appeared vulnerable and sentimental. Parathas, freshly made, were brought in, along with the delectable laddoos from his hometown Mirpur.

'You are all like my sons. That is why I have asked you over. What are you going to do breaking away? Will Kavitaji, that hysterical aurat, get the party funding? Is she going to finance your election campaigns? It is all very well to talk about clean politics. We are men of sense in this room. What bakwas is this,' he ended emotionally.

There was silence in the room. 'Answer me,' exploded Sethji, this time with an angry thump on the table. 'You chootiyas, what did she promise you all? Without me, where is the money? Who is going to look after you? And there is news. Very good news. Arun Mehta has agreed to set up an educational scheme with us in UP. We'll set up free tuition centres for secondary students across the state. I have an excellent slogan for it, "A tenth class pass in every home. Har ghar mein ek dasvi pass." Good, isn't it?' he said with a laugh. 'It's exactly what we need to win the youth base before the elections. We should be planning for this instead of worrying about Kavitaji's damn politics. Is she going to win us the elections? You know very well she is not.'

Suddenly Sethji changed the tone of his voice and said slyly, 'Maybe we should not be this harsh towards poor Kavitaji. After all she is a woman. Maybe she is suffering from some woman problem. Maybe she is in the middle of her menses or menopause given her age. Let us be more considerate. Women's brains are in their wombs. And her womb is drying up fast.' This was Sethji's classic tactic. To use gross, offensive humour to undermine his enemies. He understood that if you laughed at someone, you took them less seriously.

The four men stayed silent, not knowing what to say. But the foremost emotion in their minds was grudging respect. A few hours ago, Sethji's position had been as precarious as a one-eyed juggler's. Now in the blink of an eye, he had turned the tide against him with aggression, brashness, humour and a masterstroke. He must have pulled some hefty strings for Arun Mehta's unexpected generosity, but if it worked, their flagging fortunes in UP might revive. Besides he was right, would Kavitaji really be able to fund their campaigns? Who'd back this emotional, unpredictable woman? Money had never been a problem for Sethji.

The conversation had carried on late into the night. Sethji had gone to bed tired but confident. He knew the key votes were going to be with him and that the announcement of the tuition scheme would do the trick. The party had been

floundering with its strategy in UP. This was exactly what
they needed. Even with the news about Suraj, Sethji was
certain he would win this round. He would survive. Uske
baad? Dekha jaayega . . .

CHAPTER 17

Star anchor Akshay Tiwari's cologne was heady. Amrita guessed this freshly showered, tall, athletically built, heavily made-up peacock of a man with a permanent sneer across his face and the supercilious air of a person who knew he could get his way around almost anyone or anything was ready to grill her like a breakfast sausage. She squared her shoulders and pushed a strand of hair off her damp forehead. She had had just enough time to go home and change into her trademark pastel-coloured sari before rushing to the studios and now she felt another wave of exhaustion. Would the day's dramas never end? 'Coffee?' he asked smoothly. 'We still have . . . let's see . . . seven minutes before we go on air. Black?' Amrita shook her head and declined his offer. Even though her mouth was dry, she wasn't going to let on just how nervous she was. She knew his type – conceited SOBs who strode around the cold, intimidating lobbies of Delhi's posh hotels like they owned them. She'd watched him give Sethji a hard time during a particularly tough election rally, making her father-in-law say the most ridiculous things because of the language barrier. Akshay's snobbishness was based on nothing more than his own Oxbridge credentials but today she wouldn't allow him to get the better of her.

'We have the raped girl's sister in the studios,' he said with a suggestive smile. 'No point denying anything. Suraj is a dead duck. He's over. He's history. Minimum ten years in the anda jail. Let's not play games. You have a minute and a half to touch up your make-up, dab the sweat on your forehead and mic up. Come on . . . let's go. By the way, you are far better looking in person than in your pictures! This show is going to rock!'

Amrita's face gave nothing away as she followed Akshay out of his small cabin (she'd taken in details – pictures of two kids with him and his pretty wife outside Buckingham Palace, scrawled 'We love you dad' across them, wilted red roses in a chipped vase, a Zegna bomber jacket on a hanger, squash gear crammed into a Nike bag) and into the freezing studio with people going about their tasks in silence.

He pointed to a swivel chair next to his. 'You're there,' he whispered as a man with a powder puff touched up his face and held a hand mirror in front of him. 'Brush,' said Akshay softly, as his earpiece was swiftly clipped on. Akshay was obsessive about his hair, and used far too much gel to spike it fashionably. He readjusted his Ferragamo tie (sober, for a change) and looked sideways at Amrita. 'Let the show begin,' he said with a smirk as the signature tune blared and camera-1 zoomed in for a tight close-up of the anchor's face (angled perfectly to catch a flattering light).

'Hello India . . .' Akshay began in the voice which was recognized by the majority of one billion Indians. Crisply, bluntly and efficiently he rattled off the top stories (oil spills near the coast of Mexico, some more American soldiers killed in Iraq, another landmine explosion triggered off by Maoists near Nagpur) before plunging gleefully into the Big Story. Amrita only half heard all the words which were accompanied by gory clips showing the half-naked body of the girl Suraj was alleged to have raped. Akshay stressed on the word 'alleged' several times, and Amrita picked up the text as it appeared on the teleprompter from which Akshay was reading. It was sounding and looking so awful, she wanted to shut her eyes and plug her ears. Oh god! Amrita groaned inwardly. If only that bloody Suraj had kept his pecker to himself!

She heard her name being uttered forcefully by Akshay as he described her dilemma – caught in the middle of a nasty family drama with a father-in-law about to lose the confidence of his party members and an alleged rapist of a brother-in-law! Amrita could see camera-2 closing in on her face. It was a format she was familiar with, since she watched Akshay's show avidly each day. She could feel the nation's eyes boring into her. In a flash she remembered the words of a seasoned politician who had told her, 'Madam, the camera catches everything – it never lies. You can try any trick under the sun, but if you try and fake something – you'll be instantly caught. Nobody can fool the camera.'

And then she was on air. Amrita was being asked about Suraj, what this meant for Sethji. Amrita had two choices – to lie or to tell the truth. During that do-or-die moment, Amrita instinctively opted for the second – truth. Or at least her version of it. 'Think on your feet, Amrita' was the slogan she had committed to memory as a young girl, with no resources other than her body and her brains to fall back on.

She looked into the camera, her eyes shining with tears. 'Today a shadow has fallen on our family. Yes, it is true my brother-in-law Suraj has raped this young woman. We know he has made a terrible mistake. Let the courts decide how to punish this unfortunate young man for the crime he has committed. But let me also admit here with deep shame and sorrow that Suraj needs help. For the past few years, he has been struggling to cope with a severe drinking problem that began when the deep, emotional trauma of losing his mother really hit him. While the family stands staunchly behind Suraj during this difficult hour, and will ensure he checks into a rehab clinic, we also want to extend all possible help to the victim and her family. Such a shameful thing should not happen to any woman. My heart goes out to her as it would to a younger sister who has suffered a terrible attack that could scar her for life.

'We pledge not just to assist this one girl in every possible way, but I am pleased to share with you that my dear father-in-law, the respected and admired political stalwart, has announced the formation of a national trust, spearheaded by him, that will provide financial and psychological support to rape victims across the length and breadth of India. The first cell will be set up in Delhi next week. We are hoping to get a toll-free helpline for it immediately. He has entrusted the responsibility to me, which I have humbly accepted. As we all know, Sethji is an inspiring and dynamic social worker. Our party is very proud of him and is solidly behind his leadership. I reach out to you on Akshay Tiwari's show – which the nation recognizes as the most important show in India – to help me in this endeavour. Sethji and I will welcome suggestions from you, dear viewers.

'Please pray that Suraj wins his battle against this demon called alcohol. As for the young girl, her dignity is far more important than sensationalizing this tragedy. I will not rest till she is strong enough to face the world with her head held high once again. With folded hands and on behalf of my parivaar, I seek your forgiveness for this unfortunate incident.'

Amrita had never looked more beautiful. Her dark eyes were bright with unshed tears, her face pale like the moon, her voice trembling. She looked fragile and vulnerable. Like a woman compelled to go public with her family's dirty secrets. No one could have imagined she had taken the biggest gamble of her life. Akshay, taken off balance by her performance, barely managed to make a recovery. 'Thank you, Amritaji, but here is my question to the audience. How should we clean up this mess? Should Sethji resign and take the blame for what his son has done? Has Suraj abused his power? Should Suraj face a fast-track trial? SMS your vote on . . .'

Amrita was bathed in sweat inside that 'cold storage', as Akshay called his studio. 'It's to cool down our hot-headed guests,' he teased her, before adding, 'With all the hardware in here, we need the pumped-up cooling systems. Sorry about that. By the way, you were brilliant! It takes guts to say what you did. Because, as I explain to some of those idiots who walk in here imagining they'll get away with lying through their teeth – what were you thinking, dude? Nothing is secret these days. Lies catch up with you sooner or later. It's all out there anyway. But you played it brilliantly, Amrita. Turning truth to lies, lies to truth. Great stuff! You even caught me off guard! Besides – for a virgin TV appearance, you were bloody good, a natural! Joint anchoring karna hai, kya? We'd make a hot team – swear, yaar. No jokes. Soch lo.' Amrita glared at him and looked away swiftly. She knew she was blushing.

Akshay laughed a lazy laugh. 'Coffee? Something else? I have a minibar in the cabin – never know when you need a shot of something stronger. I mix my whisky with anything, chai, soft drinks, even coffee.' Amrita reached for her bag. He held out his hand. 'Watch out. There will be reporters outside your home. In case you need a safe house to hide in for a few hours, call me. I mean that.' He hastily scribbled his cell phone number on a business card and handed it to her. A make-up man was waiting outside the heavy studio door with a powder puff, mirror and comb. The star anchor needed yet another touch-up.

Akshay shrugged. 'Showtime,' he mouthed and indicated with the thumb and little finger of his left hand that she should phone him. 'Take care,' he called after Amrita's retreating figure. Her bun had come undone and he noticed her cascading hair barely covered the silhouette of her breasts, visible through the thin material of her choli. Akshay noted Amrita was braless. He'd spotted her nipples. Hmmm. Something to gossip about during lunch hour . . .

The television show polls were overwhelmingly in favour of Sethji not resigning. On Twitter and Facebook he was lauded as an honest and brave father, standing by his alcoholic son, admitting his mistakes and asking for a second chance.

Meanwhile, Suraj vowed never to forgive Amrita for her 'grave mistake', which he saw all too clearly would cost him his political future. He wondered whether his ambitious sister-in-law had planned it all, the rape included. Perhaps Amrita wanted to seal Suraj's fate . . . and consolidate her own position as Sethji's successor. Amrita would control the party, become party president, fight elections, become a minister. All the things Suraj had taken as his birthright. She was capable of doing just about anything when the stakes were this high. Bitch! She had screwed him good and proper with this googly.

As for Sethji, his daughter-in-law's 'candour' on television saved his career.

CHAPTER 18

The internal party debate had ended inconclusively. The party was obviously divided. Sethji's final defence would swing the balance. He took a deep breath and got to his feet, ignoring the stiffness in his joints and the sudden blinding headache. 'Can you get me a glass of water?' he murmured to Santosh. As Santosh handed him his glass, he whispered in Sethji's ears, 'Sir, I think you should switch on Bharat News. Amritaji is on air. I think the outcome might be good.' Sethji looked at Santosh's face and realized something crucial was happening. 'Before I start, I would like you all to watch something,' he said to the members. There was a murmur of surprise in the room. Santosh had meanwhile switched on the flat screen and increased the volume.

Driving back from the Noida studio, Amrita called her father-in-law. 'Shabaash!' Sethji uttered just one short word. So he had seen her performance. Amrita felt like a schoolgirl, eagerly waiting for lavish appreciation from the headmaster. She should have known better. Sethji was stingy with praise, especially with someone close to him. He'd often told her not to do it herself. 'Praise spoils people. Gives them ideas. They start expecting praise every time they do something, big or small. It goes to their heads. No, no, no. Praise has to be carefully measured. Like a diabetic who calculates every

91

grain of sugar. Less praise works best. Keeps people on their toes.' Amrita desperately wished Sethji had broken his golden rule for once. She needed to hear she'd done a great job. But all she got out of Sethji after a great deal of prodding was a laconic 'Who taught you to lie so well?' Amrita took that as an oblique compliment. But there was also the question of womanly vanity: 'How did I look?' There was nobody else she could ask that question of. She anticipated Sethji's response, 'As you always look – badhiya.'

Sethji had obviously won that round of party elections. Amrita could tell from the jaunty tone in his gruff voice. Thank god! It had been such a tense, touch-and-go situation. Had Kavitaji beaten him this time, it would have driven Sethji into the political wilderness he feared so much. One wrong move at this stage would set Sethji's ambitions back by five years. And five years were like an eternity in politics. That would have pushed Sethji and his family out of the running, perhaps permanently. Sethji had struggled for far too long to get to this point where his party's support to the government actually counted. And it would be no problem neutralizing Kavitaji now. All Sethji had to do was offer her a grand-sounding position, with no power but plenty of false prestige.

As Sethji filled her in, Amrita could barely manage a response, drained after the drama of the last few hours. As the car approached the house, Amrita spotted the reporters and TV vans outside the gates. 'Turn around,' she instructed the driver in a panic. 'No, don't,' said Sethji from the other end of the line. 'You must face them. Ten more minutes, Amrita.' Amrita sighed and speed-dialled Srichand. He spoke in a low voice, 'Don't worry. Presswallas are here. But I have offered them chai-pani. They are waiting for you.' Amrita snapped,

'What? You offered those pests chai-pani? Are you mad? Why?' Srichand answered slowly, 'Poor people. They've been here standing in the sun since early morning. They must be thirsty and tired. I told them to wait for you. You are okay, na? Sab theek toh hai?' Srichand's voice was muted, as if there was someone right next to him, overhearing everything.

Amrita exclaimed impatiently, 'Oh god! Kya theek ho sakta hai? Anyway, leave it. I'm reaching in just a few minutes. Make sure the dogs are chained. We don't want more problems with a kutta biting a presswalla.' Putting her phone on silent mode, she told the driver to slow down a little.

She saw the camera crews whirling around and focusing on the car as the driver drew up. 'Ma'am, ma'am. This side ma'am. Amritaji, Amritaji!' Amrita held up her hand. 'I'll speak to all of you. Please, don't push and don't shout. I'm not running away anywhere, please cooperate. Thank you.'

Amrita took one look at the crowd and gauged there were at least thirty cameramen and as many reporters. This, Amrita thought smiling wryly, was what 'Breaking News' was all about these days. And Suraj's was the perfect story. Something those hungry channels would run endlessly in a loop, till another, equally juicy scandal replaced it. What a combination this scoop offered – it had it all. Sex. Power. Money. Violence.

A handsome, hot-headed man, an underage victim from the North-East, a politician-father battling to hang on to his shaky career, a beautiful bhabhi defending both. Wow! Brutal sex combined with political repercussions was the kind of fodder television channels thrived on. It was up to Amrita, how she played this one. 'No comments' was a cop-out that never really worked. Antagonizing reporters, who after all were only doing their jobs, could only misfire and was the worst strategy. Amrita decided to play ball. A good decision as it turned out.

Squaring her shoulders, Amrita faced the onslaught of questions without flinching, repeating what she had said on the show earlier. That was the other thing she had learned from Sethji – stick to the story, repeat yourself ad nauseum if you have to. But do not stray from what you have stated earlier. The original script was sacred and supreme. The smartest thing to do was bore the press. Speak monotonously. Appear mechanical and robotic. After a point the press gives up and moves on. Unable to bait Amrita to reveal anything more, the presswallas turned away to look for material elsewhere. This was a story they'd been instructed to chase relentlessly by their bosses.

It was whispered that a powerful politician was determined to embarrass Sethji. And he had persuaded his friends in news channels to go after Amrita. 'The bitch will crack under pressure,' he'd confidently stated. Instead the reporters were being stonewalled by this cold woman whose expressionless face gave nothing away. If their main source was refusing to cooperate, they would have to look for other leads. Damn. Now they'd have to interview the servants, drivers, Suraj's loafer friends and, of course, wait for the victim to go public with her version of the rape. That would be the biggie. Till then, the story would have to be kept alive somehow. It was time to chase the cops investigating the crime . . . Strange, nobody was interested in talking to Sethji. Amrita figured her father-in-law would have noticed that. Would it bother him that he was being sidelined so obviously? Would he resent Amrita's newly acquired star status and grudge it? The tables had turned a bit too suddenly.

Amrita needed the breathing space the presswallas' lack of interest provided. She knew they would return. It was too salacious a story to give up on this easily. But by then, Suraj would be safely out of the country. And Sethji, back in the saddle.

CHAPTER 19

Srichand was inside the house, waiting anxiously for his wife. 'What has happened?' he asked. 'Where is Suraj? I woke up and found you in the news. I didn't know if I was dreaming.' Amrita looked at him in a daze and fell on to a chair. Phoolrani, who understood her mistress's moods better than anyone else, immediately put a pillow behind her tired head and fetched some nimbu pani. 'Srichand, I can't talk, I am so tired. Suraj is in deep trouble. He has raped a girl. The cops are looking for him. But we have arranged his escape. Your father has won the party vote, by the way. Phoolrani, Babuji will be hungry. Make sure there is someone in the kitchen waiting for him in case he needs something.'

'You must be hungry too, let me order food,' said Srichand hastily and left the room. Amrita could be so sharp and abrupt, especially when she was exhausted like today. She terrified him! She had that effect. Even on their wedding night, when he had wanted to show her how crazy he was about her, by making love tenderly and slowly, over four or five hours, Amrita had rejected his overtures. Srichand had wanted to undress her like those bridegrooms in Hindi films, starting with lifting her heavy ghungat, and kissing her forehead. But that was not to be! In his clumsiness, he got Amrita's maang-tikka hopelessly caught in the net fabric of her raani-pink designer lehenga ensemble. Soon, her heavy jadau earrings, bangles and necklaces were also entangled in all the fabric. And Amrita was protesting in pain, calling out to Phoolrani to help her remove her wedding finery. Srichand was stricken and embarrassed as he offered to help. 'Don't touch me!' Amrita screamed angrily. Srichand obediently took her word for it and crept to a chair in the corner of their flower-bedecked bedroom, while Phoolrani gently extricated her enraged mistress from all the pins and fasteners that had held her together through the eight-hour-long ceremony.

Their disastrous wedding night had set the future pattern for the relationship. Srichand longed to just stroke his wife's beautiful breasts, rest his head on them once in a while. But he didn't dare. He fantasized about her slender, athletic thighs and imagined them wrapped tightly around his waist as he entered her smoothly, rocking her body rhythmically. But that was not to be. After a few nervous attempts, Srichand gave up altogether, and reconciled himself to a life of near celibacy. Relieved by the occasional listless, loveless, passionless sex granted by his wife and frequent masturbation on the pot with porn magazines, where he would superimpose his wife's face on the porn star featured on the centrefolds.

Touched by his devotion and passion, Amrita felt a little guilty that she could not find it within her heart to reciprocate. 'Love will come – take it from me, some day you will start feeling something for your husband. It takes time, don't worry. Eventually, feelings become a habit. Husbands also become a habit. You may not feel exactly what he feels, but you will experience your own version of love,' Amrita's mother had assured her early in the marriage. All these years later, Amrita was still waiting for 'that' feeling to happen.

But yes, Srichand was now a habit. Just another habit. Life with her husband was a lot like eating rajma with chawal on a Sunday afternoon. And today, in particular, as they sat down to a quiet dinner – after the long, difficult, exhausting day – it felt equally comforting.

CHAPTER 20

Sethji's last stop of the night was at Arun's. 'If you drank champagne, Sethji, I would have opened a bottle of my best. Today began as a disaster but it ended as a triumph. Wah! Congratulations, you have done it yet again. And as for Amrita, words fail me. She didn't listen to a single word of advice that I gave her, and she rocked.' 'Yes, Amrita was quite good today and it all went according to plan. We were lucky,' responded Sethji in his usual staccato way.

'Sometimes I think that like Draupadi she must be married to all three of you in the family, Sethji. All you three men revolve around her, whether you admit it or not, and she is devoted to you. What a woman! How fantastically she handled that cocky Akshay and all those annoying journalists,' said Arun Mehta, offering Sethji a double peg of rum, adding, 'Come on, Sethji, drink it. You need a strong one after all you've gone through today.'

Sethji shook his head and declined the offer. He chose to ignore the Draupadi reference, saying instead, 'Amrita was okay on TV. She could have been better. She is an obedient bahu and safeguards the interests of our parivaar. But she is still learning . . .' Arun laughed, 'What a guru she has. You will make a champion out of her with your training. Seriously, I have seen her mature over the years. She should think of contesting the next election. Amrita is your biggest asset, Sethji. Use her well. Amrita is the one who can easily oust that horrible creature Kavitaji. That woman has the world's worst breath. And body odour! I pity all her lovers.' Arun shuddered in an exaggerated way to underline his revulsion.

Sethji waved away the comment. 'Arun, we don't have to sleep with Kavitaji or smell her armpits. Forget it. I have come here to thank you. Suraj is a good boy. He gets a little carried away sometimes and goes a bit too far.' Arun helped himself to his Cuban Rum and said thoughtfully, 'Sethji, our relationship does not require the formality of saying thank you. That is for strangers. We are family. Our understanding is based on trust and respect. You can always count on me to stand by your side. Just as I know you will stand by mine. Right?'

Sethji grunted before replying, 'We have a good understanding, you and I. I have understood your words well. The contract will be yours. A little bit of additional pressure is needed. Some party workers are creating hurdles. But I'll manage them. There have been lower bids, but we can control all that. I need some more time. In any case the government is very happy that the coalition is intact. They will want to show their gratitude. As for Kavitaji, don't worry about that woman creating trouble. I know too much about her and those telecom contracts her nephew manages so stupidly. What are friends in the IB for? I can pull out her files any time and shut that stinking mouth for good.'

Arun's expression remained exactly as it always was – quizzical and amused. But his heart was thumping wildly at the thought of sealing this one. With the highways contract in the bag, Arun would shoot to the top of the richest Indian list – which was his ultimate if childish ambition. Nothing else mattered quite as much. If only he could see his name heading that bloody list! The most coveted list in corporate India – the much-discussed Billionaires List. Arun didn't care if it stayed there for just a few short months. He'd die a happy man. Toppling his bete noire, Jaiprakash Jethia, from that hallowed position had been Arun's obsession for years. This was his chance, and he wasn't going to miss it.

The crickets in the garden were creating a cacophony as Sethji left Arun's farmhouse and headed home.

CHAPTER 21

'Have you followed today's events?' Jaiprakash Jethia's voice was thin and sounded as if it were an adolescent's, just about to break. His falsetto was his signature. Nobody needed to ask 'Who's speaking?' when Jaiprakash called. Certainly not Bhau. 'Calm down,' commanded the man who ran Mumbai, his own voice as raspy and gravelly as ever. 'You get overexcited for nothing! What is the problem?' Jaiprakash squeaked, 'I am told that the bloody bastard Mehta is going to get the contract. It's apparently a done deal. A thank-you present from the government to that Sethji. That's the problem. Now do you understand why I'm upset?'

Bhau stroked his straggly beard and laughed. 'Bas? Itney mein teri phat gayee? Jaiprakash, have faith in me. When I give my word to someone, not even god can stop me. This is all a game. And you have fallen for their tricks. Grow up, bachchu. Your father would not like to hear you crying and complaining like a woman. We'll handle that madarchod. My sons are on the job. What did you think? We were all sleeping or what? We knew Sethji's plan well in advance. Unfortunately, that bloody bitch Kavitaji was not able to do her part well, even after taking five crore in cash from us. Not only has Sethji outsmarted her, but he has also managed to buy over one of our men in Delhi to secure his own post in the cabinet. So what. We will show them what we can do, now that it is an open yudh. You don't take tension, Jaiprakash. Your late father had high BP. You also suffer from that. Take a tablet, screw a rundi, have a drink and sleep well. Our fight begins tomorrow.' With that Bhau hung up on Jaiprakash, his old friend Jitendra Jethia's only son. A person Bhau often called his own 'third son', much to the annoyance of his biological progeny, who did not trust Jaiprakash and resented their father for 'pampering' the businessman whose interests covered mega real-estate projects along with several other industries.

Jaiprakash was born into immense wealth. He took money for granted. And he had a sense of entitlement that made him believe it was only a matter of negotiating the right price. That nothing or no one in the world was 'unpurchasable'. Honesty and uprightness genuinely puzzled him. Why would anyone want to be honest and pass up an opportunity, he'd wonder, shaking his head in astonishment.

Jaiprakash was not a handsome man (it was his grandfather who had had the matinee-idol looks), but he was vain enough to make the most of his better attributes – height and build. He worked out like a fitness fanatic twice a day. Had a phalanx of personal trainers on call round the clock (in case he felt like working on his abs at 3 a.m.), and ate like a bird – fastidiously and delicately. If he could, he would have carried tiny weighing scales with him into posh restaurants, to make sure the fancy chefs got their weights and calorie counts just so. He dressed fussily, preferring to seek out the services of a humble tailor in Old Delhi to buying designer brands or Savile Row suits. He'd laugh when asked, 'Why wear what any chootiya with money can order or buy off the peg? I like to customize my wardrobe. That way I know I am the only man in the world to possess what's on my back.'

His rivals mocked him behind his back and called him the 'Salman Khan of Corporate India'. He mocked them right back by pointing out his undisputed position – 'If I flex even one muscle, the Sensex rises or falls.' Which was largely true. Along with the rotund Mahesh Shekhawatwalla, an influential Mumbai-based ally who ran the most aggressive wealth management company in the country, Jaiprakash managed to manipulate stocks and send shock waves through the markets each time he wanted the government to pay more attention to him. Whenever the Sensex soared or tanked, investors would automatically either praise or curse Jaiprakash.

Bhau and Jaiprakash's father, Jitendra Jethia, had started their respective lives together, drunk water from the same village well in the small Konkan town of Salegaon (an unlikely place for a trader's family), and even launched a political party that didn't survive for too long. But the friendship had become cemented the day Jethia Senior saved Bhau's life during a nasty revolt within the fledgling party and taken a bullet from a country rifle in his own leg. It was an injury that led to a permanent limp – a reminder of his days as an enthusiastic, idealistic greenhorn political leader who wanted to change the world, start a revolution and gain power. Bhau stayed true to his cause and calling. But Jethia Senior moved on swiftly, after establishing a small factory to manufacture corrugated cartons for a businessman producing agarbattis for export. He grandly named his tiny manufacturing company 'Prithvi Industries', telling himself one day he would dominate the business and establish his company as a global leader in corrugated cartons.

Bhau had played a key role in helping Jethia Senior set up his first unit, by getting him the land at a throwaway price and arm-twisting the agarbatti man to place a big order with a novice. Bhau's control over his village only got enhanced over the years, as the party he had launched, abandoned and relaunched became a prominent party in Maharashtra and a key ally in the era of coalitions, when every seat counted both at the centre and in the state and was worth a lot in the formation of the government. Bhau's party could be counted on to align with just about anybody who needed those precious eight or ten seats. His powerbroking skills were legendary.

Successive prime ministers courted him time and again, with money and cabinet positions for his people. If there was one thing nobody could teach Bhau, it was the art of the deal. Though he claimed he was not a businessman but a mere party worker striving for the good of his state's abjectly poor farmers, in reality Bhau was perhaps one of the richest people in India, with an unimaginable amount of wealth, created mainly through land and mining deals and his relationship with Prithvi Industries. He had flirted briefly with telecom but realized he wasn't cut out for it, being, as he himself put it, 'a kisan and not a sciencewalla'. It was rumoured Bhau owned half of Konkan, most of Pune and nearly all of Mumbai.

Because of his relationship with Jethia Senior, Bhau regarded Jaiprakash as a member of the family. Someone he looked out for, and someone who would look out for him. Both Jethia Senior and Bhau had grown together and the more wealthy they had become, the more formidable a team they made, each enhancing the other's power. Theirs was not just a business relationship. Bhau was one of the first people to

learn of Jaiprakash's birth, and one of the last people to see
Jethia Senior on his deathbed.

Both he and Jethia had set their heart on the highways
deal. It was the most lucrative contract in the country and
could spawn countless other deals. Bhau had also planned
to divert the first part of the construction to Maharashtra
and time it for the next state elections. This megadeal would
have made them both unimaginably, obscenely rich, but this
wasn't only about wealth.

Perception was everything. Prithvi Industries was widely
regarded as the most powerful company in the country,
but with this windfall that bloody Dilliwalla Arun Mehta's
construction business would now be the biggest in the
country. Jaiprakash simply couldn't afford to be number
two in anything. This lowering of prestige would have
financial effects. Impact share prices. Valuations. His foreign
collaborations. Besides there had always been a more private
rivalry simmering between Jaiprakash and Arun Mehta over
a beautiful starlet who had left Jaiprakash to warm the bed
of the more debonair Arun. Since that debacle, Jaiprakash
had vowed to destroy both Simran and Arun.

As for Bhau, the harsh truth was that his hold over
Mumbai was dwindling rapidly. It had been dwindling for a
while. His loyal followers were aware of his eroded power
and reputation, but had nowhere left to go and nobody to
turn to. Bhau's fragile health was also a matter of concern
to the vast number of party workers who had stuck by him
for over forty years. Rivals were laughing at him openly at
rallies. Younger contenders to important party positions
were rebelling and challenging his diktats. The old methods
of bringing the city to a halt by burning buses, indulging in

arson and looting were no longer working, especially with 'uncooperative' police and stubborn municipal officers. The new chief minister hated his guts, and didn't really require his party's support in the forthcoming elections as badly as his predecessors once had. Even faithful satraps had started to question Bhau's old-fashioned style of functioning and raised a cry for younger blood to take over the party's reins. Bhau knew that was not an option. The question of abdicating his throne simply did not arise. He was realistic enough to figure out that once he was dead, so was the party.

Bhau needed to send out a strong signal that he was still the undisputed boss of Mumbai. That he still called the shots. That he was not ready to be written off. For that, he needed to shake up the city and make Mumbai take notice of him once more. Bhau needed one major development to reassert himself in the metropolis that at one time would quake at his every threat and crawl to do his bidding. The national highways project, starting in Maharashtra, was going to be his trump card. The tables had turned – so swiftly he hadn't had time to respond. But he had to. Both he and Jaiprakash had staked everything on this project. 'Let's discuss this tomorrow. We must do something, but I need to think,' was how Bhau concluded his conversation.

CHAPTER 22

There were several theories as to why Jaiprakash was such a 'pain in the ass', as his bolder business contemporaries liked to describe him. But one of those involved a stern, almost sadistic father, whose relationship with his wife and son had bordered on the psychotic. The other was his mother – Mrs J as she was called. Some said she resembled the beautiful Maharani Gayatri Devi. Others insisted Mrs J was even better looking than the legendary beauty. Both ladies conveyed class, style and good breeding in generous measure. Jaiprakash was too besotted a son to be a devoted husband to his carefully picked wife – the pale, distant and frosty Priti Rani.

It was only after Jethia Senior's death, when Jaiprakash was just twenty-four and not yet done with his studies in America, that the fortunes of their company – the Prithvi group – changed dramatically, and Mrs J came into her own. She made it her mission in life to groom the young man for his destined role as chairman of the many companies that came under the Prithvi umbrella. That she did so with enviable stealth and without ruffling the feathers of uncles, cousins and other family members was seen as her personal triumph.

Mrs J won the admiration and grudging respect of those who'd been certain the companies launched and nurtured by her husband would collapse without his dynamic leadership.

Mrs J had not just succeeded in keeping the lot together, but had consolidated the group by shutting down the non-profitable arms and reallocating resources where the returns would be substantially better. Above all else, she had shrewdly refused the chairmanship when all the members of the board unanimously voted for her to head operations – and insisted on Jaiprakash assuming that position, despite the resistance tabled by everyone, shareholders included.

But what few outside the family knew was Mrs J's deep, dark secret. For several years, even during her husband's lifetime, she had embroiled herself in a passionate relationship with her own nephew – a much younger man, whose mother was Mrs J's sister. Family elders aware of Mrs J's closeness to the intelligent, good-looking Raj worried about the role Mrs J would eventually assign to him. A role that could supersede her own son's. Mrs J had nurtured Raj's every ambition, ever since he was a teenager. Raj had moved into Mrs J's mansion when his father's small business collapsed and his mother sank into clinical depression. There he was treated like an adopted son, pampered and fawned over by the staff, adored by Mrs J's coterie of bridge-playing ladies, who'd flirt outrageously with the boy while pinching his cheeks or slapping his bottom playfully. Mrs J ensured the best for him and eventually sent him to a top American university. If Raj's presence bothered the old man or Jaiprakash, nobody ever got to hear about it.

The boys grew up in the same environment, but the age difference between them (Raj was twelve years older) kept them significantly apart. Jaiprakash, sent off to Doon School at the age of ten, came home just twice a year during vacations and that was the time Raj would return to be with his parents.

This carefully orchestrated pantomime suited everyone. Raj became the darling of Mrs J's household almost by default. His easy charm and relaxed manner, his stylish ways and sense of humour appealed to the bored men and women in Mrs J's entourage who'd indulge Raj by inviting him on their outings and holidays. As Mrs J's constant companion and escort, Raj found instant access – even acceptance – into the best circles, much to Mrs J's delight.

The exact nature of their relationship ('were they or weren't they sleeping with each other?') was not known to anyone, even though they occupied adjoining suites when they travelled, and Mrs J had stopped sharing her husband's bedroom two years after Jaiprakash's rather traumatic birth (a difficult pregnancy followed by an even more difficult delivery, given that Jaiprakash was a breech baby). Mrs J had suffered gracefully during those terrible months and when she finally delivered a son there was much celebration in the mansion. But Mrs J had also made it abundantly clear that after producing an heir to the empire, her duty towards her husband's family was over. She would continue to play a key role during festivals and other important functions, but other than 'keeping up appearances' (as she put it to her husband), she would lead her own life – discreetly, of course.

It suited everybody just fine. Her mother-in-law was the one least surprised. She had been the one to pick Mrs J as a bride for her son. And she had picked well. She knew the young girl would 'manage' and 'adapt' without embarrassing herself or anybody else. And she was right. Her own son was as passive and meek in the bedroom as he was aggressive and volatile in the boardroom. It had taken a great deal of medical intervention for Mrs J to conceive. Her mother-in-law was grateful – low sperm count ran in the family. She herself had had to work exceedingly hard in order to conceive. The two women understood each other well.

Mrs J never crossed paths with her saasuji – she didn't need to. When Jaiprakash was a teenager, the senior Mrs J more or less renounced the world and took to the foothills of the Himalayas, where she established a sylvan ashram near Ranikhet. She came down once a year during Diwali only to disappear after the last puja. If she suspected anything about her daughter-in-law's close attachment to her nephew, she said nothing at all, and treated Raj as she would her own grandson.

It was Jaiprakash who could never figure out his mother's equation with his cousin. Even as a young boy of ten or twelve, he could tell his mother's attitude towards Raj was not strictly that of a fond aunt. He'd resent the fact that Mrs J would automatically turn to Raj and not his father whenever she needed something – anything. There was nobody Jaiprakash could ask what the hell was going on.

Why was his mother so dependent on this person? Why was he living in their house? Why did his mother prefer to travel abroad with this man rather than with her husband? And why did they touch one another in such a familiar manner when they thought nobody was looking? His adoration of his mother and his confusion about her sexual mores branded his character for life. Jaiprakash never trusted anyone and he rarely imagined that things were as they appeared to be. This was what made him so powerful in business. But it also had given him a fatal flaw. Jaiprakash couldn't bear being number two to anyone.

It was only after Raj's mother committed suicide and Mrs J decided it was time to find Raj a bride that things changed in the mansion. A predictably pretty but painfully docile girl was located by lackeys for Mrs J's approval. The marriage celebrated in subdued but hugely expensive style, on the lawns of the mansion, was a signal to all those who might have wondered that the Mrs J–Raj saga was officially over. Raj and his young wife, Jwala, were packed off to set up home in Ludhiana. And Jaiprakash was officially anointed the 'Favoured One' by his mother at a lavish party during which Mrs J hung on to her young son's arm like it was an iron pillar. Jaiprakash should have felt proud and needed by the one human being whose love he craved above all else. But he'd noticed the deep pain in his mother's eyes and knew she would never ever emerge from her mourning. Her emotional life was over for good. And no matter what Jaiprakash would go on to achieve, he'd never replace Raj.

He had lost the battle for his mother's heart but he could, no, he had to, win this new battle. But how? He had tossed and turned on his black silk sheets all night, full of anger and humiliation. But it wasn't to the highways project that his mind kept returning to. It was to Simran, the beautiful, irresistible, 'Sexy Simran' who had haughtily discarded him for Arun Mehta.

CHAPTER 23

Jaiprakash met Simran at Lalji Agarwal's birthday party. Lalji was turning fifty and had decided to host 'the most lavish party on earth'. This was what his massive golden invitation card said in bold red letters. It was accompanied by a brocade-covered box filled with kaju barfi covered with a fine film of gold varq. Nobody was sure what exactly Lalji's core business was – nobody asked. But Lalji's tentacles were in diverse fields, from a budget airline to solar and wind energy. He had established a mini city named after his beloved daughter Suhani, who had died of leukaemia at the age of seven, just a few days before she was to be shifted for treatment to America.

Lalji had blamed himself for her untimely death – he had postponed the trip by a month since he had local elections to deal with and a fresh government contract to negotiate. 'I killed Suhani, my precious Suhani,' he would wail after consuming his fifth Red Label (not Black, his valet would smirk and inform first-time visitors to his marble palace built on the edge of an artificial lake which had artificial swans and flamingoes dotting it rather ludicrously). After Suhani's death, Lalji had focused aggressively on becoming the biggest player in the markets, trading in mining stocks and rapidly expanding his assorted businesses.

Soon enough, his son Ajit Pratap had been married off to an Agarwal girl from a 'good' family and produced a grandson to carry Lalji's name forward. But it was Suhani's memory that haunted him. It was Suhani's name that was used for all acquisitions. It was Suhani Nagar that Lalji developed. It was Suhani Airlines that offered cheap fares to passengers flying across India. Getting into Bollywood with Suhani Productions was just another business for Lalji.

On the night Jaiprakash arrived at Suhani Nagar he had joined a queue of over five hundred 'well-wishers' waiting patiently to get inside the heavily guarded venue, past the sniffer dogs, gun-wielding guards, metal detector screens and special booths reserved for women. He'd noted with interest the helicopters as they hovered over the helipad especially created beyond the car park for the party. 'Big, big people are coming from Delhi,' someone whispered. 'Madamji has promised to grace the occasion . . . so has the CM.' Overhearing this awestruck chatter, Jaiprakash had smiled to himself.

Once inside the venue, Jaiprakash had got quickly bored as he always tended to with the small talk and chit-chat. He had wandered around the immense lawn and found himself in a small enclosure where a stage was being set up. What is that for, he asked someone. The man's eyes lit up. 'Oh . . . don't you know? Lalji has hired top Bollywood stars to dance at his birthday. All big-big names. He has spent ten . . . no . . . twenty crore on this.' Even Jaiprakash with his vast fortune had been impressed. Seeing his expression, the man nodded his head thoughtfully. 'Yes, yes, yes, I know, I wouldn't . . . you wouldn't . . . others wouldn't . . . but that is why we are who we are . . . chhotey dilwaley . . . chhotey log . . . not

Lalji. Unka kya style hai! He is larger than life . . . this is just the beginning. Today he owns all this . . . tomorrow he will own Bollywood. Mark my words.'

Technicians were testing the arrangements, doing sound and light checks near the stage as Jaiprakash strolled around. The worker grinned. 'You can watch the dancers getting ready backstage if you are interested.' Jaiprakash pretended he hadn't heard. 'Did you hear what I just said? But these are just those groupwalli girls. The big stars are getting ready in those vans over there.' Jaiprakash followed the man's gaze. Five long, sleek vans were parked in a row that blocked off the path leading to a sugar cane field nearby. Tracks of tall cane had been cut to create the space for the vans. Just as another field had been cleared of its mustard crop to carve out a makeshift helipad.

Jaiprakash walked slowly towards the vans, aware of the heavy police protection positioned on both sides of the narrow, rough road. When he was more than fifty metres away, he was abruptly stopped by a large man wearing a blue safari suit. 'Who are you? Where are you going?' the man demanded. Jaiprakash folded his hands and smiled. 'I am Lalji's special friend. I have been sent to welcome our guests from Bollywood.' The man stared suspiciously at Jaiprakash and talked into a walkie-talkie, 'Is your name Durgadas? Are you the man from Suhani Air who handles Lalji's private jet schedules?' Jaiprakash smiled mischievously. 'Thank god you at least know that much. Now please, let me pass. I have a lot of responsibility. Mehmaan jo hai. Chai-pani, vaghera. And there isn't much time left.' He moved swiftly past the man and towards the vans. Jaiprakash enjoyed playing pranks. He'd done it in the past, impersonating strangers. He'd tell himself it was a harmless diversion that amused him. But this time it was different and Jaiprakash was caught off guard for once. For he ran into Simran just ahead of the security cordon.

'Hato . . . saaley kuttey. Take your hands off me, you bloody rabid dogs. How dare you touch me? Don't you know who I am?' Jaiprakash's eyes fell on a young, over-made-up girl, dressed in a funny-looking blue outfit. She was striking in an odd sort of way, with a mop of wiry curls. He noticed she was wearing knee-high boots with metal heels, and while struggling with the guards, one of the heels had broken, making her limp as she tried to get away from the jeering men. Her blue handbag was lying on the ground, and some tinsel flowers pasted on it had broken off and were lying scattered over the muddy field.

Jaiprakash walked up briskly towards her, shouting, 'Yeh kya ho raha hai? Kaun hai yeh aurat?' The security men turned to him and said brusquely, 'She's some bloody whore who's trying to lagao a line on the heroes inside the van. Do paisey ki rundi . . . we are here to protect the stars. But this kutti is an untamed bitch . . . she won't listen.' Jaiprakash looked at the woman and said in an authoritative voice, 'I am Durgadas. I represent Lalji. You can come to me and tell me your problem. Are these men troubling you? Who do you want to meet?' Simran screamed, 'These dogs are mad! I don't want to meet any hero-sheero. I am Natasha's school friend. Tell her Simran from Savitri Devi Mahavidyalaya wants to meet you. She will remember for sure. We used to share our lunch, sit next to each other on the same bench and pluck raw mangoes from the tree in the compound. Tell these dogs I am a dancer from the superhit *Mithi Mithi*.'

Jaiprakash laughed. 'You look too young to be doing all

this, but leave it to me to sort it out.' He turned to the guards and asked sharply, 'Which one of you is Miss Natasha's bodyguard? Step forward and take this girl to madam's van immediately. Please tell madam that Durgadas is here. I was the person who flew Natashaji from Mumbai this morning. Jaldi karo. Jao!' One of the burly men approached Simran and hissed, 'I am doing this because this sirji has told me to, varna toh . . .'

Jaiprakash looked at Simran and smiled. 'Don't worry, babyji. Ask for Durgadasji if anything goes wrong. I'll be somewhere around.' He smiled to himself. How easy it was to fool the world if you played the role convincingly enough!

As Simran walked away, Jaiprakash felt a strange, empty feeling in the pit of his stomach. Suddenly, he had no further desire to be at the party. His heart had been stolen. He walked out of the glittering venue without bothering to meet anybody else – not even the birthday boy. That night, as the coloured laser beams from Lalji's party criss-crossed the sky, Jaiprakash found himself awake, next to his sleeping wife, wondering whether Simran had managed to meet Natasha.

His thoughts were on Simran's broken heel. How would the poor girl dance with those shoes? Would she end up twisting her ankle? That slim, fair ankle he'd glimpsed beneath her stunning blue dress, which had climbed up to her thighs during that unnecessary struggle with those bullies. Poor thing. Life was so tough for her. Jaiprakash wanted to help her in whichever way he could. But in order to do that, he would have to locate her. Immediately. There was no time to waste. Simran must be saved, he told himself.

CHAPTER 24

The first time Jaiprakash slept with Simran, he was a bit surprised to note the tiny size of her breasts, which were pert with taut nipples, but belonged to a pre-pubescent girl. Simran noted his expression when she took off her shirt, and laughed. 'Small! My tits are really, really small. That's what you are thinking, I know. Most men react the same way.' Jaiprakash waved his hand in embarrassment as if to say, 'Oh, don't be silly. Why would I think that?' Simran continued to remove her clothes slowly while chattering animatedly. 'You know why men feel so surprised? Because they look big when I'm dancing on the screen. Stupid fellows! Haven't they heard of padded bras?' Jaiprakash was instantly attracted to Simran's infectious candour. Later in their relationship, he generously offered her a boob job. 'You can do it in London. Nobody will find out,' he said quietly. But Simran surprised him yet again by turning him down. 'No, no no. I like my sweet little titties. Why should I change them? But if you want to pay for a nose job, I'm game.' Jaiprakash laughed. 'But I like your button nose! It's so cute!'

Simran was no beauty. But she managed to stand out because of her overtly sexy body language and provocative attitude. Like most compulsive attention-seekers, she knew her inadequacies ('small tits, big butt') and camouflaged

118

them expertly. Her wild, untamed curls framed a heart-shaped face with large, lustrous dancing eyes and lips that were so prominent men could only think of oral sex. Simran was proud of her narrow waist ('my patli kamar'), and accentuated it with broad belts. Her hands were tiny, with well-shaped, expressive and elegant fingers. They didn't go with the rest of her wildcat personality. And if there was one trait that men either loved or loathed about this spirited wench it was her refusal to remove body hair – bushy armpits, pushy pubes, hairy arms and legs. 'Forget it!' Simran would retort if someone pointed out the obvious, 'Love me, love my hair.'

On that first night, Simran had looked thoughtfully at him and asked seriously, 'Do you like to do it doggy style? I'm told I'm good at it. But I'm cool with whatever . . . the idea is to fuck, right? Front, back, sideways, who cares?' And that established their pattern. They did it any which way that grabbed their fancy. Simran was entirely uninhibited and giving. Jaiprakash had never encountered such openness, such invention. Simran introduced him to sex toys and recreational drugs which she insisted would lead to 'phataphat orgasm. Guaranteed, boss.' There was nothing she wouldn't do to make sure both of them emerged from sexual romps feeling energized and wonderful. 'That is why Bhagwan has given us bodies. To enjoy them and have fun. Why keep anything in cold storage? You like fucking. I like fucking. We make a good match.' She was right. And Jaiprakash was getting addicted to her body with the small tits. This was dangerous.

For the next two years, Simran became something of a regular in Jaiprakash's entourage. She was known as Jaiprakash's special assistant. Nobody questioned the absurdity of such a claim. If Jaiprakash's staff or even family found the pantomime more than ridiculous, they knew better than to open their mouths. Simran would flit in and out of his office (though never his home). She often travelled with him and played an attentive hostess. Since her status was nebulous and undefined she could be whatever anybody thought her to be – Jaiprakash's mistress, relative or personal assistant. After a point, it didn't matter. Simran became family. An integral part of Jaiprakash's inner circle.

His cronies were beginning to worry. Simran could become inconvenient in the future. Maybe she had been sent by enemies to spy on him? Get secrets out? Place bugs and recording devices in the hotel suites they met in for their sex romps? Tap his phone calls? Anything was possible these days. And what was Simran? Just another item girl from Bollywood, trying her luck with a big fish. They needn't have worried for too long. The Simran chapter would end soon enough.

It was the day before Jaiprakash's wedding anniversary. Jaiprakash had a cordial but unamorous relationship with his wife, who allowed him to have his affairs as long as they weren't thrown in her face. One thing was clear. Jaiprakash's lovers never came home nor met his close-knit group of friends. That was the understanding. His wife's restraint and quiet dignity reminded Jaiprakash of his own beautiful mother, and although he felt no passion for her, he had always treated his wife with respect and affection and played by her rules. Theirs was a good marriage if not a faithful one. On his tenth anniversary Jaiprakash had bought her a superb jewellery set from Van Cleef and Arpels at a Christie's auction in Hong Kong. Enormous emeralds, with a dark fire in their green depths, surrounded by flawlessly cut diamonds. These were the jewels of a European aristocrat and he had planned a large party for her to display them for the first time.

When a malicious secretary told Simran all the juicy details about Jaiprakash's anniversary plans, the young woman couldn't contain her anger. Jaiprakash had just a weekend ago taken her off to a private island off the coast of Malaysia where they had barely got out of bed. He had never been so aroused by anyone, he had said to her that weekend in a fit of passion. Heady with the power she had over him, Simran foolishly decided to push her luck and break the ultimate rule – she stormed into his house and confronted him over the anniversary plans even as the Parisian florist was haggling over the price of off-season peonies. Luckily Jaiprakash's wife was away when 'Sexy Simran' arrived.

Simran had miscalculated. And miscalculated badly. She didn't realize the inappropriateness of her demand, thrown brazenly at Jaiprakash just as he was mentally gearing up to pay homage to his marriage and his gentle wife. Simran had burst into the room and hollered in a voice that startled the dogs, 'How dare you buy that bloody bitch those jewels? Has she done some jadu on you?' Jaiprakash, an extremely controlled man, couldn't contain himself. 'Shut your filthy mouth, you slut. How dare you spoil my mood, that too on a day like this? Don't you have any shame?' Simran stood with her arms akimbo, chin defiantly out and said, 'Suddenly you remember your precious wife and belittle me? Where does your memory go when you weigh me down under your body and shove it in, huh? You forget your wife at that point, don't you? Or when you ask me to suck, suck, suck, you bloody swine!'

Jaiprakash lunged at Simran with all the force of an enraged bull. Simran deftly ducked his swinging right arm. Jaiprakash lost his balance and came crashing down against the glass tea tray on which lay his untouched tea, with a handful of almonds. The florist had hastily scrambled out by then. The sound was loud enough to attract the attention of a passing servant who rushed in to find Jaiprakash sprawled across the worn carpet, groaning loudly and cursing Simran, with his dogs licking his face sympathetically. That closed the Simran chapter; but not for long. Simran, who had walked out without a backward glance, had already started thinking about Plan B.

The day after the big anniversary party, Jaiprakash had gone to Simran's flat. In his hand was the unmistakable blue Tiffany's box with a set of exquisite rare coloured diamonds. He'd assumed that was all the apology he needed. Instead Simran's maid had insisted she wasn't home. Jaiprakash had charged inside, barging into Simran's dressing room. To his horror he found her in the arms of another man – Arun Mehta. As he stormed out, Simran's coarse and triumphant laughter and the image of Arun's smug smile played in his head over and over again. Arun Mehta would have to be finished, Jaiprakash had vowed that day. He'd need his family friend Bhau's help for that.

CHAPTER 25

Bhau had reluctantly agreed to meet Jaiprakash at a farmhouse off the Mumbai–Pune expressway to discuss their next move. It was widely known that Bhau did not like to leave his sprawling rajwada in central Mumbai. Some said he was paranoid that his enemies from Mumbai's dreaded underworld would kill him. Others thought it was arrogance ('Let the world come to me'). But this time even Bhau was shaken enough by Sethji's audacity to leave his heavily guarded den and climb into a sturdy SUV accompanied by four gunmen and his younger son, Aadesh. The three-hour drive to Pune was kept top secret from party aides and loyalists ('Why take a chance?'), and when Bhau arrived at a modest farmhouse on the outskirts of the city, nobody could have guessed a crime was being planned, or that Jaiprakash would be forced to stoop to this level in order to bag a contract. Bhau laughed at his misgivings. 'That man Sethji is a nuisance. We have swatted bigger flies without a problem in the past. We can do it very easily . . . I have a plan. So there is only one question to answer. Kill or kidnap?' Even though Jaiprakash was used to Bhau's abrupt ways, he was startled into silence.

Bhau continued, 'Why kill him? A dead Sethji is of no use to us. His party will break up. They will be worth nothing to the coalition. And the contract still won't be in our hands.

We need Sethji to cooperate and join hands with us. He will
have to throw Arun Mehta into the nearest kachre ka dabba.
After that, we can celebrate Diwali. Let Sethji come into
our territory, and then we'll see how he opens his mouth.
Saaley ki gaand phata dengey.' Jaiprakash wasn't entirely
convinced. But he was in a blind rage, his judgement clouded.
Reluctantly, he said, 'Okay, Bhau saab. If it has to be done,
why waste time?'

As it turned out, the plan to abduct Sethji was not all
that simple. It involved an immediate kidnapping. It had
to look like the slightly clumsy work of local adversaries.
Petty rivals put up by the Kavitaji faction, perhaps. Nothing
terribly sophisticated or high-tech for this job. Nothing that
could link the kidnapping plot to the bungled-up contract,
which had fallen into Arun Mehta's lap with such ease.
Bhau had already identified the men who would carry out
the job.

There were any number of desperate fellows from Uttar
Pradesh, Bihar, even Orissa, who'd undertake the mission
and execute it well. This was a brand new profession now.
An exciting career option. Unemployed, frustrated men could
be hired to do almost anything – kidnapping, blackmail,
murder. And his plan didn't end with kidnapping Sethji alone.
His two sons had to be taken care of as well. Including
Suraj, that rapist who had managed to escape across the
border. Bhau's men would track him down wherever he was
hiding. The other fellow, Srichand, was a harmless fellow.
A sitting duck. He could be picked up any time. It was that
woman, the imperious Amrita, who'd be harder to control.
But Bhau concluded that he'd leave her with no choice. She'd
have to cooperate, and join the men of her parivaar. Or get

killed. Bhau was ready. Nor did Jaiprakash hesitate for a second. 'Let's do it!' was all he said.

* * *

When the goons descended on Shanti Kutir late in the morning, Sethji was sitting on his favourite moodah, feet tucked under his bottom. He looked comical perched so precariously on that frayed stool made out of river reeds. But oddly enough it had always been his favourite seat, especially in that vast open corridor outside his bedroom. This is where he got his hair cut, his toenails clipped. This is also where Bholanath his old barber gave him all the gossip while he shaved him with an old-fashioned cut-throat razor. Whoever wished to talk to him at this hour was compelled to stand around the moodah and nobody was allowed to pull up a chair – that was Sethji's rule.

After the drama at the party headquarters, Sethji wanted a break. And the only break Sethji ever took was to visit his village. 'Let's go back, I'm missing Mirpur,' he told Amrita that day. 'Tell Srichand he'll have to miss golf this weekend. We'll drive there. It's the mango season. Get the SUV ready.' Amrita had gone looking for Srichand but hadn't found him anywhere. 'Have you seen your son anywhere?' she asked her father-in-law. But he had no time to answer.

A car drove into the driveway at great speed. Four men emerged from the vehicle and rushed into the office room. Amrita walked up to them briskly and asked, 'May I help you?' They ignored her completely and started to ransack the place, flinging chairs around and throwing the contents of the desk drawers on the floor as if they were looking for something specific.

Amrita had witnessed these scenes earlier and concluded this was nothing but an act to intimidate and terrorize their victims. For men of this kind already had the information they needed in hand. Vandalism was an old tactic – sometimes she even thought Sethji himself orchestrated these periodic 'incidents', perhaps to buy time for some bigger deal, or even just to send out a strong signal to his sons, especially the 'motherless boy'. But somehow, this time round, it didn't look staged to Amrita and her confidence suddenly turned into fear.

In the meantime another two cars had driven up and four more men had got out. The goons moved swiftly. In a few short minutes they'd bundled Sethji into one of the waiting Ambassador cars with tinted glasses. He'd shown neither surprise nor rage. Nor had he struggled. As Amrita began to scream for help, someone grabbed her from behind, gagged her mouth and dragged her into the second car. Within ten minutes, the cars had zoomed out of the bungalow, leaving the terror-struck servants gaping from behind the khus curtains. It was the perfect operation.

In the midst of the chaos and terror, Amrita noticed two things. Sethji's personal security guards had timed their chai break perfectly. Not one of them was around when their employer needed them the most. And she thought she recognized one of the men who'd hustled Sethji into the car. She remembered him from a late-night meeting she'd attended with Sethji in the Presidential Suite of a five-star hotel where a high-profile industrialist from Mumbai was staying. The man she'd spotted had been a part of Jaiprakash Jethia's entourage. Why and how was Jaiprakash Jethia involved? And what did it mean?

If he had personally led the attack on Sethji, the matter had to be serious, and somewhere in this complex maze, it was Suraj who was going to pay for it. For it had to be Suraj, impetuous and hot-headed, who'd started the war. A war that would spare nobody. Least of all Sethji.

* * *

Jaiprakash's call to Arun Mehta was brief and to the point. 'Sethji ko bhool jao. Forget the bloody buddha. Forget whatever he has promised you. The deal's off. So, Mr Mehta, you can go back to your laundas and get them to jerk you off, you bloody homo.' He didn't give Arun the chance to respond. One sharp click and the conversation was terminated.

Arun tried to call Sethji, then Amrita, then Sethji again, then Amrita. Even that buffoon Srichand. All three phones were switched off. This was serious. He called his cop contact. Blank. Nobody knew what had happened to Sethji. Bad news, Arun concluded, banging the onyx coffee table with his fist. 'Fuckkkk!' he hollered and Tinu, his favourite valet, danced up to him gracefully to ask, 'Sirrrrji, everything okieeee?' Arun bellowed, 'No! Dammit, nothing is okieeee. Shut the fuck up and get the hell out. I have to find Sethji.' Arun suppressed the urge to throw a Ming vase at the French windows. Instead, he reached for the phone and called one of his legal eagles. 'Fix that bastard Jethia. Block him, whatever it takes. Go through the highways contract thoroughly. If there are any loopholes, plug them.' All he could do now was wait.

Part 2

'There is poison in the fang of the serpent, in the mouth of the fly and in the sting of a scorpion; but the wicked man is saturated with it.'

—Kautilya

CHAPTER 26

The last city in India Sethji wanted to be in was Mumbai – he loathed the place. It was too vast and too fast. Mumbai also had a special smell that you either hated or loved. It smelt of rot. Rotting fish, rotting garbage, rotting buildings, rotting people. The stench hit you as soon as you made your acquaintance with the largest, most bewildering and chaotic metropolis in India.

But here he was. In a city he had always detested. A city filled with alien 'budtameez' people who spoke a crude language they insisted was Hindi. For the first time in his life Sethji was stumped. He felt like someone had dragged him into a blind alley and was about to rape him. He'd gone over the kidnapping in his mind. It couldn't have been Kavitaji or her supporters. He had sorted her out very generously. He wasn't obliged to create a post for her, but he had done so without her even asking. She also knew her time would come one day, she could wait. The method involved in the kidnapping was deliberately misleading. Too obvious. Too staged. Too amateurish.

If not Kavitaji and her cohorts, then who? More important, why? Weary and annoyed, Sethji shifted uncomfortably in the back seat of a far-from-spacious car. He was blindfolded but his senses were on full alert. He knew it was an extremely

131

professional and sophisticated job that had been made to look like a rough raid. Insiders would have had to have been involved; otherwise why hadn't any of his own security guards come out to help? He'd slice off their balls on his return, and hang them up in the durwan's cabin, he swore to himself. Bloody namakchor, haramis of the worst kind. Paid off by some passing pimp. Ready to sell their employer . . . he'd show them. They had wives and daughters. Yes, he'd show them the meaning of betrayal.

No one spoke to him during the car ride. Nor was he manhandled in any way. These men were clearly out to deliver him to someone. And lastly there was one man in the car who was using very expensive, imported aftershave – the sort of aftershave Suraj or his friends would have worn. But Sethji knew two things. These were no ordinary UP hoodlums. And there was no point protesting. The men in here were killers. Hitmen who wouldn't hesitate to blow his brains out if he didn't cooperate.

Sethji groggily tried to reconstruct a few of the details after he had been picked up from Shanti Kutir in such a dramatic way. His mouth had been gagged, his feet and hands tied, and a rough gamcha had covered his eyes. The convoy had sped off at such a speed, there had been no way of judging where it was headed. But one thing Sethji could remember clearly was that the car he was being held in, judging by the decreasing sounds of traffic, seemed to have moved away from Central Delhi and, after an hour and a half of high-speed driving, it had stopped. He was led out, gently but firmly, and from the sudden gust of wind that lifted up the edge of his kurta, and the sound of powerful engines purring, he sensed he was on an airstrip, very close to an aeroplane . . . not a chopper. No doubt a private one. Sethji preferred trains (he was afraid of flying). Soon he was inside the plane, and before he could react, someone had jabbed him with a needle. Saaley kuttey. Drugging an old man, he'd fix these bastards, too, he thought to himself as he drifted into sleep.

When he awoke, he was in this car, still blindfolded. But the driver had opened his window briefly and he knew instantly where he was. The smell! It had to be Mumbai. The stench was exactly as Sethji remembered it from that trip long ago, when Mumbai was Bombay, and the bhais ran the show. Sethji had been a maamuli hired gun at that time. And somehow, Bombay's bhai culture hadn't appealed to him. One minor hit later, he was back where he belonged – Delhi. He began to try and piece the earlier events together and figure out who was behind this audacious act.

It was someone with power, influence and money – a private plane was involved – and someone who was unhappy about his victory of the previous day. The timing of the kidnapping was too much of a coincidence. This person had to be someone who hadn't gained by Arun's bagging of the highways contract. But that still didn't explain this ridiculous journey – what was the Mumbai connection? In his semi-conscious, doped-out state, his thoughts turned to Amrita. Where was she? Was she all right? He had a feeling that she had also been on the flight with him and was being brought in another car. And what about Srichand? At least Suraj was safe in Dubai, no doubt drinking and whoring his way through the night. That reckless boy still had to learn a lesson.

Soon the car stopped, he was led up some stairs and then he was in a cold, dank room. His blindfold was taken off. Slowly orienting himself, he saw that it was a small space with a bed and a fan and an attached bathroom. There was an unknown man standing by the door. He was tall and was dressed neatly in a clean shirt and trousers. The stranger was smirking, like he was getting a kick out of Sethji's obvious discomfort. After a minute or two, Sethji drew himself up to his full height and bellowed, 'Do you know who I am? I am Sethji. Suna? SETHJI! A very powerful man. You won't be spared.'

The stranger shrugged carelessly. 'Don't waste your time trying to scare me. And don't fuck with me, old man. The tables have turned. You are now in my territory, this is my mohalla . . . and you will do as I tell you. I have thrown away your dabba of a cell phone and you no longer have access to anyone – not even your beloved bahu! Understand? I have ordered food for you in the room. You will go nowhere and speak to nobody till I tell you. That could take two days or two months. This is not Dilli, Sethji. Nobody cares and nobody knows who you are here. In Mumbai things work differently. You are in Mumbai. Understand? MUMBAI!' 'Where is Amrita? I want my bahu.' The man sneered. 'Don't worry, Sethji, your bahurani is fine – and so are your two sons. We have great respect here for our netas and their families, don't worry!' With these words, the man left. Alone in the smelly, dimly lit room, Sethji experienced a brand new emotion – fear.

CHAPTER 27

The skyline outside Sethji's small window in that seedy place was all he had for company. He had still not come close to knowing who was behind the act, but he learned a few other things. He knew he was in some cheap guest house and his shrewd guess was that Amrita had been dragged along with him and was in another room. He hadn't once been beaten up or abused in any form – and since that brief exchange he had had with the tall stranger on the first day, no one had spoken to him. His hope was that Amrita too was being given the same treatment. And so were Suraj and Srichand – wherever they were. Sethji waited. He knew better than to make a hasty move. The stranger was right. This was Mumbai. Sethji knew nobody. Worse, he was a nobody here.

His mind was restless and his body reluctant to adjust to the small, dank room. He looked out of the window, and saw sheets of rain pelting down. It was going to be the worst mid-monsoon storm of the season. Year after year, Mumbai would be caught off guard on days when it rained torrentially, choking all the drains. High tides would add to the mess, with water from the turbulent sea flowing right back into the low-lying areas of the city and flooding the suburbs with the thigh-high rivers of filth.

Sethji wondered what was going on in Delhi during his

absence. What about the party? Elections? Money collection? Had most of his workers defected, now that there was nobody to lead them? Had Kavitaji dared to raise her head again? Usurped his kursi and position? What was the speculation in Delhi? That he had run away like a scared bloody chootiya? At other times he'd switch off totally and stare moodily at those gleaming high-rises in the distance, wondering what sort of people lived in such tall buildings. Didn't they feel giddy when they looked down from that height? What a life it must be, he sighed.

He would gaze at the labyrinthine lanes of the gigantic slum which had crawled right up to the very edge of the high-rise complex. He'd watch people going about their chores which often started before daybreak. Mumbai was such an insanely busy city, Sethji concluded. Do people here ever stop? To live a little? Love a little? Where's the time for that? Even tiny kids with oversized bags on their narrow backs were rushing off somewhere – to school? To work? There wasn't an idle human being in sight. What about those men in brightly striped underwear sleeping in the shade of their hand carts at noon?

They looked like they were taking a shockingly short break before resuming back-breaking, tedious labour, loading their haath-gaadis with all sorts of goods and delivering them several kilometres, negotiating those long, cumbersome wooden hand carts past the craziest traffic in the world! Sethji wondered how many people got killed on those dangerously congested roads. Did anybody even notice or care? Aah . . . life was cheap in Mumbai. Dirt cheap. But at least it wasn't boring! The way he was. He was boring now. Even to himself. Never before in his life had he felt this helpless, this powerless, this useless!

But even as he looked out of the window in despair, he was thinking of a way out. He noticed that the kidnap operation was efficiently run. Regular vegetarian meals were well taken care of – but any attempt to engage the young waiter who brought him his food in a conversation was abruptly cut short. The instructions were clear – conversation was not allowed. Once Sethji overheard the waiter telling the cleaning boy, 'Buddha paagal hai. Don't talk to him or he may turn violent.' So that was it! The staff had been told that Sethji was a dangerous lunatic who had to be left strictly alone! Sethji began to marvel at his captor's twisted thinking. 'Ulti khopdi,' he termed it. Secretly he was pretty impressed. At least this fellow had brains and balls.

The only person who could help him was the only person who had any contact with him – the young waiter who gave him his daily meals. On the second day, Sethji tapped the young waiter who had brought him his thali and said, in Hindi, 'I want to get out of here – help me.' The boy pretended to be deaf. Sethji tried again. This time the boy said nervously, 'My orders are to not speak to you. Please, saab. Don't ask me for anything.' Hearing the boy's distinct accent and his giveaway diction, Sethji asked him, 'Are you from Uttar Pradesh? Border of Bihar? That small town called Sonapur?' The boy looked startled as he said, 'Yes! Yes! But how did you guess, saab?' Sethji knew he'd made a breakthrough. 'From your sweet tongue! The way you speak! I have been longing to hear our language ever since I've come to this horrible city where nobody speaks shuddh bhasha. I am from a nearby village myself, Mirpur, do you know it?'

The boy nodded with a faraway look in his eyes. 'You are too young to be so far away from your people, your village, your home, your mother. Tell me, son, how did you get to Mumbai?' The boy shrugged. 'I came to see my favourite star – the man I can give my life for – Armaan Khan. I had to run away from home in the middle of the night, spend three days taking buses and trains. That's how I came here.'

Sethji made sympathetic cluck-cluck noises with his tongue, pointed heavenwards and declared dramatically, 'God's will!' The boy stared nervously at the door. 'I have to go. They told me you were a paagal buddha. But you are not mad at all. Please hurry up and finish your food or the boss will send someone to look for me.' Sethji smiled. 'I would have given you a good tip, but I don't have any money.' The boy said, 'You are like my grandfather. I wouldn't have taken money from you. Okay. See you tomorrow. And please don't tell anyone I spoke to you or I'll lose my job. As it is we North Indians face so many problems here in Mumbai.' Sethji shook his head understandingly. 'Don't worry, son. You can trust me.'

As the boy was cleaning the table with a duster he'd been fiddling with nervously, Sethji leaned forward and whispered urgently, 'If you can get me out of here, I will reward you handsomely. Do you have a mobile phone?' The boy shook his head. 'Saab, I cannot afford such a luxury!' Sethji caught him by the shoulders. 'Get me a mobile phone, son! I need to make just one phone call – one! If you do this much for me, I will personally go to your village and build a new house for your mother! A new temple for the village. I am a very rich man. That is why those badmashes have taken me prisoner. They are after my money. I have lots of it. Lots! You can work for me once I get out of here. I'll double your salary. Kasam se!

'You may not realize it, but I am a very powerful man. And

listen, I will also make your other dream come true! Armaan's chachu is from my village – really! Kasam se! Once I have a phone, all it will take is a call to chachuji and he will fix up a meeting for you with Armaanji – that too, in Armaanji's house, not in a studio.' The boy was shaking. Sethji couldn't tell whether this was out of excitement at the prospect of meeting his superhero or the fear of being found out as the stupid waiter who spoke to the 'paagal buddha'.

Sethji impatiently waited for the next day and the young waiter he'd befriended to show up again. But the boy who brought up his food was a stranger who refused to acknowledge him. 'Where's the other fellow?' Sethji asked in desperation. The waiter ignored the question, banged down the steel thali and left the room.

CHAPTER 28

There was just one way out of this hell, Sethji decided. And that was to declare a fast unto death. He'd stop eating. And that would bring them to their senses. Total hartal. Non-cooperation. Just like Gandhiji. Sethji's resolve collapsed on the same day itself, when the waiter produced piping hot gulab jamuns in the evening. Someone had done their homework and knew Sethji's weakness for the syrupy, sickeningly sweet speciality, and given the waiter extra money to walk across the street and get a plate of gulab jamuns from the halwai's shop.

One look at the dark brown, deep fried balls of flour – plump and soaked in rose syrup – and Sethji's willpower collapsed instantly. He pounced on the sweetmeat and polished off both gulab jamuns in under a minute. The waiter laughed. 'Sir was absolutely right. He knew you wouldn't be able to say no to this!' Sethji glared at the light-skinned Nepali boy and hollered, 'Bloody chikna, saala gandu, teri phata doonga. Get out of here.'

The fast may have ended but something worse happened. Sethji's body that night was racked with high fever. He couldn't stop shivering even under two heavy blankets. The fan was off. The hot air inside the small rooms was oppressive in its stillness. Sethji felt drained of all energy as he tossed and turned. He was breathing with difficulty and

140

sweating profusely. The thin bedsheets were soaked with his perspiration. He needed water. He needed someone. He needed Amrita.

The hazy image in front of his half-shut eyes was that of his bahu. She was smiling for a change. Her gaze was softer than he'd ever known it, as she looked at him and gestured with her hand, as if to say, 'Follow me.' He could sense her presence. He could smell her fragrance. He could feel her touch on his fevered brow. Amrita was there. He knew it. She was close by. She had come here to save him, protect him, take him away, take him home. Rescue him from a demon. Sethji was delirious. Malaria had claimed one more victim in Mumbai.

Had it not been for the immediate medical care, Sethji would have died that night itself. When he opened his eyes, all he could see was a grimy ceiling fan whirring noisily over his head. His first word was: 'Amrita.' His head was spinning and he'd never felt this weak in his entire life. Even the small effort required to keep his eyelids from falling over his eyes tired him out. He tried lifting his hand and gave up. In any case, it would have been difficult, given the IV that was dripping into his vein.

He was delirious, and dehydrated. As he lay still, his mind playing games with him, he imagined his dead wife was pottering around the room scolding him for neglecting his health. He thought he could smell gobar drying outside the old village home. He was sure he heard the crackle of dried wood burning as the evening meal was being prepared on an open choolha. He longed to taste home-made ghee made from hand-churned white butter. At times his wife resembled Amrita. At other times, Amrita was wearing his wife's old cotton sari. Was Srichand crying? Was nobody guarding the baby as he played in the baked mud courtyard? Was Amrita the woman who was pregnant with Suraj? No. That was not possible. It must have been his wife. But she was dead. Was she dead? Or was it Amrita who had died?

Sethji's head was getting heavier. He was feeling drowsier. Now there were voices in the room. The voices were getting closer. He felt a cool hand on his forehead as a stranger's deep voice said, 'It's okay. He'll be fine. But he needs complete rest. Good, clean food, a full-time nurse, fruits. He needs to eat. If he won't, then keep him on the drip. Remember he needs to be kept alive no matter what. Bhagwan ne bachaa diya, nahin toh buddha mar jaata. Mumbai ka malaria is khatarnaak – just like the city. One bite kaafi hai.'

There was a piece of singularly good news, however. He overheard a scrap of a vital conversation inadvertently. It was when the waiter talked about the 'madam' next door repeatedly demanding nimbu pani. It had to be her! Amrita! Suddenly, Sethji felt stronger, more optimistic, even elated! She was here! Amrita was just a few feet away from him. What a relief. She would think of a way out. Amrita always did. With her next to him, he could take on the world. He had nothing to fear. This nightmare would end soon enough. And they'd go back to Delhi together. It would be fine, they'd resume their lives, and Amrita would take care of him in Shanti Kutir – their home.

CHAPTER 29

Sethji had guessed correctly about Amrita. She was indeed in the adjoining room and it was she, and not Sethji, who left the pokey guest house first. At the end of the week, a man walked into her room in the early evening and handed her a mobile phone without a word. Amrita put the phone to her ear and asked urgently, 'Where is my husband? And my father-in-law? What have you done to them?' The stranger at the other end of the call laughed. 'Missing your men? It's only been a week. Shall I come and get you from that all-white prison?' Amrita said quickly, 'What do you want from us?' The man replied, 'I'll meet you in the underground car park in an hour and answer all your questions.' With that the line was disconnected.

Amrita was taken down to the car park at the appointed hour. She heard the low purr of the engine before she spotted the metallic grey car smoothly taking the turn into the underground parking lot. She'd surveyed the lot earlier – it was empty, with just three cars parked in assigned slots. Even the attendant was missing. The left-side door of the car opened slowly and she slid gracefully into the seat next to the driver. It was Jethia's associate, the man she had spotted pushing Sethji into the car during the kidnapping. He was reeking of Cool Water, one of Amrita's favourite colognes. Amrita ignored

his greeting and asked sharply, 'Where is Sethji? Where is
my husband?' The man laughed. 'First, let me get you out of
this hellhole! What fun! It's like being teenagers again – all
this secrecy, meeting in an abandoned parking lot. Mazaa aa
raha hai, agreed? All we need is a bottle of beer and roadside
bhelpuri to complete our date. Let's go.'

The car sped into the night, smoothly negotiating its way
past narrow lanes and abandoned mills, avoiding naked
slum children bathing at that hour in water gushing out of
a punctured pipe, till it hit the Western Highway, close to
the airport. 'Where have we come?' Amrita asked as the
car stopped. 'Stupid question! To meet your husband, of
course! You do want him back, don't you?' The car stopped
in front of a hotel and the two got out and stepped into the
foyer. The lobby was tacky enough. She knew it was what
is called a 'Gulf-style' hotel close to the Chhatrapati Shivaji
International Airport. She could hear the sound of the
powerful Airbuses flying low over the building.

The two of them silently took the lift up to the third floor.
As the lift door opened, Amrita noticed that the corridor was
full of security guards. Walking briskly past them, the man
ushered her into a dark room. 'Now . . . stay quiet,' said
Jethia's associate with a finger to his lips. 'I want to surprise
that husband of yours . . .' Amrita was relieved. At least
Srichand seemed to be all right. Controlling her emotions, she
asked coldly, 'He is unharmed, I presume.' The man laughed.
'Worried about your hubby? So sweet! You'll find out in a
minute, but ssshh. Like Rajesh Khanna's character in some old
phillum said, "Pushpa, I hate tears." I'm telling you, "Amrita,
I hate noise." Kya karoon? I'm very sensitive, darling.' The
man went towards a door that led to an adjoining suite. He

turned around, stared at Amrita and smiled, 'Interconnected. Convenient, no?'

He clicked the latch softly, opened the door a crack, gestured to Amrita to come closer and whispered, 'Look at your beloved hubby . . . I told you he was fine!' Amrita walked over quickly and stood on tiptoe to look beyond the man's broad shoulders. In an instant, she drew in her breath and stepped back. The man laughed. 'Shocked? Didn't expect to see such a scene? This is Mumbai, meri jaan. Everything happens here. Anything is possible. Do you think he's missing you, huh? Tell me? Does it look like that? Be honest.' Angry tears were threatening to spill out from Amrita's eyes. 'You filthy pig. Why have you brought me here?'

He shrugged. 'I thought you'd want to meet your hubby. Thoda pyaar-vyaar ke liye, no? Once you see him, hug him, kiss him, squeeze his balls, make him happy. This may be the last time you are together. Honeymoon manao. It's on the house. But if you'd rather leave right now, it's up to you. Before you meet that no-good fellow, let me tell you one thing. We want to close the deal. We do business very differently in this city. Your Delhi tactics won't work with our Mumbaiwallas. Your father-in-law may be a big shot in Delhi, but he's a nobody here. If your family is to survive in Mumbai, it has to be on our terms. Get it? Achcha. Go inside. Fuck him or don't – it's your wish. In case you are wondering whether I'm going to fuck you after that, forget it. I don't reuse toilet paper.'

Amrita was about to slap him. She raised her hand and screamed, 'How dare you?' He caught her hand roughly and twisted her wrist. 'Mind your words. You are in no position to insult me. Keep your temper for that hijra husband – in

any case he can't do it. Can't get his bloody tool up. Don't
we all know who keeps you happy in bed?'

Without another word, Amrita walked into the adjoining
suite and said, 'Srichand, I have come to take you home.'
Before her husband could respond, the naked woman on
the double bed with him giggled and said, 'Helloji, my, you
are so pretty! Naughty boy, you never told me you had such
a pretty biwi . . .' She moved closer to Srichand, patted the
vacated space on the king-size bed and cooed, 'Come, come,
join us, no problem.'

Amrita took one look at her husband and knew he'd been
sedated – his eyes were dull and when he raised his right
hand to greet her, the movement was slow and strained. He
slurred and asked groggily, 'Babuji? Theek toh hain? Aur
aap? Hamarey pyarey kuttey?' Amrita suppressed a smile.
Srichand was missing the dogs. And why not? They were the
only two who greeted him enthusiastically when he got home.
And followed him around from room to room, wagging their
tails wildly. He kept a jar of their favourite biscuits by his
bedside and invariably carried a few in his pockets to toss at
them whenever they barked.

Wryly, Amrita thought how sad it was that her husband,
the eldest son of the family, received love and respect only
from his pet dogs. They were the ones who missed him when
he travelled, moped during his absence, refused to eat their
normal meals, and howled at night, as they lay on the carpet
near his bed. The dogs looked up to Srichand. He was their
master. They made him feel good about his wretched life.
And today, it was the dogs he was thinking of much more
than his father or wife.

Amrita ignored the naked woman and asked Srichand to

get dressed. Her voice was soft and far from hostile. Srichand looked at her goofily and said, 'No, no, no. Why get dressed? Why leave? I am happy here. Really. See, look, sab kuch theek hai idhar. I prefer being here. You go back to Babuji, go, go, go. It's okay.' Amrita sighed and looked around the dimly lit room for his clothes and belongings. The woman, who had been refixing her smeared lipstick in a tiny mirror, giggled and said, 'Meri jaan, how can your mard get dressed? They've taken away his clothes.'

Without a word, Amrita left the suite and walked back into the room. She found Jaiprakash's associate smoking on the balcony. He placed a finger on his lips and said, 'Don't say anything. Don't spoil the mood. Look at Mumbai. What a city! Just look at it, glittering like a kingdom of jewels. You belong here, Amrita! Forget going back to Delhi. There's nothing left for you there. Suraj was last seen in Dubai. They'll get him wherever he is. They have all of you! Your only hope is to cooperate. Got it?' 'What do you want me to do?' asked Amrita, trying to keep the desperation out of her voice. 'We know you are the only person Sethji listens to. Make sure he cooperates.' With whom, about what – Amrita knew she would get her answers soon enough.

CHAPTER 30

Jaiprakash's associate didn't bother to drop Amrita to the waiting car. She was escorted to the elevator by another man who drove her back to the guest house. But instead of being shown to her room, she was taken to another one. As soon as Amrita entered the room, Sethji let out a roar from his bed. 'Saalikuttirundiharamzaadi . . .' all the abuses were clubbed together as he spluttered with rage. Then seeing it was Amrita, he became silent, not quite believing she was here, standing in front of him.

'Are you all right? Where is Srichand? Not with you? What happened?' Not getting a response from Amrita, he bellowed hoarsely, 'Have you lost your hearing, woman? Did you not hear me? I said I want to go back to be with my son in Delhi. What is there for me to do in this place with its fake trees? Get bitten by another machchar?' Amrita answered steadily, 'It is only for a few days while you recover fully. We'll take a decision after that. Babuji, I am here, so don't worry. You are getting better. Babuji, can you hear me? Please say something, Babuji?'

But Sethji had drifted off yet again. It was Srichand's voice that he was hearing – unmistakably Srichand's. What was he doing here? He was not supposed to come to Mumbai. If Srichand had left Delhi, then where was Suraj? Amrita? Sethji struggled to keep his eyes open. He was slipping in and out of sleep. But even in that state, he could tell something was wrong. He gestured to Srichand to come closer. When Srichand leaned over, Sethji asked, 'Is he . . . is Suraj . . . dead?' Srichand placed a hand over Sethji's arm and shook his head. 'He is fine. Don't worry. We are there to look after you now. You must eat, Babuji, you are very weak. How long can the doctors keep feeding you through your nose, your veins? Don't be stubborn. I have checked with the nurse. They said you refuse to listen to anyone.' It wasn't Srichand. It was Amrita talking to him. It had all been a dream. There was no Srichand in sight. But Amrita was here. Not in a dream but in flesh and blood.

'My bladder will burst! I couldn't do peshaab with that rundi around. I hate that woman. Calls herself a nurse! What nurse? All she did was talk on her cell phone.' Amrita wordlessly tidied up the room and helped Sethji from the bed. He hobbled to the tiny bathroom and she could hear him urinating like there was a geyser bursting inside his body. He emerged, shaking the last drops of urine from his penis. The leucoderma patch on his groin was visible. But he didn't care, nor did he bother to cover himself. Amrita settled Sethji in bed and forced him to eat some dried fruit and nuts. Then she sat by him as he drifted back to sleep.

Later in the night, the old man recovered enough strength to sit up in bed. Amrita began to speak. 'Babuji . . .' she said with urgency in her voice, 'Babuji, things are bad. Really bad. I have no idea where Suraj is. Srichand has also been picked up, like us, but he is somewhere else. He is . . . he is . . .' Her voice cracked at the memory and she managed to whisper to Sethji what she had seen. Sethji stiffened with rage at her words. And then he shouted.

It was a sound that emerged from his very core, a primal, guttural sound. 'I will kill them all,' Sethji swore, as Amrita tried to calm him down by placing her hand gently over his. When his heavy breathing came back to normal, she said softly, 'We are finished, Babuji. Finished. Do you understand?' Sethji stared at his daughter-in-law, his expression perplexed. 'Nonsense!' he snapped dismissively. 'Nobody can finish me. You hear that? Nobody! My deal is directly with Bhagwan. He told me there is still time. I have faith in him. Only him. And my dead wife. She also told me last night in a dream that there is a lot of time before she and I can be reunited in heaven. So, my dear, forget all this talk of finished-winished. Nobody finishes Sethji.'

Amrita realized Babuji was on one of his megalomaniacal, delusional trips. When Sethji was stuck in such a frame of mind, he believed he was indestructible. He also believed his dead wife was right there, next to him, offering sage advice. Amrita had often watched him conduct lengthy conversations with her garlanded portrait in his room. He did not feel embarrassed if Amrita came in and witnessed his monologue. He'd carry on for the next few minutes, until he was satisfied with the solutions he sought from the mute portrait. Amrita was not surprised by her father-in-law's reaction to the crisis. She decided to wait a few more hours before raising the topic again and her suspicions about Jaiprakash Jethia being involved. But that didn't happen. A few minutes later, after persistent and loud knocking on the door, two men in spotless white kurta pyjama stormed into the room. Saffron scarves made out of shiny satin were draped casually over their shoulders. 'Jai Bhawani Mata! Bhau has sent us. Bhau is waiting for you. Come on.'

CHAPTER 31

Suraj looked around the gigantic suite on the ninety-sixth floor of Dubai's latest showpiece – a dazzling seven-star hotel on the edge of a man-made lagoon with dancing fountains that swayed to Mozart's music every fifteen minutes. He checked the sleek new gun that had just been delivered to him. It looked lethal and sexy. Would do the job, he concluded. But before he got down to business, he needed a massage. He called to fix an appointment at the lavish Lotus Blossom Spa on the premises. A ninety-minute deep tissue special would do the trick, he'd figured. That would be followed by ten minutes in the sauna, another ten in the steam room and then a quick dunk in the chill pool. Yes. He had earned it.

Suraj checked the suite – checked the heavy, double-latched door, large windows with spectacular vistas of Dubai, and examined the space behind the huge LCD TV. He expected the room to be bugged, of course. Nobody took chances in Dubai – the desert destination of the world's most deadly thugs. But he was not going to be there long enough to make any conversation. The spa receptionist told Suraj over the phone that she had no slots left. He could try later. Perhaps tomorrow? He snarled, 'Make a slot happen. Cancel someone else's appointment. I need that massage badly. I need it now.' The young Filipino girl started to stutter that it wasn't possible. Suraj banged down the receiver and headed out of the room. He'd go straight to the spa and make sure he got that massage. As he left, he took his brand new, loaded gun with him.

The spa was semi-deserted at that hour. The men would saunter in later. Their arrival would be preceded by the heady aromas of sickeningly strong ittars – musky, sexual, the raw smells of the desert combined with the fragrance exuded by lissome habibis dancing naked under the stars. Dubai was not Suraj's scene. He couldn't understand the way it functioned.

Dubai had changed since Suraj was last there, two or was it three years ago? These days it was the Russian mafia that called the shots. Earlier, it had been the exclusive domain of exiled bhais from India, who shuttled between Karachi and Dubai. Suraj had no problems dealing with them through his middlemen in Delhi but the Russians were a different breed. The city too had changed. The place looked depressing and deserted, with hardly any of the frenzied building activity that had once made it the crane capital of the world.

Driving in from the airport, even the famous Dubai Creek had looked dried up. Most of the subway work had been stopped a long time ago, and he spotted several unfinished building complexes that seemed abandoned and empty. Suraj's Kerala taxi driver had watched him observe the ghost townships and said, 'Saar, Dubai khallaas!' But Suraj had been in no mood to chat with the man, whose bloodshot, sad eyes kept staring at him from the rear-view mirror. 'Saar, travelling alone? Saar, I can arrange fun. Blonde girls from phoren. Ukraine girls very popular. Cheap, also. Cheaper than our desi girls from India. Many Mumbai bar girls here. You from India, no? I can tell. India best country, saar!' Suraj grinned. 'Then why are you here?'

The driver seemed delighted that his passenger was ready to chat. 'What to do, saar? Money not enough in India. But now, Dubai also same-same. Money, big problem. Two more years here, then I retire. I will stay with you as your driver in Dubai, saar. I know roads, shops, bars, girls, even boys. Work very slow, saar. I'll give you good daily rate. Discounts for shopping. Discounts for girls also. Okay, saar?' Suraj leaned forward and asked, 'Discounts for guns, too?' The cabbie laughed. 'Sure, saar! This is Dubai – you can buy anything here. Come on, let's go. My friend is the best gun dealer in Dubai. Lebanese. Clever! Good contacts with police.' The car had swerved abruptly at the next turn, and Suraj found himself heading right back towards the creek and Bur Dubai. It was a useful if long ride.

CHAPTER 32

In Dubai, ensconced in the lap of synthetic luxury, Suraj felt uncharacteristically distracted and alone. Abandoned. The same feeling when Babuji had broken the news to him about his mother's death. Suraj had been close to Maaji. As close as he'd ever be to anybody. When she died, he had known he was on his own. He'd watched his father and Srichand, as they performed the last rites of a woman who demanded absolutely nothing from anyone. Not even their company. Maaji existed. That was enough for all of them. She barely spoke. But when she did, it was basic good sense. Even though Maaji was consulted before any single major decision was taken, there was no doubt in anybody's mind that Babuji's word was the final one.

Suraj had never seen tears in his mother's eyes. She was born to smile. Sometimes he wondered what she was smiling about! Did she even know she was smiling? Or was it a reflex? The same reflex displayed by infants with little control over their facial muscles? It didn't matter. She was universally liked and respected by all. The servants worshipped her and when the time came for them to bid their mistress the last goodbye, they wept unselfconsciously, even the men. 'Ram naam satya hai,' the chant started from the oldest member of the staff, who was immediately joined by several others. Suraj felt dizzy

154

and nauseous. The chanting, the incense, the garlands being heaped on her body, even the sight of the generous smearing of sindoor in the parting of her thick hair, made him ill. He vowed he'd never attend another funeral – not even Babuji's.

With Maaji gone, the running of the house was left to senior servants. Babuji had no time between political meetings and incessant travel. Their home had become the party headquarters . . . something Maaji had resisted when she was alive. Now, it was no longer possible to tell whether that person sleeping on a vacated bed, close to the air cooler, was a party worker or family member. The kitchen functioned round the clock. Lunch, dinner, snacks, meals blended into siestas, dinner became breakfast, or lunch was skipped altogether. Nobody bothered about timing, nobody was there to supervise what was cooked or who ate it.

Suraj missed his mother more than he cared to reveal. He had always been the chosen one – her favourite son. And now Babuji's, but that was irrelevant to the lonely boy who stopped eating jalebis the night he watched the flames of his mother's funeral pyre light up the sky on the banks of the Yamuna. Glistening jalebis, heavy with ghee made out of cow's milk, sticky and sweet, hot and succulent, became his personal offering to his Maaji's memory. Perhaps nobody could understand the enormity of his gesture. Perhaps giving up jalebis was considered too trivial a sacrifice. But for Suraj, those jalebis represented love.

He could eat fifteen in one go! He'd stay put in the kitchen on jalebi-making days and refuse to move till Maaji fed him mini-jalebis made from the leftover lightly fermented flour. Other members of the household, especially the kitchen staff, would laugh as Suraj stuffed one jalebi after another into his mouth, his cheeks bulging comically, making him resemble a monkey. Maaji would tweak his ears and say, 'Bandar!' and then wipe his sticky mouth with the corner of her sari pallu. No more jalebis for Suraj!

Strange, that bloody hill girl he was accused of raping had offered him jalebis, too! He tried to recall details of that evening. He remembered her chipped metallic blue nail polish and the prominent mole over her upper lip. Shiny, poker-straight hair down to her narrow waist. Small boobs, like golf balls. Smooth, hairless limbs. Silky pubés. Lightly freckled back. Tiny, pouty mouth. Teeth like a cat's – sharp, small, white. Darting, dark eyes beneath scanty brows. Pretty thing, but so dumb! Not his type, at all! He'd even said so.

He shut his eyes briefly, and pictured her as she squealed with pleasure when he pinched her nipples (pink!). If only she hadn't ruined everything by offering that jalebi! Even after he told her he had stopped eating jalebis after his mother's death! Stupid girl. She laughed when he told her that. Laughed! That was it. He saw red. She was obviously making fun of him . . . of Mataji.

How dare she – this bloody slut from nowhere. He'd been nice to her. He had smiled and asked her politely to take her clothes off. He hadn't torn them off roughly or anything. Well, not at that point. He had even asked her permission about not using a condom (offering to pay extra for the concession). Had negotiated for a blow job as a bonus (two thousand bucks more). It was only after her insulting laughter that he had struck her, and then he had carried on striking her, entering her roughly, just to teach the bitch a lesson.

He'd told her, 'Respect se baat karo.' But no! Would the bitch listen? She must have been on something, all those

Pahadi girls were on something. Drugged-out bitches. Dope-heads! And then they blamed men for 'taking advantage' of them. By the time he was done with her, she was lying in a motionless heap. Suraj kicked her a couple of times to check whether she was faking injury. Yes, there was blood, but maybe it was from her cut lip. Saali, she'd tried to bite him! What was he supposed to do? Let her continue biting like a rabid bitch?

Suraj sighed and shook his head. It was all because of that wretched chinky girl that this had happened. What a seasoned actress she was! The whole thing was a game. He'd been set up. Framed. Those jalebis must have been laced – that was it. It was an elaborate trap to drug him . . . poison him . . . abduct him. Bach gaya! Had he been offered laddoos instead of jalebis, he would have eaten at least one! God was on his side! Definitely. It was beginning to make sense to Suraj now.

***

As Suraj tried to unwind in the sauna, attempting to fit all the pieces together, his mood darkened. Arun had sent him a link to Amrita's 'performance' on Bharat TV. Suraj may not have possessed the long vision of his father but he knew instantly that any possible political career for him was finished with this news report. He had always imagined he would take over his father's constituency at some point – that is, if Babuji ever slowed down. But Amrita had fucked all those plans. A slow flame of anger began to burn in him. His life would be about the backroom, cutting deals, making money, but no glory, no fame, no real power. She had ended those dreams in a stroke. And maybe created a brand new dream for herself!

How shrewdly Amrita had sidelined him! Suraj marvelled at her cunning. He couldn't help feeling a grudging respect for his sister-in-law. How had she pulled it off? Amrita was just like Babuji – the two of them together were unbeatable! The best combo. Like McDonald's and Coke.

Suraj often thought about his Bhabhiji, the great Amrita. She was someone he hadn't been able to decode. Everything about her was a little mysterious. But the one thing Suraj could never understand was why she'd agreed to marry his brother. She could as easily have married him! They were far better suited, and they both knew it. At least he did. And he'd said so to Babuji, who had laughed, patted his head indulgently and said, 'You are wrong. She will finish you off in one gulp. She's better for Srichand. He needs someone like her. Someone strong and fearless. We'll find another beauty for you. You need a lamb, not a tigress.'

Suraj had often wondered about Babuji's relationship with Amrita. Initially, he had put it down to Babuji's fascination for an attractive, modern woman. Just her proximity must have been a turn-on. Amrita was the kind of woman his father could only have fantasized about till that point. But he knew Babuji for the rogue he was. He may have loved and respected Maaji in his own eccentric way. But she was dead. Had been dead for a very long time. Babuji had his rundis. His favourite prostitutes. But of late, he seemed less and less interested in what he called 'bazaari aurat'.

It was obvious his father had lusted after Amrita from the moment he'd set eyes on her. But even Suraj did not want to believe Babuji slept with her. Oof! Ugh! Suraj pushed the image of Babuji humping Amrita out of his head. It was too distasteful. There was talk. He'd overheard comments from servants. But Suraj had dismissed what was so apparent, unable to confront the sordid truth. Unwilling to accept his father's loathsome behaviour. Or perhaps, even envious and resentful at the thought that Babuji was enjoying something he himself was denied. Suraj would have loved to screw his Bhabhi! It was hard for any man to resist Amrita's sexual power.

But whatever the relations between Babuji and Amrita were, there was no doubt that it was his Bhabhi who dominated their household. It was Amrita who oversaw the smooth running of not just their sprawling home, but Babuji's chaotic daftar and all their crazy schedules. Without Amrita, their lives would have remained disorganized and scattered. Impersonal and cold. If there was hot food in the kitchen at all times, it was thanks to Amrita's meticulous planning. If the sheets and towels were changed regularly, it was because Amrita made sure the dhobi did his job. Amrita was the pivot. All the three men needed her. Suraj included.

Suraj had participated in the wedding with a great deal of resentment in his heart. He danced half-heartedly in the baraat, taking frequent swigs from his vodka-filled hip flask. He couldn't bear to visualize Amrita in bed with Srichand . . . even the idea revolted him. Not that Srichand was ugly or anything. He was just nondescript and boring. Uninspiring like watery buttermilk minus the rock salt. Thinking of his favourite summer thirst quencher made Suraj nostalgic. He wondered when he'd be able to get back to Delhi. There was so much unfinished business to take care of. And the delivery of his new car – the powerful, sleek Maserati he'd booked through his regular car dealer. What would happen to the car? And why had that bloody bastard Shakeel not been in touch?

Shakeel, his best friend and shadow. The man Babuji hated and blamed for all Suraj's misdeeds. Suraj's lips curled into a twisted smile as he thought about those wild nights with Shakeel as they raced towards a farmhouse party in Chhattarpur. What fun they used to have. Models, designers, starlets, cricketers, socialites, lawyers, tycoons, diplomats, politicians and, of course, a mad cocktail of several pills.

But that was always Shakeel's department. He knew where to score virtually any drug consumed in the world. Suraj recalled coming back home at 7 a.m. and meeting Babuji after one such orgy – and an all-out orgy is exactly what it had been. Babuji had waited patiently for Suraj to emerge from his low-slung CLS Mercedes Coupé before asking sarcastically, 'Anything I can do for you, bade saab . . .? What is your hukum?' Suraj's faithful retainers had rushed forward to help their master before he staggered and fell down the steps, landing at Babuji's feet. Suraj had caught sight of Amrita watching the scene from a distance – her disdainful expression had said it all. Suraj had attempted a greeting, his words slurring, 'Bhabhiji . . . good morning . . . no, no, no, good afternoon . . . good night.'

Amrita must have instructed the servants to carry a pitcher of freshly squeezed lime juice to his room. He had thirstily glugged it down, before collapsing on the large double bed. Babuji had turned and walked away, his disgust apparent to everyone present. Shakeel had called just then to ask if all was well. And today, when all was far from well, there was no Shakeel.

***

The heat in the sauna was getting to Suraj as the heavy gold chain around his neck almost singed his chest hairs. It was time to get out of the spa, and out of the hotel. Suraj dressed quickly and walked to the reception area. All the girls from before were missing. A burly Arab in a spotless white dishdash smiled as Suraj looked around the place to tip the young woman who had signed him in. 'The car is waiting outside for you. Keep your hands out of your pockets and follow me,' he instructed, in heavily accented English which sounded more like French, with an exaggerated rolling of the r's.

There was just one exit, Suraj noted. And behind the reception counter, a heavy glass wall with water flowing through fortified pressed sheets. He had no choice. Suraj moved swiftly, like a panther fleeing from a hunter, and shot the glass wall with his new 'toy' – the heavy-duty gun sold to him a few hours earlier by the green-eyed Lebanese dealer. But even as the glass shattered around him, and sheets of water poured out, flooding the reception, Suraj was surrounded. He thought to himself, 'This is plain crazy, man! What the fuck!'

There was no way he could make a run for it. The Arabs were armed. Four barrels were pointed at his head. 'Drop the gun,' one man told him sharply. Suraj did as he was told and raised his arms. Another man patted him down expertly, checking for hidden weapons – knives, another gun. A third produced handcuffs, pushed Suraj against a wall, pinioned his arms behind him and clicked the handcuffs firmly. Suraj's mind was racing furiously. This wasn't the fucking deal he had made with Arun! What the fuck was going on? That Arun – Babuji's Arun! Arun had obviously stabbed Babuji in the back after agreeing to help him – is this what that fucker called 'help'? Suraj vowed to kill him . . . kill Arun in a way

that would make him repent this act of betrayal as he begged
Suraj to spare him additional torture. He'd gouge out Arun's
eyes first . . . feed them to crows. He'd . . . he'd . . . before
Suraj could think of more ways to punish Arun, a hard crack
of a pistol butt on his left temple knocked him out cold.

CHAPTER 33

Bhau was much smaller in stature than his pictures indicated, Amrita noted when he walked into the room. He appeared diminutive, shrivelled up and sickly, as he coughed into a large towel draped over his sloping, narrow shoulders. 'Call that madarchod . . .' he rasped, as he took his place on a gilt-edged throne behind a large desk covered with pamphlets with his picture on them. His body nearly disappeared behind the papers piled up on the desk as he groped around the mess to locate his reading glasses. He pretended he had not noticed Sethji or Amrita all this while and carried on like they were not in the room. The 'madarchod' turned out to be an unlikely person dressed in a sharp suit.

'Sir . . .?' the man said, his accent polished, even clipped. Bhau stared at him belligerently. 'Arrey you, bhadwa. When will you stop pimping for those useless cunts and start working seriously for me? Where is the municipal clearance I had asked for three weeks ago?' The man's expression remained calm and unruffled as he started to fiddle with his laptop. Bhau exploded, 'Shove that bloody machine up your arse. Just give me an answer. I don't want to see all those, all those . . .' he fumbled, as the man answered smoothly, 'Spreadsheets, sir. But I have to show them to you, take you through the plans.' Bhau turned to one of his cowering assistants and said wearily,

163

'Throw this bloody bhadwa out before I strangle him with my own hands. I don't want to see all those fancy things on a machine. I want results . . . not, not . . .' The man smiled. 'Spreadsheets, sir. Spreadsheets. Don't worry. Everything is on schedule. I am meeting the chief minister tomorrow. All signatures within a week. Jai Bhawani!'

Bhau finally looked in the direction of Sethji and Amrita. 'Bring tea. Good tea. Separate chini, doodh. In good cups, not stainless steel glasses. We have important visitors.' He smiled, revealing teeth stained by tobacco. 'And yes, get me a whisky. Big and not what I give to my pigeons. Get fried fish. Go tell Vahini we have guests from Dilli. Let us show them some Maharashtrian hospitality. I know these show-off Dilliwallas think we "ghatis" are chingoos and don't treat our guests well. Get some komdi also. These two look hungry.'

'Look here,' Sethji began, ignoring Amrita's attempt to restrain him. He was extremely weak but too proud to show it. Bhau held up his left hand, weighed down by countless gold bracelets with religious medallions dangling and said sharply, 'Chup karo. Speak when I allow you to open your mouth. Remember your position and place. Your sons are in my custody. Do you want to see them alive? This is not the time for us to argue. I need you. You need me. Simple. But let me tell you one thing – you need me more than I need you. If you understand that much there'll be no problem.'

His voice grew menacing as he continued, 'Remember one more thing. This is my city. Mumbai belongs to me. Everything you see here is run by me. Everything. Make no mistake. I too have sons. One is clever. The other is not. Just like your boys. I also have grandchildren – unlike you. Your family name can end here in Mumbai. Right now, in fact. I can kill you and your daughter-in-law. My men can finish off your sons. The one in Dubai is with my local partner there. Why get into all this bad stuff, jhanjats and unnecessary lafdas when we can work together, kyon? Have tea. I won't offer you any whisky, I know you don't drink much, Sethji. Eat komdi. My wife makes it very well. After that we can discuss business. Okay?' Amrita answered before Sethji could react, 'Sir, anything you say is okay, sir. We are ready to work with you.' Bhau laughed uproariously. 'Jhakaas! Smart woman. Just like my own daughter-in-law. But small correction, madam. You and your baap there won't be working *with* me but *for* me. Chhota sa difference.'

Both men were silent, as Bhau's man Friday shuffled around the place pretending to tidy up papers. Sethji noted with some satisfaction that Bhau's den was pretty shabby – shabbier than his own daftar in Delhi. The tea placed in front of them was served in tiny cups. Saala! Kanjoos about chai? What sort of business would such a man do with badey dil ke aadmi? Small cups, small mind, small ambition, Sethji concluded, as Bhau spoke to someone on the phone in Marathi.

Bhau seemed far more fragile and weak in person than he appeared on television. His voice was thin and it quavered when he chatted animatedly. Sethji had expected a roar. He glanced sideways at Amrita, who had after her little outburst put back her icy, expressionless mask on. As usual. That was her trademark. Fuck her or beat her, the eyes stayed stony, emotionless. Sethji had seen his bahu cry inconsolably only once when her pet dog Bahadur, a magnificent German Shepherd she had brought with her to her marital home, had been run over in the driveway as Suraj's SUV took a sharp turn at a crazy speed. Amrita had rushed out of her quarters

hearing Bahadur's piercing cry as the heavy front wheel
crushed his strong body.

   Suraj had tried to apologize, but Amrita had brushed past
him without a second glance and cradled Bahadur's limp body
in her arms, weeping silent tears, her body shaking with grief.
Amrita had stopped talking to her brother-in-law for months
after the incident. Sethji had wryly wondered at the time
whether Amrita had wept as much or been filled with such
sorrow when her own father had died. Bahadur's accident
had robbed Amrita of her rare smiles, Sethji had noted. She
had lost weight and worn plain white saris for a year as a
mark of respect. Amrita in mourning had touched Sethji's
heart more than he had imagined it would. He had respected
her feelings and arranged an appropriate burial spot, with
a marble tombstone for Bahadur, under Bahadur's favourite
jamun tree in the compound. Often, he'd spot Amrita sitting
on a bench close by, lost in her own thoughts, pretending to
read a book without turning a single page.

***

Today, in Bhau's ugly office, Amrita looked dead to the
world, but Sethji knew her mind was at work, trying to figure
out Bhau's game plan for them. Bhau was in no hurry to
spell it out. After several phone calls, with the conversation
conducted in Marathi, Bhau finally turned to the two of
them and asked abruptly, 'Don't like tea?' Amrita didn't
respond. Sethji answered briefly, 'Diabetes.' Bhau rang a
bell and shouted, 'No sugar. Diabetes patient. I had told you
bhadwas, chini, doodh separate. Gandus! Don't listen to
instructions! Make new tea.' Sethji grimaced and said, 'No

need for tea. We are not here to chit-chat. Let us talk sense and not waste time.' Bhau laughed. 'Seems my men didn't look after you properly. Maybe a few days somewhere a bit nicer will improve your health and mood.' Sethji tapped the glass top of the large desk impatiently and waited.

CHAPTER 34

'You have been creating some maha problems for me, Sethji,' Bhau said, finally breaking the tense silence. Sethji didn't respond, observing every move of the frail-looking man in front of him. 'The highways contract to Arun Mehta? That was a shock. Big shock! How did it happen? We had been promised it, you see. It is most unfortunate that this was taken away from us.' Sethji wondered who the 'we' was and who had made the promise, but remained silent.

Bhau continued, 'Never mind. It is still not too late. The contract can be managed. Everything is possible in this world, if people try. I'm sure you will try. Try very hard. Because if you don't, I will have to finish you off. Kill you. All of you. Understand? No choice, baba. Our dirty world is like that. You and I didn't create it. No need to feel bad. It is very simple. The contract hasn't been announced officially yet. I think you can call the FM and tell him you have changed your mind about Arun. The FM is a good friend of yours, isn't he? But I cannot work with that man and those lungiwalla Annas of his. Nor those Bunts from Karnataka. I understand neither their language nor their secretive and hopelessly clannish dealings. Don't you agree?

'And you know what they say about me? They think I am no better than a crude paan chewer whose spittle is filthier than Delhi's gutters. The FM ignores me in public and pretends we are strangers, even though he has no problems accepting cutbacks from other contracts. Everybody knows that third-class fellow and how he works. He gets a cut of all the tasty things, greedy bastard – from infrastructure to outright rokda crores for fixing cases. Saala, he has amassed enough to take care of five generations of his family during his term as FM but even then he is not satisfied. Anyway, who am I to throw stones at anybody? Matlab ki baat hai. Let's get down to business.

'Call your minister friend and say you have a better plan. Tell him you have found a bigger party and would like to pull Arun Mehta out of the contract. Make up a story about being double-crossed by Arun. Say you have material on him that you'll give to the media if he doesn't cooperate. These days, everybody has material on everybody else. It depends on whose dirt is dirtier, that's all. After all, the highways project was given to you as a favour and there were lower bids. Perhaps you can say your conscience has spoken and won't allow you to get into any illegal activities?' said Bhau, laughing loudly at his own joke.

'. . . and I have one more "request",' said Bhau, while Sethji and Amrita were beginning to digest his threat. 'This is very simple. I need a few hundred outsiders to vacate a plot in Tardeo, which was once a textile mill. The Gujarati family that owned the land is willing to hand it over, but the mill workers are refusing to get out. Their union leader has to be "managed". At the moment my man is working on clearing it, but it's taking time and my boys are getting impatient. There are other interested parties working on acquiring the same land including a powerful cabinet minister, operating

through his relatives in Mumbai and Pune. He has an army
of well-armed workers, but zero local support.'

Bhau paused for effect, then continued. 'I need manpower.
But nothing that can be traced to me. Men from the north,
who can be hired to muscle out and terrorize the few mill
hands left on the premises. The operation will have to be swift
before the Mumbai police get into the picture. Those Mumbai
cops are the worst. And as of now, they are on the minister's
payroll but negotiations are on with the top representatives
of the cops. But you know what they are like – as always
demanding too unrealistic a cut from the deal. I want you to
send your men. Simple.'

It would take very little to mobilize a team to carry out
this operation, Amrita mused. In fact Bhau didn't need Sethji
for such a small job at all. This was merely a diversion. An
additional something for Bhau to play with, a little extra
burden to place on Sethji's shoulders. Amrita knew that Suraj
had conducted countless such operations in the past. But they
couldn't count on Suraj this time. Amrita wasn't even sure
whether he was still alive. Sethji, too, had listened to all this
quietly without interruption. He continued to remain silent,
his mind ticking and his restless right foot shaking – a sure
sign of impatience, Amrita noted as she tried to unravel the
conversation. The pieces finally fell into place. She understood
now why Arun Mehta had been so helpful about Suraj . . .
about Srichand, and the tuition scheme.

Sethji in the meantime was thinking through the
consequences. The out-of-town thugs were no problem at all.
But in demanding the highways contract, Bhau was asking
for the impossible. No doubt it was for Jaiprakash Jethia,
his 'third' son and Arun's enemy number one. As soon as he

realized that Bhau was behind the kidnapping, he guessed that Jethia was the big money involved. But the contract had been all but finalized, after many delicate negotiations, and overturning it would make many enemies, not least Arun Mehta. Sethji decided the plan was not sound enough and too risky. He said so firmly.

Bhau laughed. 'I like you. Refusing the only offer you have in hand! Good, good. If you don't take it, what will be your fate? And the fate of your family? Or don't you care? Let me tell you, your precious Suraj will be finished off by our men in Dubai. They are waiting for my orders. If you don't agree to this, your son will be chopped up into kebab-sized tukdas. Even the dogs in Dubai won't eat his drug-filled polluted flesh. Then what? Then, we'll take your bahu on a picnic. Mazaa aayega. We'll shoot a video for you and her husband to watch and enjoy aaram se. After that, we'll decide what to do with both of you. The nullah you passed a few minutes ago is choked with bodies of people like you. But why am I boring you? You have filled the nullahs of Delhi in the same way. You know how these things are done.'

Sethji thought quickly. 'If I agree, how much time do I have? And what will I gain? You know this is the most valuable contract in the country and that I am the only person right now who can overturn whatever has been finalized.' Bhau laughed. He laughed so hard that what followed was a prolonged coughing fit. His man Friday rushed forward with a spittoon. Bhau wiped his mouth on a towel placed on the arm of his throne, before saying, 'Wah! Facing the gallows and still asking for a cut. Once a bhadwa, always a bhadwa.' Sethji continued impassively,

'If I had no value, I wouldn't be here. Moofat mein kaam koi nahin karta.'

Bhau smiled and looked at Amrita. 'Your father-in-law will fit in very well here. Mumbai needs people like him. But what about you? What can we do to make your life in our great city a little more enjoyable? Tell me? Do you want to join Bollywood? Not as an actress. No, no, no. You are too old for that even though you are more beautiful than many of our heroines. Sadly, Bollywood needs taaza maal – sixteen-, seventeen-year-olds. They like juicy Aapoos mangoes here . . . fresh murgis. Preferably virgins.

'Someone like you would do well as a producer. My son Yashwant invests money in those hopeless dishum-dishum pictures they make. It keeps him busy. As an investment, Bollywood gives zero returns. I never get my money back but that's okay. My son has a position in society because of this. He's invited to important awards functions and woh Page 3-walla parties. He's happy. His mother is shaant. I am happy. Only his wife cries. What can I do if her husband prefers whores and starlets to his own spouse – tell me. You know the story well. You just met your husband with that naughty doll . . . what is her name? Yes, Silky. But you are not crying over him and his rundi, na? Why? Because you are smart. I like smart women. Not crybabies. Welcome to Mumbai. Now, finish your diabetes-tea, and get out.'

'We will leave but you too must think of my offer,' said Sethji softly. 'Surely we can work out something in which we both gain without upsetting Arun and involving the FM? There are many other big, big contracts, big, big projects. Forget this one . . . I'll get you something much better.' Bhau's face darkened with rage. 'Do you not understand your

position, Sethji? Chhee chhee chhee – and they call you Delhi's
smartest dalal! I want that contract. Baat khatam. You have
one night to fix it. Jai Bhawani! I'm tired now . . . my drink
is over. Get out . . . jao . . . jao . . . jao.'

CHAPTER 35

In the car Sethji slumped back in exhaustion. The meeting had taken a toll on his fevered body but his mind was in overdrive. He knew they were stuck—all of them. And for now, Bhau was their only hope. But Sethji had noticed something else during their exchange. For all of Bhau's big talk and aggression, Sethji's instinct, the instinct that had saved him time and time again, told him that there was more to this. He could sense ill-disguised panic in Bhau's actions. The man had overdone everything – not just brazenly kidnapped him and Amrita, but also drugged Srichand and surrounded him with whores. Bhau's performance today was equally overdone and amateurish, as if he were pulling out every trick to childishly frighten him and Amrita.

These were the actions of a man desperate enough to try anything. Bhau himself seemed to have staked something on the highways contract. That would seem more likely. In any case, Sethji knew one thing. Panic was not good for business. Panic made you weak. Panic impaired clear thinking. And Bhau was clearly panicking, no matter that he strenuously tried to hide it behind all the big talk and bluster.

Sethji went over everything he knew about Bhau. The man had virtually disappeared from public view ever since his paralytic stroke and the inevitable slowness that followed.

Even today, some of Bhau's words emerged slurred and he was frequently incoherent. His left hand appeared lifeless and limp as he obsessively turned the beads of his jap-mala. His followers had sensed his vulnerability and knew it was a matter of another two or three years before Bhau would be forced to hand over charge to his boys. His party had weakened, because of Bhau's diminishing star power. The two sons were not considered effective successors. Sethji grimaced at the irony of it all. His situation was no different from Bhau's. How strange it was that the political world could make such easy winners and losers of everyone. It was enough to make you believe in destiny.

He remembered hearing that there had been a strong bid from Mumbai for the highways contract with a proposal that the building of the national highway would begin from Maharashtra. If Bhau had engineered the bid, then of course he would have used the project as political capital, no doubt ensuring that Jaiprakash launched it on a grand scale with Bhau presiding over it. Landing such a prestigious contract for his state would be a spectacular behind-the-scenes way to show his enemies who still called the shots. No wonder he couldn't afford to let this slip through. It was Bhau's last-ditch attempt to regain his former glory and control the state as the unquestioned, unchallenged supremo.

As he thought about Bhau and his ramshackle offices, he felt sure this must be the reason. He had learned that in a negotiation there was no such thing as an empty hand. Everyone came with their own strengths and weaknesses, and the better you knew them, the likelier the chance of you getting what you wanted. Today he was sitting imprisoned, his sons captive, his entire family close to death. But Bhau couldn't afford to have him killed, because Sethji had something he desperately wanted. No wonder none of them had been hurt yet. But the minute Sethji gave Bhau what he was demanding, his value would become zero. Khatam. Bhau would finish them all. It was important to keep Bhau dangling. Sethji would have to buy time somehow. As he worked it all out, he felt a wave of exhaustion and pain hit him.

Amrita too was quiet in the car. She knew Babuji's mind was ticking in the dark. She'd heard Bhau's plan in silence and watched her father-in-law wriggle out of an impossible situation yet again. She realized that she felt lighter in the last few hours than she had in a long time. Whatever would happen next, at least Babuji was there by her side. She knew Babuji would have to pull it off. Or they could both forget about staying alive, in Mumbai or Delhi.

She was jolted out of her thoughts by a small groan. Babuji was doubled up in pain. He turned to Amrita and said, 'Something is wrong. I can't bear it any longer. Ask that man to stop the car.' She held his hand firmly. 'Babuji, be patient. There's no bathroom close by . . . and this is Mumbai and you can't do it on the road. We will be back in the guest house soon and the nurse is there. Be strong, we will soon be there.' Babuji's voice came out in a thin wail, 'This is not about my peshaab. I am dying of pain. Please, do something.'

Sensing Babuji's urgency, Amrita leaned forward to instruct the driver. Without taking his eyes off the traffic, the guard sitting next to the driver pointed the barrel of an automatic straight at Amrita. 'Shut up and sit back. No stopping. No talking. If you move again, I'll shoot you.' Amrita turned around to see if Babuji was okay and found him slumped on the seat, his hand still clutching his crotch, his eyes rolled back into his forehead, his breathing heavy.

Amrita let out a scream. Startled by the sound, the driver swerved the car sharply and the next thing Amrita knew it had hit a road divider, spun around and crashed into an S-Class Mercedes which was behind them. It was the sturdy, tank-like Merc that saved Amrita and Babuji that night. Both men in the front died on the spot. Amrita scrambled out of the car, and tried to drag Babuji through the half-open door. His weight in that state seemed to have doubled, as Amrita struggled to lift him.

'Allow me,' said a male voice, adding, 'Please get into the car and let me handle this before the cops get here.' Amrita gasped in shock at the sound of the familiar voice, a voice she hadn't heard in years. 'What the hell are you doing here?' she said as she struggled to get inside the car. 'Following you,' the man replied. Idle pedestrians had started to walk towards the accident site. Amrita heard an urchin shouting, 'Abbey aajao, saala mar gaya, khoon khoon, bandook bhi hai. Lagta hai koi gangster tha.' An elderly man had taken it upon himself to play traffic cop and was waving other cars to drive past the mangled vehicle.

In less than two minutes, Amrita was speeding off towards South Mumbai and safety. Babuji was groaning and calling out to his dead wife, 'Leelaji, Leelaji, main aa raha hoon. Hey Bhagwan, Leelaji.' Amrita wasn't sure he'd make it this time. And underneath her panic were the questions. Why was he here? How had he known where she was? Who was he working with? The questions would have to wait.

Babuji had stopped groaning. His head was on Amrita's lap. She touched his brow. It was cold and damp. She turned to the man and said, 'I don't think Babuji's going to last

. . . Oh god! I think Babuji is dying!' The man replied firmly, 'Relax, baby, Sethji is not ready to die just yet. I'm taking you to my trusted polyclinic in Colaba. Sethji will be examined by the best. Don't worry. And if required, I'll fly in a specialist I trust, from Chennai. But Sethji must stay alive. For you and for all of us . . .'

CHAPTER 36

The polyclinic was located in a dark bylane behind the Taj Mahal Palace Hotel, opposite the famous Gateway of India in South Mumbai. Amrita was tense as the Merc pulled up and a sleepy guard opened the door. The burly durwan nodded wordlessly and helped the two of them carry Sethji to the elevator – an ancient one with a rusty, creaking grille. 'Are you sure this place is good enough?' Amrita asked anxiously. 'The best. At this point. There is really no other option. The cops will be looking for Sethji. Worse, so will Bhau and his men. I need to switch cars once I leave you upstairs with the doc. I don't want to be traced here. Let's be really, really quick.'

The clinic was far better from the inside. The nursing staff knew the man and led them into a waiting room next to the doctor's chamber. One of the nurses whispered something to the man and he nodded briskly. He walked up to Amrita and instructed her to keep quiet and leave the talking to him. Within minutes a young doctor appeared and asked without any preliminaries, 'Age, blood group and symptoms of patient?'

He spoke with an incongruous American accent. Sethji's breathing was uneven, while the doc examined him. The nursing staff got busy with blood pressure apparatus. The doc turned to the man and said, 'He'll pull through with luck.

Most of the parameters are stable. It looks like a particularly virulent case of malaria. He needs a blood transfusion and must be put on glucose. He is very weak. I'll put him on a central line so we can get the required medication into him much faster. You guys, go chill. Have a coffee at Shamiana. I'll work on him. And keep you posted.'

They decided to walk to the Taj. The driver was instructed to follow closely. Amrita looked over her shoulder and thought the silent Merc resembled a gigantic bat as it trailed them in the night. She was still too shaken by the sequence of events, by this man's sudden appearance and felt as if she was sleepwalking. They walked into a deserted lobby. An airline's crew was idly hanging around near the long reception counter, behind which hung a magnificent M.F. Husain canvas in flaming orange. The crew was taking time to check in. Amrita stared longingly at the bright red uniforms of the flight attendants and remembered her schoolgirl dream to become a stewardess one day and jet to unbelievably fantastic destinations. Her mother had promptly shot down the idea. 'Oooof! You want to become a glorified ayah and clean toilets? Is that what we have sacrificed so much for, you silly girl?'

The man's voice interrupted Amrita's reverie. 'I have a suite here. We could go upstairs for that coffee or a cognac. There will be more privacy and it's safer.' Amrita nodded as they walked towards the elevators, past the Starboard Bar and India's most famous restaurant, the Zodiac Grill. On entering the suite, Amrita let out a long sigh and reached for the nearest support – a luxuriously stuffed sofa – before losing her balance, sliding off the edge of the two-seater and collapsing on the carpet.

When she opened her eyes, she was propped up against three large pillows on a king-size bed. 'Better? Soup?' he asked from an armchair near the large bay window overlooking the Gateway of India. He was wearing trendy Armani spectacles and glancing through a copy of the *Economist*. Amrita smiled wanly and shook her head.

'How is Babuji?' she inquired. 'Out of danger,' he said and came over to the other side of the bed. Wordlessly, Amrita held out her arms and lifted the quilt to invite him next to her. She hadn't seen him in all these years but it only felt like five minutes. She didn't want answers, she just wanted to be in his arms, the only place she had ever felt safe. Was this a dream? The man removed his Dolce & Gabbana fitted tee with a V-neck, climbed out of his Levi's and got into bed saying lightly, 'There. I've done it. I'm naked. Now it's your turn.' Amrita whispered, 'Undress me and switch off the bedside lamp.' The man said, 'Yes, to the first request. And no to the second. I want to see your body. It has been too long.' Amrita snuggled up to him, her fingers tracing the long length of his torso.

Amrita was startled to discover MK still had so much power over her. It was almost frightening. She ignored the warning bells, as her body willingly went along with MK's demands, falling easily into their old lovemaking routine. She didn't want to 'think'. She just wanted MK. Her body had waited all these many years for that single touch that would awaken it – MK's. And Amrita was not going to let anything stop her from drowning in the moment. Not even the thought of Babuji.

'Show me your birthmark,' Amrita said as she tried to turn him around. 'Still a butt girl, I see,' the man laughed. 'Still a voyeur, I notice,' she commented and pulled him over her supple body. 'I love your smell. Always have,' he said, nuzzling her neck and nibbling her earlobe. 'Liar. This is a brand new smell. New perfume.' He laughed. 'You can switch perfumes but you can't switch your own fragrance. That doesn't come out of a bottle. It comes straight from there.' He reached between her legs, touched her gently and kissed her mouth, using his tongue to stab her lips which remained pursed.

'Obstinate as usual,' he smiled, withdrawing his body, propping himself on an elbow and staring at Amrita with a strange fondness and longing. The kind ex-lovers share and instantly recognize. Amrita stuck her chin out. 'But you still haven't shown me your birthmark. Turn around. Show me! I'll kiss you after that.' The man got out of bed and stood close to her, his erect penis inches away from her face. 'Do we have a deal? I'll show you mine, if you show me yours. Back to playing our old game. You first. Go on, face me and open your legs. I'll find it.' Amrita drew the quilt over her head and muttered, 'That's not fair. I was so much younger then. I can't do that now.'

The man tugged the quilt off her, and the next thing Amrita knew he was inside her, his impatience matching his passion, his mouth over hers forcing it open with a powerful push of his tongue. Amrita felt her breasts swelling up against his chest, her nipples erect and tingling in anticipation of his touch. Just at that feverish moment – limbs, tongues, skin, brains and hearts tangled deliciously, the man's cell phone started to ring. 'Leave it!' Amrita instructed. 'I can't!' the man replied, disentangling himself and grabbing the phone. Amrita could hear a little girl's voice, lisping, 'Papa, where are you? Why aren't you at home? I am scared, Papa. Please come back quickly. I'm so scared. Mama's not at home either.'

Without another word, the man got dressed. He muttered, 'I must leave. Stay here as long as you want. Do not use the phone to call anybody. Lock the door. Keep the curtains drawn. Don't worry about Sethji. We need him alive. That doc will make sure of that. Oh . . . keep this. Just in case . . .' Amrita stared wordlessly at the snub-nosed gun and the cell phone he'd tossed on the bed. When she looked up, he was gone. And Amrita had still to see the birthmark.

CHAPTER 37

Amrita wondered whether to get out of bed and have a shower – a real shower in a real bathroom with real bath products and real towels. It had been a week but it felt like a lifetime. And suddenly in the middle of this new-found comfort, she felt a deep weariness. She was sick of this life-on-the-run. She was sick of Sethji and his roller-coaster political games. Sick of her role in an unfolding saga that had nothing to do with her dreams. Amrita felt trapped and angry. This was so bloody unfair. When she'd married Srichand, she knew she'd be giving up a lot – but this much? How could her mother have imagined she'd 'get used to it'? Why do so many mothers say that to their daughters? At times, Amrita thought it was spiteful of her mother to have talked her into this alliance. Spiteful, and selfish. Seeing MK again brought out the same rush of painful emotions she had felt when she had given him up and chosen to get married.

At such times, Amrita thanked her stars she hadn't produced a child. Now, of course, such an eventuality was ruled out. Amrita had gone along with all the 'treatments' suggested by Sethji including seeing various vaids and performing all sorts of pujas. Sethji had consulted astrologers and gurus but not once had he thought of asking his son to consult a doctor.

'Mere betey mein kuch dosh nahin ho sakta. No fault. No fault in him. He has my sperm after all,' he'd boast, implying the 'fault' was Amrita's. Five years of trying had left Amrita exhausted and devoid of any desire to become a mother. She hated the thought of sleeping with Srichand to begin with.

What made it even worse was the enforced timetable prescribed by fertility experts. Sethji, who monitored his daughter-in-law's menstrual cycles as closely as the takings of his party workers (and going as far as to keep a chart in his bedroom), would demand over parathas at the breakfast table, 'Kuch hua? No? Kuch kiya? No! How can you get pregnant if you don't sleep with your husband? When did you last bleed? I know, it was on the twenty-third of last month. Chalo, let's wait for another week and see. Shall we go to the Ajmer dargah and offer a chaddar? I know it will work. That man Talwar ki aurat went to Ajmer and, phat, she got pregnant. The pir there is very powerful.' Amrita knew better than to argue with Sethji when he was stuck on this topic.

Once, when Srichand angrily left the table, Amrita asked Sethji exasperatedly, 'Why don't you give up, Babuji? Or ask your son to see a doctor?' Sethji furiously pushed his plate away and hollered, 'Hold your tongue, woman! There is nothing wrong with my son. We are a family of asli mards – we are real men! It is your womb that is weak, it is your bloodline that is tainted. I have checked up on your family tree. Now I am beginning to wonder about your paternity. Maybe your father was impotent.'

Tears of rage stung Amrita's eyes, but she bit back her words. She had blocked all thoughts of her liaison with Sethji. Or else she would have asked him why, despite their own couplings after her marriage to his son, she hadn't conceived.

But of course, she also knew what his retort would have been. He would have pointed to Maaji's portrait and taunted, 'Look at the mother of my two sturdy sons – she had no taqleef conceiving. Her womb was perfectly fertile.'

The force of the shower invigorated her tired body. She thought about MK's birthmark and smiled. What a strange world they both occupied. And how very different it was from those early days when they knew each other – he, a brash, dashing student leader, and she the reluctant beauty queen of her college – a title she was still so embarrassed about. The first time they'd 'done it' was in the back seat of a borrowed car. He'd wanted to see her naked body, and she had been paralysed at the thought of peeping toms turning up and interrupting their lovemaking. The tension had made her tighten her muscles, making his entry difficult and painful.

'Relax, Amrita, relax. Trust me. I won't hurt you,' he'd instructed, as he stroked her inner thighs. Just as he was about to penetrate her, Amrita spotted a man's face outside the rolled-up windows of the Ambassador car, and let out a scream. That was it! He had reacted with admirable alacrity, jumping nimbly to the front seat, switching on the ignition, putting the car into reverse gear, and backing out at top speed from the dark, narrow alley, as the intruder hurled stones at the car.

MK had turned to Amrita with a rakish grin, once they'd hit the main road, and teased, 'Oh ho, kamaal hai, Miss Beauty Queen – what a way to save your virginity! How much did you pay that fellow? Next time, darling, just say a simple no! But let me tell you right now, I'm the guy who's going to have you first. That's a promise, not a threat. You are going to love it and you will love me forever after that. Kasam se.

I am not boasting. Just telling you straight. So, darling, keep yourself for me and me alone. I'm the best! And you're the best, meri jaan.'

Amrita smiled at the memory. Of course, he was right. He was the best. And when they finally did have sex, it was in the perfect setting – a plush hotel suite, just like the one she was in right now. He had 'borrowed' it from one of his father's hotelier friends and like he had promised, 'full filmi-style romance' marked the big occasion, complete with a post-coital popping of champagne, and clinked glasses while lying on a canopied bed covered with rose petals. He'd smirked, 'I feel like Shah Jahan.' She had laughed, 'With his favourite nautch girl or Mumtaz Mahal?' He'd answered seriously, 'That's a sad love story, ours will be happier. You wait and see.'

In the background hovered the marriage that had been arranged for him with a wealthy family friend's daughter. He had promised to break his engagement. She had waited. For five long years. Till she heard about his nikaah from a common friend. On the day of her marriage to Srichand, she had received a large, decorated tokri filled with mogras. She didn't have to check the identity of the sender. Mogras were 'their' flowers. Whenever and wherever they met, he made sure there were mogras around. Sometimes strung into garlands, often unstrung and placed in glass bowls at strategic places around the room. These he would scoop in the palms of his hands and pour over her naked body, scatter them into her hair streaming over plump pillows, place between her toes, and arrange carefully around her pubes. It was a ritual both enjoyed. Mogras defined the mood of their intense lovemaking. The crushed flowers, left to die on the bed at the end of their frenzied coupling, told their own sweet story.

After marrying Srichand, Amrita stopped wearing mogra gajras in her loosely tied bun. She stopped buying mogras at traffic signals. She wanted to obliterate any memory of those fragrant blossoms from her life. A life she had started to despise. A life she saw as wretched. She had deadened herself to beauty and that happened the night Sethji came to her room, about a year after her marriage to his older son. But now, as she caressed herself under the shower, tracing her fingers lightly over her breasts, she felt an unaccustomed arousal. She reached for the hand shower, placing its powerful jet between her legs, her body shuddering with longing. As she slid to the floor of the shower cubicle, she opened her legs wider, and increased the pressure of the water till she climaxed over and over again, her thighs squeezing together to maximize and extend the delicious tingling that had taken over her mind, her body.

Memories, long suppressed, were flooding back now. Memories that she had locked up because they were so dangerous. She remembered the days when she used to be so sensitive to the slightest touch – her own, or his. She recalled vividly those restless nights she'd clamp soft pillows between her legs and imagine it was him, as she rubbed herself rhythmically against them till she felt the tiny little bud between her legs exploding with indescribable pleasure. Not once but over and over again. In those days, she would miss his body so acutely, it made her wonder whether it was a sickness.

She'd touch herself in the middle of the day and then place the fingers under her nostrils inhaling the smell of her own sex – the way he used to before saying goodbye after a tryst. 'I want to smell and taste your musk on my tongue, on my fingers, inside my mouth till we meet again. I long for you, Amrita. Your breasts, your nipples, those tiny moles surrounding them. Your calves and the soft folds of flesh behind them. I can't spare even your eyelids. I must be mad! But I even want to fuck your eyes – literally! Your eyes, your navel, your ears, every bit of you . . . I wish there was some way I could remain inside you always and forever.' His hot-blooded words came rushing back to her now. Words that she had so determinedly shut out the day she had got married. The day when she had transformed from his fiery goddess to the inscrutable ice princess that she was today. But in a stroke he had turned back time, and melted her.

Amrita reluctantly raised herself up from the floor of the shower cubicle and emerged from under the shower. She wiped the stickiness that was dripping down her wet thighs and smiled. It had been a long, long time since she had felt this uncontrollably aroused. And it was a warm, wonderful feeling she wanted to cherish as she waited impatiently for him to return – avoiding the questions that desperately needed answering.

CHAPTER 38

Hours later, sitting silently next to Babuji's bed in the polyclinic, those stolen hours seemed like a strange dream. Babuji needed blood – a lot of it. Amrita was very worried. His blood group was rare enough not to be instantly available. The only persons she knew who shared it with him were his sons. One was out of the country, the other, doped out of his skull. And both were in the hands of Bhau.

When MK didn't return to the Taj suite, she wasn't surprised. He had appeared all too suddenly, and left a trail of unanswered questions and she imagined that he had his own complications to deal with. One part of her believed that he'd make sure he'd see her through this particular crisis, no matter what. They owed each other this much. He'd know just how desperately she needed him in this strange, unfriendly and impersonal city where she was a nobody, a stranger. Amrita in Mumbai was just another beautiful woman without a man by her side. Worse, she was stuck with a seriously ailing father-in-law, in a shabby clinic, with no money and absolutely nowhere to go. But the other part of her wondered if MK could really be relied on. What was his connection to Bhau? And was she being sucked into another deeper, darker game?

MK finally called late at night. The exchange was brief and

to the point. 'You'll have to move soon. You and Sethji. I'll make all the arrangements. Leave it to me. And don't use the phone I left for you. I will call you, okay?' She knew better than to utter a word. All she said was, 'Ji.' 'Is he better?' 'Still weak but yes, he has improved. Thank you,' replied Amrita ending their brief conversation. She didn't feel reassured after hearing MK's voice. Things were still too uncertain. Sethji and she were safe for now, their location still undetected. But she knew it wouldn't remain that way and yet how and where could she move the old man in his condition? The nurse came in to say his pulse was low and that he needed blood immediately.

There was one thing Amrita could do – pray. Pray hard. At times like this, she'd remember her mother telling her, 'When you give up on God, you give up on yourself. Don't do that. There is always a way. There is always hope. And no matter how discouraged you feel, turn to the Almighty. But remember, don't curse what He gives you. That is His will. Accept it, and you might survive the worst. Fight it and you're finished! Bas khel khatam. Picture over. The End on the screen.' Amrita was not prepared for 'The End' – not for herself, not for Sethji.

She asked the nurse calmly, 'Is there a Shivji temple close by?' The nurse replied, 'I know only Colaba Church. I am a Christian from Kerala. My village is near Kochi.' Amrita wanted to scream, 'I don't want to hear about your fucking village in Kerala. Just lead me to a temple, any temple.' But she knew better than to scream at a nurse in whose hands she had entrusted the life of her father-in-law. The nurse spoke again, 'Madam, you won't get blood in a temple or a church. If it is okay, I have my source. He will arrange. But too much money he is asking, too much. You are having money, no?

Then, no problem. I am making phone call now only and telling him. That way, he's reliable. Saves lives, also. Last minute, where people can go, no? Say fast-fast. You want blood or no? I'll arrange. But not to tell doctor saab. You tell him your relative came and gave, okay? Otherwise, my job gone. Boss is strict. Okay, shall I phone? Costly but life is also costly. What we can do?'

Amrita snapped, 'Yes. Call. But my money is not with me at this moment.' The nurse put down the receiver promptly. 'Oh-ho. Then no blood. He don't take credit card, no? What about ATM? You have ATM card?' Amrita shook her head. The nurse stared pointedly at her throat and wrist. 'Gold you are having, no? Thick-thick chain, bangles also. At least fifteen tolas. That is enough. You give gold. He'll give blood. Decide fast-fast. Old man sinking, no? Waiting, waiting not good. Patient off ho jayega.' Amrita removed one bangle off her right wrist. The nurse shook her head and said, 'All! What will one bangle fetch? Half a bottle of blood? He will need at least five. Madam, hand over the other bangles, and I'll make the call.'

CHAPTER 39

Dawn was breaking over the Gateway of India, as Amrita dozed off on a rexine chair next to Sethji's bed. She was awoken by a familiar roar, 'Saaley, haramkhor. Kya ho raha hai?' Amrita reached over and held Sethji's hand. 'I am here, Babuji,' she said softly. 'Don't worry, there was a small accident. A car accident. We are in a clinic, it's okay.' Sethji tried to sit up but fell back on his pillows, demanding impatiently, 'What's okay? Nothing is okay, samjhi? What happened to Bhau? Where is that haramzaada? Why are we here? Wasting time for nothing. Niklo idhar se quickly. Chalo, chalo. We must leave immediately.'

He tried to roll off the hospital cot, quite forgetting he was hooked up to an IV feed. Amrita stood over him and firmly held his shoulders down. 'You are weak and seriously ill. Please stay still. I am waiting for the doctor to come and examine you.' Sethji raised his voice to the extent he could. 'Are you mad, woman? Which doctor? What doctor? We are in Mumbai, not Delhi. These people are khatarnak, the doctor will kill me. That is his job. That bhadwa Bhau must have sent him for me. Now you do as I tell you. Get me out of here, that is the first step. Do it! Now!!'

Amrita didn't know whether to be frustrated or amused by Sethji's behaviour. Here he was, just out of a serious medical

crisis, still extremely weak, and raring to go. And maybe
he was right, it might be better to use this opportunity and
disappear. MK could come later. Besides, was he to be trusted?
Whatever Amrita felt about her father-in-law, she always took
his razor-sharp instincts seriously. If he wanted to leave, they
should. Not that she had a say in the matter. He'd probably
yank off the drip going into his veins if he had to and drag his
body down those old, wooden stairs, past the lurid tin signs
advertising a local version of Viagra. The picture on the tin
plate was of a stallion with a monumental erection. Even in
this semi-comatose state, Amrita knew Sethji would notice it
and smirk, 'Saala, dekho, ghodey ki lund dikha ke mardon
ko bewakoof bana rahey hain.'

Amrita rang the bell for the nurse. Fortunately, her 'saviour'
from last night had left after finishing her night duty and
pocketing a fat commission from the 'bloodsucker'. Her
replacement looked more like a bar dancer wearing a nurse's
uniform – the make-up! The obviously stuffed bra! 'Yes,
madam?' she inquired, her eyes blank, her voice, a babyish
lisp. 'We want to leave immediately. Please take the IV needle
out. We are in a hurry.' The young girl stared at her with
zero comprehension and repeated, 'Yes, madam?' Amrita
said sharply, 'Do you not understand what I am saying? We
want to be discharged. Right now.'

The nurse ran out of the room, her eyes wide with fear.
A minute later, a young man who looked like a model for
trendy Friday dressing strode in casually. Before he too could
go into the 'Yes, madam?' routine, Amrita told him briskly
they were leaving and would he please do as asked. Sethji
shouted, 'Arrey kuttey, can't you understand simple language
in this bloody city? We want to leave. Samjhey? Come on.

Do as you are told.' The cocky fellow stood there grinning, playing with the stethoscope around his neck. Then he drawled, 'Sorry, sir, madam, but I don't take orders from my patients. I have instructions to keep you here till you recover fully. According to me, you are far from being declared as fully recovered.' Amrita spluttered, 'Instructions? Who from? What are you talking about? You'll listen to Sethji, if you know what's good for you.' The doctor grinned some more and shook his head. 'Sorry, madam. That's not happening.' Swiftly, noiselessly, Amrita reached inside her handbag and pulled out the snub-nosed gun, enjoying the way it felt in her palms. MK would not have anticipated that Amrita would have to use it so soon.

CHAPTER 40

Within minutes, Amrita had bundled Sethji into a dilapidated cab with rusted doors, electric blue curtains with yellow frills and slippery plastic-covered seats. 'Main nahin marney waala. You think I'd die so easily, huh? Like some weakling? Why all this fuss? I think you enjoy seeing me suffer. All of you get a kick out of it – admit it. You want me to die, don't you? And that useless fellow who calls himself your husband. You want him to die, too. Then you can grab all that we own. Become a maharani. Live like a queen. Let me assure you – I am not ready to die. I have a lot of work to complete . . .' Sethji's words faded away, as he fell back on the seat. Amrita quickly checked – alive! He was alive but had passed out. Even the short journey from hospital cot into the cab downstairs had been too much for him.

She told the taxi driver to head for the airport. The cabbie looked out of the car window at the worsening weather and said, 'Two thousand.' Amrita yelled, 'What? What did you say?' The cabbie shrugged, 'Flooded roads, rain is not going to stop. Two thousand or find another cab.' Amrita checked herself. 'Why only two thousand, bhai saab? I'll give you two thousand plus an extra three hundred. Chalo. We are getting late. I have a heart patient.'

The driver made eye contact with her and asked, 'Saab mar

gaya, kya? I don't want any police lafda. Let me drop you to Jaslok Hospital. It's on the way.' Amrita told him to keep driving. She assured him Sethji was tired and taking a nap. The driver looked unconvinced but said nothing. He switched on the car radio. She had no idea how she'd pay the fare, but she had to keep moving and thinking. The drive would take close to two hours, even if the driver decided to use the Sea Link. She needed more time than that. She instructed the man to avoid the Sea Link as she was not in a hurry. Besides, who'd pay the pricey toll?

The cabbie changed gears and took off noisily, after switching on the car stereo, pumping up the volume and shaking his head to the latest Bollywood item song. Amrita noticed the 'Jai Mata Di' sticker on the windshield, the tiny plastic shrine above the ignition key, with a bright red, tinsel-bordered scarf and a tiny bulb designed to look like a flickering flame. 'Jai Mata Di' she said loudly and folded her hands as if in deep prayer. To underline her faith, she muttered a few mantras, closed her eyes, touched her forehead and kissed her fingers. She noticed the cabbie observing Sethji in the rear-view mirror. 'From Dilli?' the cabbie asked. 'Haan. New to Mumbai. Heart patient treatment. We've heard Mumbai's doctors are very good. Best in the world.' The cabbie laughed. 'Everything in this city's the best in the world, memsaab. Even the cabs!' Amrita forced a laugh out of herself.

The cabbie was warming up. 'I am also from Dilli . . . not the city, but close by. I am from Mathura. Been there, memsaab?' Amrita wondered whether or not to fib and say she had. She decided it might be wise to lie. She needed to keep the man on her side. 'It is lucky for you, madam. A truly holy city. Radhey! Radhey! Krishna! Krishna!' The cabbie looked pleased and started discussing kachoris and kulchas. 'Mumbai is all right, but you can't get good kulchas here,' he complained. 'No? So what is good in Mumbai?' asked Amrita. The cabbie grinned wickedly. 'Maal!' he chuckled, 'best maal comes to Mumbai.'

The phone MK had given her suddenly rang. Amrita pounced on it. MK said, 'What are you doing? Didn't I tell you not to move anywhere? I know you don't trust me, Amrita, but don't be foolish. It's no longer your life that is at risk. I have staked everything too. Tell the driver of the cab to make a sharp right turn when he reaches the Haji Ali crossing. There's a white Honda City parked in front of the large shopping mall across the road. Get out of the cab and get into it. The man in the car will help you and pay the cabbie. Don't waste a single minute.'

Amrita was about to argue but stopped herself. She recognized the urgency in his voice. Whether it was their old love being ignited, or the panic she heard, something told her to give him a chance. She turned to the cab driver, saying, 'I am not going to the airport. Please drop me where I tell you, near Haji Ali.' The man grinned. 'Appointment hai kya? Chalo, theek hai. Take care of the old man. He looks seriously ill. May not last too long.' Amrita grinned back. 'You don't know Sethji, bhai saab. He may outlive both of us.'

The white Honda City was waiting for them exactly where he'd said it would be. Leaning against the car, someone paid the cabbie. By that time Sethji had awoken, though he was still groggy. 'Where are we? This is not the airport, is it?' 'No, Babuji, we are going somewhere else where we will be safe. The man who saved us yesterday is making all the arrangements.' 'Who is he? Do you know him?' asked

Sethji, his eyes suddenly alert. 'Why is he helping us?' 'No
. . . yes,' blushed Amrita, hoping that Sethji was too ill to
notice her discomfort. 'Babuji, the time for answers is later.
Come, let's go.'

They were taken to a service flat in Lower Parel. It was
comfortable with a living room, cable TV and two bedrooms
with views of a busy complex. Sethji had fallen into a
stupor again once he was in the car, and had to be carried
with enormous difficulty to his room, where a nurse was
on standby.

MK was waiting for her in the other bedroom. He was
dressed in a sharp suit, and smelling of Nomad. Amrita found
all tiredness drain out of her. Seeing him, she forgot all her
suspicions of him, all the questions in her head. She hadn't
realized that she had been staring at him hungrily without
the slightest embarrassment. MK smiled. 'That good, huh?'
Amrita hastily looked away and reached for an apple. He
approached her, pulled her to him by her waist. 'It was good
that night, wasn't it? Could have been better. I hate unfinished
business. It's time to complete what we'd begun . . .' he said
and kissed her. Amrita allowed herself to be drawn into his
kiss, but she quickly moved away.

There! MK had done it again. Mesmerized her into losing
her mind. Amrita tried vainly to fight him off, struggling
to wriggle out of his embrace. MK pushed himself against
her almost aggressively. She could feel him hardening, as
MK placed his right hand over her buttocks and pulled her
closer. This time, Amrita told herself, she was not going to
give in . . . she would find the strength to resist . . . to fight.
But her knees were beginning to buckle and MK was trying
yet another trick to soften her. He began to utter her name

hoarsely . . . over and over again. Muttering, 'I love you
. . . I love you . . . I love you.' Amrita hated MK at that
moment with an intensity that surprised her. Or maybe, she
just hated herself for being in such a ridiculous situation –
caught between two men who desired her body.

One of whom revolted her. The other who obliterated
reason. Either way, it was sickening and demeaning. Amrita
had had enough! So many lies, so much deception. And MK
was still swearing love . . . dying to make it too. Right there
. . . under grotesque circumstances. No. Amrita had made
up her mind, as she managed to extricate herself from his
embrace and say, 'MK, stop it! Stop it this minute. We need
to talk.' Caught off guard, MK backed off and held up his
hands dramatically. 'Okay . . . so talk! What the fuck do you
want to talk about?'

'MK, what the hell is going on? How are you involved in
all this? How do you know Bhau? Why did you disappear
last night? What do you want from me? From Sethji? Who
do you work for? I am going crazy. I refuse to believe you
just turned up out of nowhere to help me. After all those
many years of zero contact. So stop playing games. Just tell
me!' MK sat her down on the bed and holding her hand he
began to talk. Amrita listened stonily. MK had always been
an outstanding bullshitter. How would she know whether he
was telling her the truth?

CHAPTER 41

Bhau was on the terrace of the bungalow drinking his first cup of tea ('There's nothing like Mai's tea, she has magic in her fingers') when his son Aadesh broke the news of Sethji's escape to him. Bhau threw down the cup, his hands shaking. 'What is this nonsense you are telling me first thing in the morning – I have yet to finish my tea. You couldn't wait to give me bad news?' Aadesh stared at his feet and said nothing. Bhau roared, 'Round up all those jokers we employ. Ask them. I want an explanation immediately. No! Stop! No explanation. I want to kill the man who botched up this job.' Aadesh said quietly, 'Both men are dead, Baba.' Bhau demanded, 'What? Who killed them? How? The plan was perfect. We had taken every precaution. Where's Yashwant? Sleeping in the arms of some rundi? Get him!'

Aadesh said quietly, 'It has nothing to do with Yashwant, Baba. We know a car deliberately crashed into our car, in which Sethji and his bahu were, but unfortunately that's all we know.' Bhau shook his head in disbelief. 'Kya bakwas keh rahey ho!' Whose car was it – the one that crashed into ours? Nobody knew about our plan. There has been a bloody double-cross here – a leak! Do we know if Sethji is alive? Where the hell is he?' Aadesh hesitated. 'We don't know, but our men are on the job. We'll find them.' Bhau caught his son by the shoulders and said evenly, 'I thought you were reasonably smart. Not very smart, mind you, but chalta-hai smart. That's why I had handed over their transport arrangements to you. Now I know you are an absolute asshole!

'But let's play this to our advantage. There's no point concealing Suraj's death any more, is there?' Bhau hissed. 'We must let everyone know. But let us make it seem like it was deliberate. Whoever helped Sethji escape will surely give him the bad news about his son as well. Sethji will know that my threats mean something, they aren't empty ones. I want Sethji to realize I can do to Srichand what I have done to Suraj. He may be the less precious son but he's the only one left now. Sethji may run, but he will come back. He needs us. I am the snake, he the mongoose. Let us prepare ourselves better this time.'

***

While Sethji and Amrita had been struggling in Mumbai, and Srichand was entrapped in a drug-induced haze, Suraj had been treated surprisingly well by his captors in Dubai. He was kept in a sleek-looking house, and his room had a view of the sea and the sports cars parked below. He would be given food and allowed out for a short walk once a day. 'Suraj . . . saala . . . you should be in Bollywood, yaar! Kya acting-shacting karta hai!' Suraj recalled Shakeel's words as he planned to fool his lazy, indifferent guards. Theirs was a boring job, made worse by the searing loo from the desert, each time they stepped out for a smoke.

Suraj, forced to spend hours in their company, watching

mindless Hollywood action films, strenuously strained to establish a level of communication by asking for a few puffs or admiring their uniforms. Nothing worked. Most times, it was a monologue that received a monosyllabic response or a few grunts from the guards. Till the day Suraj discovered the special passion Abdul, one of the guards, harboured for spiffy sports cars. Suraj took to talking about cars animatedly, hoping for a breakthrough. If there was one subject in the world Suraj was an expert on, it was sports cars. Fortunately, it happened when Abdul was assigned to accompany Suraj on his daily after-dinner walk.

'I have every sports car you can imagine in Delhi. I would love to look at these cars closely during my next walk. Is that possible?' Suraj said wistfully to Abdul, staring at the latest Porsche in the compound. Suraj had inherited Sethji's roguish charm. He could be irresistible when he wanted to be and Abdul couldn't remain immune. Visiting the cars soon became a regular feature of his daily late-night walk until one day Suraj pushed his luck. 'Do you think I could actually sit in the car? Do you have the keys? Just for a few seconds . . . I want to see the new dashboard. My Ferrari model is slightly old,' he said glibly to Abdul, who reluctantly agreed and opened the door of one of the many Ferraris. Suraj slipped in and in a flash leaned out of his seat, grabbed the keys, locked himself in and sped away.

It was a daring escape, but short-lived. Suraj died while on the run. Two men in a sleek, white Porsche had chased his Ferrari on the deserted highway that connected Dubai to Abu Dhabi. He'd spotted their headlights in the rear-view mirror and rashly accelerated. Unfortunately for Suraj, he'd lost control of the unfamiliar car while negotiating a sharp turn on a flyover. Suraj had crashed into the metal railings, and been flung out of the low-slung car before it burst into flames.

The hitmen who'd been pursuing him saved their bullets, as they whirled their car around and drove back to Dubai for a quick beer and shawarma. They wondered whether they'd get paid for the job with the way it had ended. They needn't have worried. A briefcase stashed with soiled dirhams was waiting for them at the guest house when they finally got back after consuming nearly a crate of Coronas. Fifteen per cent of the promised amount had been duly deducted, but they weren't complaining. Fair is fair, they babbled and slurred as they got out of their sweaty, smelly jeans bought at the Al Karama Bazaar, where every second shopkeeper spoke Malayalam and smelled of coconut oil. They laughed at the easy money they'd made and wondered whether Suraj's body was still lying in a pool of gasoline and blood.

Dubai cops were just like their desi counterparts – they invariably arrived hours after a murder had been committed in public and generally closed the investigation a few weeks later claiming a lack of evidence. Suraj's death would be recorded in an obscure police station, and quickly forgotten. Desert hits were just that – hits. Nothing personal. Dubai attracted gangsters from across the world. One gangster here and there hardly mattered. As the men put away their guns, they laughed some more. 'Saala. Gaya narak mein. Goli bhi bach gayee. Shukriya aabe, abhraha tu aur tera Khuda.' They turned in for the night, their breaths heavy with the beer, their bellies rising and falling visibly, as a small fan whirled noisily from the low ceiling. Nobody heard the two muted shots that killed them in their sleep. Nobody cared either.

Part 3

'Never share your secrets with anybody. It will destroy you.'

—Kautilya

CHAPTER 42

MK had finally begun to give Amrita some answers – though how much was true, she could never be sure. After college and Amrita's marriage, he had moved back to Mumbai and reunited with his family. He'd promptly married Tabassum, his fiancée, at a well-attended nikaah, extensively covered by the media. Both families had rejoiced at the alliance which had consolidated their respective businesses. But MK had announced other plans. He'd taken everyone by surprise, declaring he wanted to pursue further studies. Immediately after their honeymoon in the Prague, the couple had moved to Boston, where MK had got admission into Harvard Law School.

MK had done brilliantly there, throwing himself into a structured, focused life, graduating with high honours and turning down attractive offers to join any one of the top law firms in New York. He wanted to come home. He had missed Mumbai and it was time to reconnect with the city that had had such a seminal influence on him. His wife was keen on returning to her maternal home as well.

It didn't take much time for MK to set up a corporate law firm in Mumbai. With his sharp business instincts and old contacts, MK soon became a sought-after deal-maker, known to represent the best interests of his clients while making a killing – for himself and those he so ably represented. Because of his film producer father, he also became the go-to man for big Bollywood deals. A couple of years later, he met Bhau's younger son, Aadesh, who had been his friend in school. Aadesh had some routine work for him and the two quickly renewed their old friendship. Soon, MK began to play an increasingly important role in Aadesh's life.

It got to a stage where, much to his family's astonishment, Aadesh refused to take a single decision, big or small, without MK's advice. It was MK he depended on, even when it came to matters of his personal life. MK was the one who 'approved' of Ashwini, Aadesh's future wife, after Bhau had screened her. It was MK who managed to keep at bay a potential blackmailer who had dirt about Aadesh's fondness for rent boys. And it was MK who tried to reconcile him with his elder brother, Yashwant, time and time again. For all this and more, Aadesh felt indebted to MK and, over time, assigned more and more responsibilities to the canny lawyer, whose brain was as sharp as the suits he wore.

Bhau too approved of this smooth-talking, supremely intelligent family friend. In Bhau's mind, it also made political sense to deal with a Muslim lawyer, whose father had 'connections' that extended to Pakistan, Dubai and beyond. MK was the kind of gutsy mercenary Bhau enjoyed doing business with. Just like he'd enjoyed working with MK's father, known simply as 'Khan Saab' in the movie industry. Bhau noted enviously that Khan Saab had tutored his son well. MK was even more ruthless than his father. And, as Bhau often remarked when discussing the father–son duo with close aides, well educated and better looking, too. Khan Saab was an 'angootha chhap' (an illiterate man who 'signed' documents with a thumbprint) yet he had had the foresight to send his boy to a good college in Delhi, and then supported MK's decision to enrol in one of the world's best law schools, besides allowing MK to forge his own relationships.

Bhau let it be known within his party that MK was his protégé and he personally orchestrated the rise of MK, introducing him to key associates. Soon MK was doing other related assignments for Bhau. If there were issues to take care of within the builders' lobby, MK was the chosen one. It was MK who brokered the megadeals and dealt with politicians across the board. It was MK who knew all their dirty doings and commercial secrets. It was MK alone who knew how to leverage them at the opportune time. And it was MK who acted as Bhau's go-between with Jaiprakash Jethia.

To seal their friendship, MK was just about to go into a partnership with Bhau's sons and the property developer Hridaynath Joglekar to develop illegally acquired land in Tardeo as a super luxury mall. The three men had visited Joglekar in his nondescript home in Ville Parle to make their offer. Joglekar was a surprisingly soft-spoken man. Clad in trendy designer jeans and hanging on to a can of Diet Coke, he spoke rapidly, in short, sharp sentences – his language a hybrid mix of Bambaiya Hindi, murdered English and chaste Marathi.

The three men were amused to be served non-refrigerated water in tall, heavy steel tumblers, along with two overripe bananas and a few limp potato chips in a plastic plate. A box of paper napkins was positioned at the centre table, which also had a brass flower vase filled with garish fake flowers. The brightly patterned upholstered chairs were carefully protected with thick plastic covers on their backs. On the patchy blue-

painted walls, MK noticed elaborately framed pictures of
various gods and goddesses with flickering electric bulbs that
mimicked candle flames. These pictures were also garlanded
with rows upon rows of artificial flowers, interspersed with
plastic pearls and tinsel tassels. On the other side table was
a framed picture of Hridaynath Joglekar's dead wife (it
was rumoured he'd had her killed when he discovered she
was having an affair with one of his aides). There were no
pictures of his two young children who lived with their
maternal grandparents.

At one point an attack dog was led into the room for
his midday treat – Baskin Robbins ice cream, which was
personally served to the beast by his loving master. Hridaynath
grinned as he urged Hero to lap up the rapidly melting ice
cream. 'Meet my family – this handsome boy is my son. He
loves me. I love him. Come on . . . say hello.' MK grimaced
as the dog came up and sniffed his crotch. Hridaynath
laughed. 'Have you been up to some masti recently? Admit
it! You can't fool my son. He sniffs out trouble better than a
detective – ha ha ha!'

The meeting had been a very useful one. Hridaynath
Joglekar wished to own Mumbai. Own – not merely control
it. In his early forties, he was still young enough to plan ahead,
and headstrong enough to go where old hands wouldn't want
to venture. His focus remained on acquiring undervalued
land in central Mumbai, most of it entangled in complex
legal webs. He had successfully negotiated terms with over
a hundred chawl dwellers living for decades around an
ambitious residential project in Tardeo, once considered a
downmarket labour-class area.

To Joglekar, though, a plot in central, if yet undeveloped,

Tardeo was worth more than tracts and tracts of suburban land. 'My mines are pure gold,' he had laughed. 'I don't need to exploit poor tribals in Orissa for iron ore business. All I need to do is to get rid of these squatters, slum dwellers and chawlwallas, bas. This is where you men come in. I have some outstanding problems with the chawlwallas. Help me with this problem, come into partnership and then see . . . our buildings will touch the sky. Mumbai's outline will be redrawn by us. It can all happen within the next five years.' To emphasize his point further, he snapped his fingers dramatically and repeated, 'Phataphat! Five years, no more.'

MK and Bhau knew how to deal with this new breed of urban squatters. But the chawl owners today were tough. They were no longer the victims who'd willingly settle for a pittance thrown at them by property developers fronting for politicians. Today's squatter knew his price and had sharp agents to work out juicy settlements in hard cash. Aware of his rights and unwilling to go along with arm-twisting, the chawl owner was in no hurry to vacate.

Neither was he scared for his life. He knew it was a matter of setting up one goon squad against another, one politician against another. He realized only too well that if he sat tight and refused to move that piece of property was worth nothing. To counter this problem, Hridaynath Joglekar had offered them astronomical amounts and ruined the market for other builders. But to gain absolute control over the tough, hard-negotiating Tardeo chawl owners, Hridaynath's goon squad also had to out-muscle three other goon squads. The rival goons owed their allegiance to older, more established political bosses. If Bhau and his sons backed Hridaynath, many would jump ship to him.

Besides, Joglekar needed silent investors as well – Vrindawan Towers, the building complex he was planning to build, was a big dream but the big dream was bleeding him dry. Billed as the most expensive residential tower in India, Vrindawan Towers would have four penthouses on the sixty-fifth floor, a helipad on the roof, an Olympic-sized swimming pool, a state-of-the-art gym, a swanky shopping arcade, interconnected bridges and glass, glass, glass everywhere. Plus, the mandatory dancing fountains, of course! Every ambitious builder in India was after just one architectural 'statement' – à la Dubai's. Preferably, fountains that could dance to Bollywood hits. This project was to be a building that would outshine anything in Dubai. Joglekar wanted to reserve enough space for a glamorous casino attached to a seven-star hotel to be constructed at a later date once permissions kicked in. This would not only make the sprawling complex one of the priciest in India, but would set fresh benchmarks for similar projects in other destinations. Hridaynath was already offering flats at a heavily discounted price to Bollywood stars and sports icons, 'By invitation only'. Just that announcement had seen real-estate prices rocket.

After the deal was inked, MK leaned back and said, 'Why call such an ambitious, modern tower by such an old-fashioned name? Let's think of something more global . . . like Boston Towers. Boston is as historic a city as Mumbai, and I have a special connection to it.' 'Wah,' said Joglekar, 'good name, good name. Achcha laga. Boston Towers . . . wah! This is why I need people like you, MK. We make a good team.' For MK, this was his big, independent entrée into Mumbai's complex real-estate world. If he pulled off this project, he would be laying the foundation for future joint ventures that would consolidate his position in Mumbai. For Bhau, Yashwant and Aadesh, it was the most profitable deal of their careers and it came at a time when Bhau was most vulnerable within his own party.

The deal had made MK even closer to the family, for he had conceptualized, structured and seen it through. But construction activities aside, it was their joint deals with Bollywood and MK that Bhau and his family most enjoyed – he and his sons were obsessed by the movies. Using his producer father Khan Saab's connections, MK helped set up a futuristic production house specializing in 3D technology in which Bhau was the silent investor. If his party workers resented the crores of party funds that were diverted into the production of several duds that lost money, they were smart enough to keep their mouths shut. Besides, Bhau's sons were totally enamoured of Bollywood and Yashwant in particular had made no secret of his love for a married starlet, a former beauty queen, and had informed Bhau of his plans to leave his wife and marry her, whether or not Bhau approved.

That had come to nothing, after the starlet was discovered with a few deep gashes across her arms, a fracture on her left leg and a black eye that took months to fade. It was dubbed an accident on the sets of the action film she was shooting at the time. But the message had gone out to Yashwant, who had sheepishly crept back to his distraught wife. MK had been involved . . . behind the scenes, of course! The more troubling liaisons were those Aadesh conducted secretly with aspiring young men from the modelling and movie worlds. It was such a closely guarded secret that even Bhau remained unaware of it. In the earlier days, Aadesh was discreet enough to conduct his gay encounters while holidaying abroad. But over the years he had become more daring, taking the sort of chances that were not just risky but downright foolish.

His latest obsession was the upcoming young star Shoaib K., son of an ex-superstar, famous for his 'sharabi aankhen' and his exquisitely sculpted body. He had made his name in Aadesh's latest production, titled *For My Eyes Only*. Shaazia, Bollywood's hottest item girl, had swung energetically with Shoaib to its hit dance track 'My body . . . your body . . . who needs anybody?' and their chemistry had made the song a chartbuster. Everybody assumed Shaazia was Aadesh's current mistress. They were wrong. The person who had caught his fancy was Shoaib, not Shaazia. And Shoaib was refusing to play along.

Aadesh was thrown by the unexpected passion he felt for the handsome young actor. Rebuffed by Shoaib, he was going all out to court him, sending gigantic bouquets to his vanity van, with invitations to dinner. Thwarted but not defeated, Aadesh decided to up the courtship game by including expensive gifts with the flower arrangements. The latest offering was an impressive Panerai watch, with a note: 'Just in case you forget the time when we are together.'

Shoaib was flattered but uneasy about Aadesh's attention. However, the young star was also looking for another big hit and a great deal of PR to stay in the game. He knew Aadesh was in a position to fix both. If Aadesh signed him on as the main lead for his next big film, *Jab You Left*, opposite Anamika Singhvi, the daughter of another former star, his career would remain on track and all those commercial endorsements his manager was pitching for would automatically follow. It was just that Shoaib wasn't prepared for this new romantic development with Aadesh, who had, so far, managed to keep a straight reputation in Bollywood. What had changed? Why had Aadesh picked him? Shoaib was shrewd enough to figure that sooner or later he would have to give a little, to get some back. Till then, he would keep Aadesh panting.

Aadesh himself couldn't quite understand his attraction to Shoaib. All he knew was he wanted the boy with 'those' eyes, and that slim, golden, hairless body. Whenever they were together, Aadesh would almost stop breathing in his presence . . . Shoaib made him that dizzy with desire. Aadesh was not going to take no for an answer. But he was not going to force himself on Shoaib either. He would woo him successfully, like he had wooed all the others in the past. Which man didn't enjoy being pampered, adored and worshipped? Aadesh was ready to admit he was smitten – fida. And he was prepared to wait. The boy was arrogant. Aadesh liked that. But he would soon be won over. Aadesh smiled smugly at the thought. Getting his way was a habit with him. And the man who helped him get his way time and time again was MK.

CHAPTER 43

The mega real-estate deal was just about to be tied up when an unexpected conversation shattered MK's ties with Aadesh. As Bhau had got older and weaker, the rivalry between his two sons had become more intense. Aadesh, the more intelligent but more volatile of the two, was determined to win his father's throne. There was only one way to achieve this – Yashwant would have to be eliminated from the race. Aadesh first approached the family's trusted retainer and security head, Subhash Sawant, who was closer to him than to Yashwant. Subhash turned pale when he heard Aadesh's audacious order. He loved Aadesh but Yashwant was also like a brother to him. How could he lay a finger on a man with whom he had played gulli-cricket for years?

Aadesh's voice was low and menacing as he outlined what he had in mind. Seeing Subhash's reluctance to execute the dastardly plan, Aadesh did what only he could – he threatened Subhash. First, by telling him he'd be sacked if he didn't comply. And later, when Subhash resolutely refused to go along, by suggesting in a sinister fashion that he would harm Suhasini, Subhash's high-minded wife. A woman Subhash not just adored (they had been college sweethearts), but deeply respected. Subhash broke out in a cold sweat when Aadesh placed a hand on his shoulder before getting into his car and said clearly, 'Your wife is a good woman. She is like a sister to me. I would be the first person to cry if something happened to her.'

In the days that followed, Subhash stopped eating, he barely slept, tossing and turning in bed all night. Finally one evening Suhasini sat him down and demanded to know what was plaguing him. She stayed out of Bhau and his family's business, but it was no secret to Subhash that his close involvement with this notorious family bothered her greatly. This time, she was not about to keep silent. 'So now you will kill a man who is like your own brother?' she taunted him over dinner. Subhash held up his hand, which was a signal for her to back off. But Suhasini was unwilling to let it go. 'I have kept quiet for too long. This time I am giving you an ultimatum. Can't you see how Aadesh uses you – are you blind? Why doesn't he get one of his sharpshooters to commit this crime – why you?'

Subhash replied wearily, 'Because he trusts me. And when I say "me", it includes you, too, remember that.' Suhasini turned away from her husband of eighteen years. 'Please don't allow him to club us together like this. I don't interfere in your affairs generally. But if you go ahead with this plan, I'll report both of you to the police – I mean that.' Subhash stared at his fiery-tempered wife in disbelief. 'You can't do that. He trusts me – us. Aadesh has not given me a choice this time.' Suhasini laughed bitterly. 'Have you already given a supari to someone? I cannot believe that my own husband could stoop to this! I didn't marry a murderer – this monster in front of me. Really, Subhash. What has happened to you? What sort of control does Aadesh have over your mind and heart? What do you owe him? Tell me!'

Subhash refused to answer. He had never seen Suhasini so agitated. To escape her verbal onslaught, he walked into their neat, tidy kitchen and found the maid watching her favourite soap on TV. She sprang to her feet and asked nervously, 'Water?' Subhash walked to the liquor cabinet and reached for a bottle of Blue Label. After pouring himself a large drink, he walked back into the dining room to find his wife missing. Thinking she was sulking in the bedroom, he sat for over an hour sipping his Scotch and planning his next move. There was just one more name on his list for the job.

And that was when the doorbell rang. It was the watchman of the building, along with a terrified teenager from the eighteenth floor. 'Uncle . . . Uncle . . . I didn't do anything. I wanted to borrow my dad's car and take it for a spin. I was about to drive it out of the compound when I saw the watchman running towards me and heard the paanwalla outside the compound shouting and screaming . . . that's when I got out of the car and . . . and . . . found Aunty. I mean, Aunty's body . . . on top of the car. I got really scared. Uncle, please don't tell my dad. He'll kill me! My dad doesn't know I take his car out at night. If he finds out, I'm dead! It's not my fault . . . about Aunty. Please Uncle . . . don't phone my dad, that's all.'

***

Aadesh was by Subhash's side at the crematorium. Subhash could not bear to look at anybody, especially Aadesh. All he could see were Suhasini's eyes, filled with accusation as he'd walked away from her to get the drink from the kitchen. He kept thinking that if he had not left the dining room, she would not have walked off in a huff to the bedroom either.

The conversation would have turned heated and ugly, the argument would have led to a fight but at least his wife would have been alive. In order to avoid a fight at any cost, Subhash had lost the one woman he truly loved – he had sacrificed Suhasini, his best friend, his lover and partner. Why? This was just not fair! He watched the flames from the funeral pyre rising high into the night sky. He could see the urchins sitting around waiting for ritual alms, once the last rites were over.

Aadesh's right arm was around Subhash's shoulders but it felt as if a snake had coiled itself around his neck instead. Subhash caught sight of Suhasini's widowed mother, sitting quietly on a chair near the parapet, her paralysed right hand resting in her lap, her left hand clutching a corner of her sari pallu, wiping tears from those sad grey-green eyes her daughter had inherited. Subhash shrugged off Aadesh's arm and rushed across to Atyaa (as everyone called her). He fell at her feet, sobbing uncontrollably, repeating over and over again, 'Forgive me, Atyaa . . . please forgive me.' There was no one to see off Aadesh as he swiftly left the crematorium and slid into the back seat of his Audi. One thing had become very clear to him – he'd have to find someone else to do the job. He had lost Subhash forever. There was no time to waste.

After losing Suhasini, Subhash had become morose and had stopped wearing the rather ostentatious 'lucky' topaz ring Bhau had given him years ago. The index finger of his left hand looked naked without the trademark ring Bhau had gifted him, after an astrologer advised Subhash to wear it as 'protection' from evil forces. But the ring had not protected him from Bhau's son. And the ring couldn't save Suhasini. Subhash had felt abandoned and entirely alone. There was just one person he felt comfortable with, now that his home was no longer a home, but just a place to exist in. Always close to Vimlatai, Bhau's sister, Subhash had become emotionally dependent on her. Vimlatai was an extraordinary woman whose advice was avidly sought by top party leaders from time to time. Bhau himself had often sought her out when he found himself on a sticky wicket either with the family or party workers. Tough, shrewd and fearless, Vimlatai rarely showed her cards, trusted nobody and lived on her own, declining repeated invitations from Bhau to move into his mansion or accept a party position. Vimlatai was an independent power centre, revered and feared by even the virulent opposition party, renowned for her impartiality and home-grown wisdom.

Vimlatai was hosting her annual Shravani Somwar feast, with traditional faraal to break the fast that was kept by the entire household. As always, Subhash too was invited and arrived at seven that evening. Vimlatai was busy arranging well-scrubbed brass thalis on the decorated floor of her modest dining room. Bhau's loyal workers were helping her with the arrangements, filling water in the drinking glasses, serving small heaps of rough sea salt, green chillies, wedges of lime and mango pickle ahead of the main meal consisting of shudh vegetarian preparations cooked in home-made ghee. Subhash had always enjoyed Vimlatai's exquisite cooking, secretly preferring it over his wife's spicier version. He knew Vimlatai would be serving either velvety shrikhand puri or the richer puran poli that night.

After observing a strict 'fruits only' fast all day, Subhash was ravenously hungry. He was heading for the washbasin in the corner of the room to clean his hands before sitting down for the meal, when he spotted Yashwant and stopped in his tracks. Yashwant smiled and rushed towards Subhash, who took a few steps backwards before regaining his composure and greeting the man he had been instructed to kill by his own brother. Subhash felt guilty and deeply uncomfortable coming face-to-face with Yashwant. In his paranoia, he felt Vimlatai was watching the two of them, as if she knew something was amiss. Did she know? Subhash greeted Yashwant politely, taking a few extra minutes to ask about the family.

His guard was up, but he kept the smile on his face and waited for Vimlatai to start serving the first course – which turned out to be basundi puri. So the menu had been changed! No puran poli, either! Subhash suddenly remembered Suhasini as he took a bite of the crisp, hot puri after dunking it into the velvety, creamy, thickened milk. Suhasini had won his young heart a long time ago when she had triumphantly served basundi on their first wedding anniversary, after slaving for hours in the small, hot kitchen, stirring the milk and sugar mixture slowly over a low flame till it thickened and acquired its final almond-coloured sheen and smooth, velvety consistency. Subhash found himself gagging, his eyes blinded by tears, tears he had been stubbornly holding back.

They streamed down his cheeks, for Suhasini, for Bhau, for Yashwant and Aadesh, and most of all for himself. He crouched over the thali, wracked with grief, his body shaking uncontrollably, his sobs escaping from his constricted throat in short, guttural spasms. Vimlatai swooped down on him and enfolded him in her arms. Held thus, Subhash felt instantly comforted and yet uncharacteristically out of control. Under Vimlatai's watchful and worried eyes, he felt like a panicky schoolboy. He didn't want anyone to know about this dangerous plot Aadesh had hatched, but he felt desperately in need of confiding in someone. And what if Aadesh had plans for him too? Subhash was broken, exhausted and terrified.

That night he went to MK's home, begging him to help him escape. 'I know Suhasini killed herself to save my life. She knew that if I didn't eliminate Yashwant, Aadesh would finish me. Even till the very end she thought of me,' he said, breaking down. 'Help me, MK, help me. Only you can help me now. I'm desperate, MK. I don't want to live. But I don't want to die at Aadesh's hands either. I know he is plotting to kill me soon. I need to go far away from this snake pit . . . away from this poisonous family.' MK had made the arrangements, his heart growing heavy and fearful even as he did so. He knew Aadesh would not give up. Aadesh would look for a new man to conduct the Yashwant hit. MK bitterly concluded that that man would be he himself.

MK was right. Shortly after Subhash's disappearance, Aadesh outlined his brutal plan. MK, who had willingly done all of Aadesh's dirty work till this point, baulked at this. On many levels, MK was an old-fashioned family man. Kali Yug had truly arrived when a man didn't hesitate to kill his own brother. Besides the task was both dangerous and difficult. Yashwant was milder mannered and reliable and therefore popular within the party – the assassination would cause a horrific, internecine war. Lastly, MK didn't want blood on his hands. He may have been involved in all kinds of shady, even slimy activities – money was money. But he was essentially a commercial person. An educated professional. A man who handled papers and negotiations. Murder was something else.

He said as much to Aadesh during their morning briefing in Aadesh's bedroom, where the two men sat on Aadesh's king-size bed while Ashwini served cardamom-flavoured tea, which was accompanied by a snack of kandey pohey and batata vadas. 'I won't do the job,' MK said flatly, throwing up his hands. 'What the hell do you mean? It has to be done! Or we are finished. It's either him or me. You know that! Don't you think Yashwant is hatching the same plot against me as we speak? And remember if I fall, you fall. You know that, too. Do you want our wives to live as widows? Come on, MK. What's the matter with you? I don't trust anybody else. Just do it, yaar. And do it quickly. The elections are round the corner. As it is the party workers are demoralized and confused about Bhau's illness. Don't you remember our dream at school? That I was going to be chief minister and you my law minister? It was our ultimate plan, even as kids. I can't believe you are backing out at this stage! The timing is perfect. If we let this moment pass, we will miss the boat.' Aadesh's plea was a veiled threat. MK had looked into his school friend's eyes and recognized the seriousness of his sinister intentions. Aadesh wanted Yashwant dead. And MK would have to kill him.

When your best friend gives you such an ultimatum, the only thing to do is cut all ties with the person. It had finally come to that. MK began to look for a way out of the Bhau–Aadesh web. The family had become too dangerous for him. Besides, Bhau's days were numbered, his health deteriorating, and MK calculated that neither Aadesh nor Yashwant would really be able to lead the party. Yashwant was too malleable, Aadesh too unpredictable. And MK was not one to support the losing side. He had to move away before it was too late, but how? He knew far too much about this family – especially their murderous instincts.

CHAPTER 44

As MK began to plan his exit strategy, Aadesh made the decision for him. The love of MK's life was a beautiful girl – a beautiful four-year-old called Ayesha. He would arrive home early so he could have dinner with his daughter every day, no matter how tight his schedule. Shortly after his exchange with Aadesh, he got an unexpected call from Ayesha as he was heading home. 'Hello Papa,' she said uncertainly. MK sensed something was amiss. 'What's the matter with my jaan, my darling? Are you okay, baby? Where's the nanny?' The little girl whimpered, 'She is watching TV upstairs. She always does that when nobody's home. I'm scared, Papa. She always scares me by saying horrible things. Tonight she told me she is going to take me away from you and Mummy as I am being naughty. I hate this nanny. I hate all nannies. They are so mean to me. Come back fast, Papa.' 'I'll be there in five minutes. I'm just driving up the hill from Chowpatty. Don't be scared.' But those five minutes were all it took for Baby Ayesha to disappear.

'Bachchi hamarey paas hai,' the corpulent man reported to the voice barking orders on the phone. 'Saaley chootiya, don't touch her or harm her, or else Aadesh will cut off your balls and sell them to the neighbourhood butcher.' The man laughed. 'Don't worry. Just tell me what to do with this expensive maal before her father finds us.' After a quick consultation, the man on the other end of the phone said tersely, 'Bring her here. One of the vahinis will look after her till Aadesh decides what's to be done.' The little girl, dressed in pale blue pyjamas, was lying in an inert heap in the back seat of the car – a stolen Land Rover. Just a whiff or two of the heavily chloroformed hankie had knocked her out within seconds.

The man whipped the car around and headed in the direction of the well-illuminated Worli Sea Link. He switched on the car stereo and made a face at the tracks blasting Black Eyed Peas. These rich people listened to such faltu foreign music! Did nobody enjoy romantic Mohammed Rafi songs these days, he wondered, as he picked up speed and tore down the empty stretch. The sooner he got rid of the girl the less his responsibility, he told himself, chewing on the contents of a freshly opened packet of flavoured gutka. He laughed out loud at the memory of the expression on that rundi's face when he poured gutka over her breasts and bit her nipples while trying to eat the tobacco directly from her body. These bloody whores were all the same – too much nakhra for nothing! He was paying her. That too, this one didn't come cheap. She was a 'top-class cheez' as her pimp had insisted. Ooof, when she danced to 'Kajraa Re', he went mad in that sadela Angel Bar. How she teased and tantalized men! Taunted and insulted her aashiques – all those besotted customers who were regulars at the dance bar. The more gaalis she hurled at them under her breath as they showered money on her, the more they lavished on her. He couldn't wait for the day he'd saved up enough cash to negotiate with her pimp.

Two hours. That's all that bitch gave him for thirty thousand in cash. Even that was taken as if she was doing him a favour. He didn't want to waste even a second on extra talk. He started to tear off her clothes but she stopped him imperiously with a flick of her delicate wrist. 'Mard hai ki jaanwar?' she asked and then proceeded to remove her clothes carefully and slowly, very slowly, folding each garment and placing it under the mattress. He knew the bitch was deliberately eating into his time but there was nothing he could do. Her pimp was just outside the ragged curtain at the door of her kholi, and he'd seen the blade of a cut-throat tucked into the back pocket of the man's frayed jeans.

The bitch wanted to jerk him off initially saying that's all customers got for those measly thirty thousand but even she recognized the uncontrollable force of an aroused and enraged bull, which is what he'd become by then. She lay down on the mattress, and spread her legs, saying, 'Jaldi, jaldi. I'm very tired and you smell. I'll do ulti if you try and kiss my mouth.' That's when he had thought of the gutka trick! He'd genuinely believed the overpoweringly sickening smell of the tobacco would kill his own foul odour. He was being considerate and nice to the bitch. But what did she do? She spat! Yes, spat right on his face to show her disgust while trying unsuccessfully to wriggle out from under his heavy body. He'd wanted to twist her neck and snap it right there and then. It wouldn't have been the first neck to break with his bare hands. But he quickly remembered the pimp and the knife and bit her nipple instead. Bit quickly and hard, just enough to leave a nishaan – a mark that would remind her of the man who had paid her full price and only asked for what had been negotiated in return – a fuck, not a hand job.

Even after all that, he longed to go back to the Angel Bar and fuck her. Fuck her slowly, once, twice, maybe fuck her ass too, that large ass of hers which reminded him of two upturned tablas.

He was hitting 160 kilometres an hour now. These imported cars were like makkhan even at that speed. He was thinking of his bitch dancing to 'Billo Rani' and flicking her dupatta across his face. He felt like he was soaring into space, his engorged, thick organ inside her, moving in-out-in-out-in-out as Mohammed Rafi sang a special romantic song for them. How could he possibly have seen the traffic cops trying to flag him down on that dimly lit stretch? And how could he have heard the sirens above the din of Black Eyed Peas blaring inside the car, as two white-and-yellow jeeps chased him all the way to the end of the Sea Link and forced him to finally pull over. Bellowing 'Madarchod', without bothering to look, he came face-to-face with the very people he had spent most of his life running away from – the police.

'Mar gaya,' he said aloud, as he placed his hands on the top of his head as the door of the Land Rover was wrenched open by one of the officers. There was no time to call and inform his handler that he had messed up big time. Either way, he was dead. He should have killed the little girl and not listened to anyone. Killed her and flung the body into the high, crashing waves at Worli. Now there was zero escape for him – if the cops didn't finish him off, Aadesh would. If Aadesh let him go, the little girl's father would. He preferred to die right now, before the cops could ask him a single question. He ran towards the railing of the Sea Link and jumped. The angry, hungry Mumbai sea didn't get to devour the little girl that night. So what? A fat, drunk, hairy man, struggling to stay afloat in those ominously dark waters, was better than nothing.

***

MK had rushed to the scene after the cops called him and found his little girl safe, if groggy. Taking her in his arms he had experienced a rush of enormous relief, but fear swiftly followed and constricted his heart. He knew this was no ordinary kidnapping. It was a warning. Only Aadesh, psychotic, power-hungry Aadesh, was capable of such a grotesque gamble. It was his way of saying he was closing in rapidly. And was certainly not in the mood to deal with delays. One false move from MK, one more show of doubt, and the people MK most loved could be hurt. MK shook his head in utter disbelief. This level of brutality from a childhood friend! A man MK had helped a countless times! A person he'd fooled himself into believing he knew and understood so well. Aadesh! What was this evil world coming to? Aadesh was willing to stake everything for a bloody position. This wasn't just greed, MK concluded, it was a sickness. No matter, MK would have to 'cure' his friend of this sickness, whatever it took. The traffic cop in the meantime wanted to take MK to the station to report the case. MK swiftly negotiated with the man without wasting words.

'Why report such a case when the child has been found and all is well? Let's not get higher authorities involved. Why not just file a report saying a child who had lost her father in a crowd was found by an alert traffic policeman? No further investigations required. Matter closed.' The price the men demanded to leapfrog the procedure was steep. But for MK it was nothing at all. He would have willingly signed over his entire fortune that instant had the cops asked. But these were lowly traffic cops, accustomed to taking bribes of a hundred bucks from speeding motorists.

What MK offered was beyond their comprehension. Five lakh! In cash. Not tomorrow, not two hours later. But right there and then if they cared to accompany him. They cared. One of them naively stammered, 'Sir, but how will we take it? Where will we hide the notes? We don't have bags.' The other one shut him up promptly. 'Lottery jinkli. Chup!' MK smiled. 'Don't worry, I have a couple of suitcases to spare. But first, my bachchi, my daughter. I have to take her home.'

*　*　*

After the kidnapping attempt, a shard of glass entered MK's heart. His best friend became his most hated enemy. If one of his closest friends could dare harm his child, then he too was capable of murder. MK knew that before he could plan any revenge, he had to leave Mumbai. He had to ensure his family would be safe elsewhere. Aadesh had sent out a lethal message – that he was capable of kidnapping and terrorizing MK's little girl, maybe even killing Tabassum, his wife. Aadesh was insane enough to actually do it! He would stop at nothing, not even destroying MK, his dearest friend, his only ally, to get what he wanted. Yashwant had carefully wooed MK himself in the past. But he was too weak to checkmate Aadesh. And Bhau would never believe MK. Bhau's one weakness was his sons. Not a word could be uttered against either of them. And something as deadly? As horrific? Impossible! No, Bhau would hear MK out, say nothing and then find a way to feed him to the dogs. The only way to deal with Aadesh was to pretend to agree with his plan and buy time, and then find a way to get the hell out. The only way to do that was to find himself another powerful patron. Someone even more powerful than Bhau and Jaiprakash Jethia put together.

CHAPTER 45

Amrita had heard MK's toneless narration without interrupting him even once. What he'd told her sounded credible enough. But what he hadn't said made Amrita's blood run cold. MK had systematically staged the entire Sethji 'escape' because he saw her and her father-in-law as the only way out of the mess he was in. The filthy, cheap son of a bitch! He had had the gall to do this to her, of all people. His original love. She stared at him wordlessly as everything fell into place. Seeing her face, MK said 'I am sorry, jaan. But let's deal with our situation like sensible adults. I am not just using you. We have a bond that goes back several years. I have never felt for another woman what I feel for you. I hope I'm not being presumptuous when I believe it's the same for you too. And now I desperately need your help. Give me what I want and we can both get out of this mess and begin to plan a future together. I can set you up easily – a flat of your choice in Mumbai . . . how does it sound? Amrita, I do love you . . . you know that, don't you?'

Amrita burst out laughing. She laughed hard and long, as MK stared at her in stupefied silence. This wasn't the reaction he'd expected at all . . . He shook Amrita roughly by her shoulders and shouted, 'Stop it, Amrita. Stop it right now. Have you lost it? You're behaving like a lunatic.' And

then MK did the last thing he should have done. He raised
his hand to strike Amrita. In a flash, Amrita caught hold
of his wrist, raised her right knee and kicked him in the
groin. Kicked him hard. 'Bitch!' MK yelped. 'Bitch! Bitch!
Bitch!'

MK wanted to hit Amrita but he controlled himself.
'What a hellcat you are, Amrita. What a pair we make.
But let's talk business. You have very few options and I
need you. I need Sethji. I need to meet Arun Mehta. I have
information he would find invaluable. Files, tapes, recordings,
contracts, photographs. All of Jethia's deals. Jethia has
been sabotaging Arun's megadeals over the past five years.
I have the proof.' Amrita looked away. She felt like there
was a heavy stone weighing her down. She felt sullied.
But more than that, she felt foolish for giving in to her
heady emotions.

MK's voice was urgent. 'Amrita . . . jaan . . . you have to
fix up a face-to-face meeting with Arun. I'll never ask you for
anything after that. This meeting is crucial – not just for me,
but for you and Sethji too. What I have is pure dynamite! But
these are delicate matters and I must meet Arun Mehta via
a trustworthy source. Someone discreet. Someone he trusts.
Otherwise he will imagine I am still working for Bhau.' Amrita
sighed tiredly. 'And that's where Babuji and I come into the
picture, right? You will use us as bait while you hunt your
quarry. You are disgusting, MK. And pathetic.' Amrita's eyes
were expressionless. Her mind was at work. Finally, she faced
MK squarely, and uttered just one word, 'When?'

* * *

MK laughed. 'You are too smart, Amrita. Yes, you are dead right and straight to the point as always. I have played along with Aadesh so far. Bhau's new production, a megamovie with megastars premieres soon. It is expected to be this year's biggest hit. It's about a fictional Maratha warrior, like a local *Braveheart*. Yashwant is the official producer. Since the content is pretty provocative in the way it depicts a Muslim traitor, it won't surprise anybody if there are protests at the theatre that turn violent and . . . you know . . . a gun goes off suddenly, accidentally. It could kill anyone . . . even Yashwant. Aadesh will use this shocking development as a way to consolidate his position within the party, by assuming charge and forcing Bhau to announce his abdication in the wake of such a personal tragedy. The premiere takes place next week. We don't have much time. I really do need you and Sethji. I have to meet Arun Mehta before that bloody premiere. Pick up the phone, Amrita. Talk to Mehta.'

Amrita's expression remained impassive, her voice frosty as she said, 'Babuji is too unwell to discuss anything like this with you.' MK said, 'Yes, yes, I know. But we really don't have much time and I have to return to Bhau's.' Amrita nodded grimly. The irony of it all finally struck her with devastating force. The only person who could save Babuji and her was MK. But right now, MK needed to save himself first. 'Will you find out about Suraj and Srichand? Are they okay?' she asked her treacherous lover. 'I shall. I'll do what I can. But I have to play my cards carefully. You understand, don't you?' He caressed her face, running his finger down her eyes, her cheeks, and then slid his finger between her lips. Amrita was filled with desire but before she could react, he had left. As he was walking out, Amrita said, 'MK, I can't quite believe what's going on. I want you to remember one thing, though. Babuji and I are a unit. We are a team. I won't do anything without him . . . or anything that could harm him. Got that?' MK nodded his head and smiled crookedly. 'Of course. And listen up, jaan, whatever deal I strike with Sethji, you, jaanu, remain the bonus.'

CHAPTER 46

Amrita rushed out of the room and into the tiny bathroom with the cracked mirror that distorted her face each time she looked into it. She heard the soft click of the front door as MK shut it behind him. Amrita steadied herself by holding on to the basin. The maze seemed to get more and more complicated. Who could she trust? In the room next door, she could hear Babuji groaning and talking to his dead wife, complaining as usual about how badly he was being treated by his own flesh and blood. Amrita smiled to herself. This was a good sign. If Babuji was grumbling, it meant he was on his way to recovery.

When she entered Sethji's room, she was surprised to see him sitting up in bed. What kind of indomitable spirit did this man possess? He made it clear he hated his new home. 'It is too chakachak,' he complained to Amrita, staring at the starkness of the white walls, white marble tiles, white faux leather furniture and white doors. There were far too many mirrors around the room, and a gigantic orange-coloured plastic plant in a brown plastic pot holder, near the tiny adjoining balcony.

Sethji mocked the plant in his bedroom and taunted Amrita, 'Wah! What a khubsoorat tree. What is it – gulmohur? Any khushboo? Or is it true what they say – only plastic flowers and trees survive in Mumbai, where everything is all dikhaawa – all faltu sho-sha, as fake as the promises made?' Amrita ignored his remarks. But Sethji refused to let it go there.

'Tell me, how often should we water this plastic tree? Does it give fruit?' Amrita snapped, 'Babuji, what is the point of such meaningless conversation. This is just a temporary flat till we find a solution. If all goes well, we shall soon get out from this place, so please be patient. And rest – your body as well as your mind.' Sethji scoffed, 'Rest? You are asking me to rest? I don't know the meaning of that word. God does not bring us into the world to rest – samjhi? I have worked all my life. From the time I was a child. I don't need rest. I need to get back to our kothi in Delhi. I want to meet my sons – they need me, those poor motherless boys. Nobody is giving me any real news about them. How do I know they aren't dead? Why should I believe you? You have lied before.' Amrita did not interrupt Sethji. She knew better. When her father-in-law got enraged, there was no one who could calm him – not even her.

'And I heard you talking to that sooer ka bachcha, saala. He is the man from the car, isn't he? I never forget voices – I'd recognize his from my grave. And you! I saw *everything*. A slut remains a slut. Shameless whore. All this chumma chummi while your husband's life is in danger. What sort of a woman are you? Behaving like a slave in front of an enemy? It must be the size of his cock. All you women are the same. How dare you cohort with that rundibaaz? You are the bahu of our parivaar. Have you forgotten that?' So this was what Sethji's anger was about.

Amrita whirled around and said with great deliberation, 'No, Babuji, I have never forgotten that – but you often have.

What is this "bahu" business? When have you ever treated me like a "respected" bahu? Shall I remind you? About all those times you have forced yourself on me . . . forced me to . . . forced me to . . . No, I can't utter such filthy words, I won't! But you know very well what I'm talking about. I will not be talked to in this manner by you, or anybody else. Who are you to point fingers at MK or me? Yes, we were lovers once. But if it hadn't been for him, we'd both be dead by now. And so would those wonderful sons of yours.'

She stormed out of the room, went into the tiny living room and switched on the television set next to the window. Sethji watched her curiously and started scratching his groin, as he did when he was trying to figure things out. Amrita imagined he was thinking of an apt retort, something sharp and cruel to put her in her place. But Sethji was more interested in something else. He had rarely seen Amrita lose her temper. Who was this man to her? 'Who is he, Amrita? What does he want? Come back here, talk to me,' he said cajolingly, trying to make peace.

After some time, Amrita returned to his room and with a sigh sat at the foot of Sethji's bed. 'I knew him before I was married, Babuji. I hadn't seen him all these years. It seems he is a very successful lawyer now attached to Aadesh and Bhau. Yes, he is the one who rescued us from Bhau but now he needs our help in return. What he wants is not all that simple. He wants us to introduce him to Arun Mehta.'

'Do you trust him?' asked Sethji, thinking ahead of the next step. 'Will he get us out? And Srichand?' 'I don't know,' said Amrita with a deep sigh. She had never felt more confused or lost. And she knew only she could find a solution.

CHAPTER 47

Amrita couldn't afford to slow down now. Her mind ticked even in her sleep. An assassination had been ordered as casually as an item on the menu of a fast-food chain. A husband and brother-in-law had to be rescued. A sick father-in-law needed looking after. Amrita required help. But who could she turn to? Her sole contact in Mumbai was Sonu, her wastrel cousin from Ujwal whom she had kept vague contact with after moving to Delhi.

Sonu now lived in a distant suburb of Mumbai, a few miles from Film City, and had changed his name to the more fashionable Bunty. He ran a small shop selling pirated DVDs. It was more a kiosk than a shop, but it paid the bills, and he was happy, since most of his clientele consisted of people from the film industry, small-time actors from TV, directors and technicians. His USP was the 'home delivery' service he provided to some 'star' homes of 'special' movies. When he got these calls, Bunty would slick his hair back with extra hair gel, wet his handkerchief and wipe grease off his sweaty face, spray on cheap, counterfeit scent from Taiwan, jump on to his fifth-hand bike and head out for a personal delivery. That 'delivery' frequently featured a cocktail of drugs.

His clients included once-famous directors like Sam, who would open the front door, clad in nothing more modest than brightly printed boxers, his pot belly (all that beer, all that food!) hanging over the waistband like an upturned matka. Bunty would greet him enthusiastically and praise his latest 'fillum' (never 'film' or 'movie', maybe 'picture'). Depending on the number of beers consumed, Sam would wink, slap Bunty heartily on the back, and give him a hundred-buck tip (same price as the hire of a single DVD for the night). Of course, they would keep their little secret: Sam was addicted to child pornography, Bunty made sure he kept up a steady supply – and kept his mouth shut.

Sam lived with his ageing parents – a paralytic father and cranky mother who chased every new servant and driver out of the bungalow, frequently throwing pots and pans at them. Sam was a good son – he never stinted on medical bills or attendants to look after his ailing father and foul-mouthed mother. His addiction to child porn was his way of de-stressing. Sam hadn't had a hit for a while. Younger, sharper, bolder directors were taking over from his generation and Bollywood was just not what it used to be. He needed an outlet for his accumulated frustrations. Child porn provided it. Bunty had many more high-profile clients such as Sam, all hooked on extreme porn. They all needed a low-key, discreet guy like Bunty to feed these needs.

Amrita called up Bunty, giving as little away as possible, and asked her long-lost cousin if he knew any retired cop. He suggested Amrita meet Sarkari. Sarkari was an ex-cop, a retired 'encounter specialist' who had his tentacles in virtually every government department. As an ex-cop, he had his informers and foot soldiers working at several levels. Bunty was one of his informers – and provided invaluable tips about the big stars of Mumbai and their incurable weaknesses.

Today, Sarkari was a tired man. His health had been failing over the years and hereditary diabetes was starting to slow him so that he hated to get out of bed, preferring to conduct his business over the half-dozen cell phones that lay propped up on a soft pillow next to his left hand. His right hand was always in reach of a gun. This was his trump card. And he planned to use it at the right time. He had a gut feeling that time was going to be soon. Besides, his doctors had warned him after his last health scare when he had to be rushed to hospital, with alarmingly high blood sugar levels, that if an enemy's bullet didn't kill him, a stroke certainly would.

The ex-cop lived to gorge on mithai. If no sweetmeats were within easy reach, he'd suck on toffees, or worse, ask for a jar of sugar, pour some into the palm of his hard, deeply lined hand, and gulp it down greedily. Sarkari's life had fascinated several Bollywood directors who had tried to capture it on celluloid. This used to make the ex-cop laugh uproariously. 'No cinema screen is large enough to contain my life, boss!' he'd scoff, after reading news reports about the latest venture.

Sethji used to tell Amrita, 'Never trust a vardiwalla. Policemen make the worst enemies. They are khatarnak. And they are the original namakharams. They know they can kill at will. Who is going to catch cops? Stay away . . . stay away. And no matter what the situation, it's better to surrender than kill a policewalla. Remember that . . . if you kill a cop, be sure to know you are dead yourself. Poori duniya mein, this is the golden rule. From Amrika to Australia. Same kanoon. Kuttey ki maut marogey!'

Amrita did not reveal to Sethji that she was meeting Sarkari. It was her decision. A risky one, but it had to be taken. Amrita had a special assignment for Sarkari. It would be expensive.

But she'd get the funds – somehow. The bigger question was: would Sarkari bite? Would he be able to deliver, even if he did take the job? She'd probably have to tap Arun Mehta for money. Arun could be killed. So could she. But if she didn't take this route, she and Babuji would be dead anyway. They were worth nothing to anyone. When she thought Babuji was asleep, she slipped out for her secret assignation.

As she was stepping outside the door, she heard Sethji's booming voice: 'Where are you running off to? To meet your aashique?' 'Babuji, if you'll excuse me . . . I have to attend to some urgent work. MK has organized an excellent hospital nurse for you. She'll be here in half an hour. I'll have the house key delivered to her so you needn't get out of bed, or worry if you hear some movement outside your room. I have to go to meet someone who can help us. The Sister will be in the room with you at all times. She will feed you, assist you when you use the bathroom. She's a trained nurse from Mumbai's best hospital. Remember – do not let her answer the door if the bell rings. This is an empty floor. The building is very new. We don't have any neighbours. And we are not expecting any visitors. Try and sleep a little. I'll be back as soon as I finish my errands.'

Responding to her bossy tone, Sethji said, 'Heroine lag rahi hai . . . don't worry,' and made the mistake of laughing at his own remark. Amrita whirled around and snapped, 'It's not a joke, Babuji! I am serious. This is not a joke! We are in a mess right now. We have to figure out an escape. At least, don't make a joke out of my life – okay? There is so much work to be done – I have a few contacts here. But not that many. We have to move quickly.'

Sethji nodded and used his most sarcastic tone, 'I don't

know where you are off to, Amritaji, I'm not asking . . . but I don't like it. And I don't need a nurse. How do I know she won't poison me?' Amrita was about to close the door behind her without responding, when Sethji stopped her. 'Are you going to a meeting or a mujra with so much heavy scent sprayed all over yourself? You can fool your dumb husband but you have never been able to fool me!' Amrita left wordlessly. She really didn't need Sethji's tantrums right now. Besides . . . she wasn't reeking of 'heavy scent' . . . it was her nervous sweating that had reached Sethji's nostrils. As she rushed downstairs, Amrita marvelled yet again at Sethji's uncanny ability to zero in on her vulnerabilities. He always hit her when she was at her lowest. What she resented most was that it mattered.

CHAPTER 48

Bunty had sent an unobtrusive Maruti car. She was driven to one of those indistinguishable suburban hotels with acrylic vaastu fountains in a cramped lobby and money plants and dancing lucky bamboos wilting in plastic vases on the cheap, laminated reception desk. The person manning the counter took one look at Amrita and clicked his fingers. 'Room 304. Third floor. Lift ke paas-paas. Sarkari Saab is expecting you.'

Amrita's mouth twisted into a smile. It was straight out of a Bollywood movie, this entire scenario. She looked around the tiny lobby and at the public phone in the corner. Three young girls with exotic Oriental features, glossy, long hair and excessive make-up were waiting patiently for an Amazonian blond clad in denim shorts, tube top and thigh-high boots to finish her call. The man at the reception followed her gaze and laughed. 'New girls. New demand.' She saw four other blonds emerging from an autorickshaw at the entrance. They were haggling over the fare. A tough-looking man who had been idling near the elevator sprang to his feet and rushed forward to help sort out the fare issue. 'These Russies are so smart and so strong they don't need anybody's help. One karate chop, aur khatam. Even I am scared of them!'

The four women entered the lobby, chatting noisily and greeted the man behind the counter with a level of familiarity.

'Any calls from Boss?' they asked, while Amrita tried to figure out their thick accent. She'd heard about the influx of Ukrainian prostitutes into Mumbai and Delhi. This was the first time she had actually seen them. Amrita had to admit they were sensational looking, with fabulous bodies, cornflower blue eyes, shiny blond tresses and great body language. They resembled fit, toned, super athletic Olympic gymnasts and not those cheaper-by-the-dozen, garden variety hookers. No wonder the Ukrainians were doing well not just as sex workers, but also as models on the catwalk and sexy back-up dancers in Bollywood movies.

Bunty had briefed her about the set-up, explaining that the girls all belonged to Sarkari's Maroushka Modelling Agency, which was nothing but a cover for an escort service that specialized in supplying Caucasian girls from the former East Bloc countries to Bollywood bigwigs, fashion moguls, industrialists, cricketers. Anybody willing to pay for their favours. The rate card was simple and precise. Party attendance fees varied between Rs 20,000 per appearance to Rs 50,000 depending on the girl's looks (there was a three-tier category – A, B, C class).

The same categories were used for modelling assignments. Fashion shows hosted by C-grade designers with limited budgets were sent C-grade girls at cut-rate prices which were far lower than the fees demanded by local models. This was how it worked across all the jobs that came in, and there were lots of those available given the way the business had grown. One-day shoots for Bollywood producers in which the girls were featured as 'guests' in party scenes were the best assignments – an easy way to make anything between Rs 20,000 and 50,000 per shift, plus oily, heavy studio food (which the girls packed to eat later), and the chance to be 'spotted' by a unit hand for other, more lucrative services – maybe an invitation to the hero's wild pack-up party, or even for a lunchtime quickie in the hero's vanity van (prices negotiable, depending on the hero's manager's mood).

The ultimate ambition for these hungry girls was to get a full-fledged role in Bollywood. It had happened to other lucky foreigners. Failing such a break, they were ready to settle for an arrangement with a producer – he'd provide a retainer for a period of three months, and the girls would make themselves available to entertain his financiers and their friends. The biggest kick for out-of-towners on the fringes of Bollywood was to be photographed with 'goris', preferably with their own hairy, brown arms around the fair, bare shoulders of the girls. Easy money, the girls and their agents had concluded after the first wave of these women arrived via chartered flights and went home with bags filled with goodies – food, clothes, toys for their kids. Amrita watched as the girls chatted and giggled. She marvelled at their enterprising spirit.

She knew Maroushka Modelling Agency was a minuscule business for Sarkari which he ran alongside his main business. She'd correctly guessed that Sarkari had set it up to gather even more ammunition for his clients – the same kind of ammunition he gathered from Bunty. Sarkari scrupulously maintained files on where his girls travelled, with whom and for how much. 'Never know when we might need the khabar,' he'd laugh, biting into another barfi.

Maroushka gave him many opportunities to 'leverage' his position. Sarkari especially got his kicks when he received urgent calls from ministers in Delhi asking for the firangs. Occasionally, the same ministers would 'request' their

businessmen friends to lend a private aircraft to ferry the
girls from Mumbai to destinations like Goa, even Bali. Sex
opened all doors, Amrita thought to herself wryly.

'Are you Amrita?' said a woman interrupting her thoughts.
'I am Lovely Singh, I have come to take you to Sarkari.'
Lovely was huge. Not fat. Huge. She was clad in a voluminous
salwar suit with a print of gigantic red poppies all over it.
Two of those poppies were positioned strategically over her
nipples. Amrita suppressed a smile but continued staring as
they got into the lift. Seeing her expression, Lovely began to
laugh. 'I saw your expression. Come on, yaar . . . admit it.
You expected me to be lovely, na? It's okay. Most people have
the same reaction – shock! I am used to it. I keep saying, my
parents have a great sense of humour!'

Lovely grabbed her pendulous breasts and guffawed.
'Poppies on my boobies – that's what you are staring at, right?
Arrey, what to do, that bloody bewakoof darzi should have
realized. In fact Sarkari hired me for my size – I am being frank!
My brain is good. I am a lawyer, but he liked my size the most.
I run the modelling agency and these size-zero girls who work
for us feel comfortable with a fatty like me. They are very
insecure, poor things! These girls can't handle competition.
They see me and bas, they feel good. I make them feel more
beautiful and sexy . . . contrast ke hisaab se. No threat – Moti
is here, ha ha ha. We have bouncers and all that in place in
case anybody tries to act funny with our girls, but I deal with
clients and handle all appointments. The girls feel comfortable
with me – I am like their mausi, a big, fat mausi. Now here
is Sarkari's room. Let me open the door for you, Sarkari can
barely get out of bed.'

***

'Bolo . . .' growled Sarkari from his gigantic, messy bed as Amrita walked in. His bloodshot, deep-set eyes surveyed her lithe frame. Amrita sensed Sarkari didn't want to waste a microsecond on niceties. She skipped saying what she'd carefully rehearsed, 'I have come to you for help,' and wordlessly handed over an earthen matka of juicy, syrupy rasgullas. He laughed uproariously. 'So your plan is to kill me with sweetness? Forget it, madam. Other women have tried the same trick and failed. Now, let's not waste time on all this. What do you want?'

Amrita looked him in the eye and said, 'I want you to do a job for me.' She indicated with a hand gesture exactly what she meant and then gave the details. Sarkari was momentarily startled. 'Achcha? That's all? Just shoot a powerful man like that as if he is a kabootar on a windowsill? Jhakaas. Easy job, madam. Like swatting a mosquito, right? Why? Because you have offered me a matka of rasgullas? With it, you may also offer your overused cunt. So? I should jump and do it? Woman, you must be totally mad. Or a she-devil who drinks blood and consumes human flesh. You really have guts! Tell me first – why should I do this?'

Amrita spoke slowly and clearly, noticing that Sarkari resisted blinking, so trained were his cop-eyes which seemed to bore holes into her brain. 'It is a job. You don't have that many jobs in hand these days. I have the money. You have the expertise. Nobody else can do it. This man has many enemies. You kill him first, several of his rivals will welcome you into their camps. You will become a big person again, Sarkari. A hero! They will all protect you. You may get caught, go to Tihar for a few years. But that's about all. Jails aren't new to you.'

Sarkari remained silent, never taking his eyes off her slightest movement, even when she swatted a gigantic mosquito on her arm. Sarkari laughed. 'Madam . . . too many machchars here. Easy to kill. But you want me to go after a magarmach, a bloody crocodile. That too, one with Z-category security. I like your boldness. How much?' Sarkari asked, his lips curling over large, uneven, paan- and tobacco-stained teeth. 'Name the price,' Amrita answered evenly.

'How soon?' he asked. Amrita replied, 'Within the week. I have all the information. His travel plans and other schedules.' Sarkari raised his left hand and fanned out stubby fingers. 'Four?' Amrita asked. He shook his head, 'Four mera unlucky number hai. Five.' Amrita permitted herself a tiny smile. 'Five,' she confirmed. With a wave of his hand, he dismissed her. 'Jao. Kaam ho jayega, madam. I will contact you through Bunty.'

Amrita slipped out of Sarkari's surreal setting and stepped straight into a pile of human excreta near the open drain right outside Maroushka agency. As she tried to clean herself, she thought back on the conversation. Strange. This man clearly had no interest in money per se, going by his abysmal living standards. Perhaps he killed for fun? What would he do with the five crore she had offered him? Move to a better home? Buy a car? Get clean clothes? Travel to a dream destination?

No. Sarkari was like Sethji. Money meant just one thing – power. Power over people's lives. Money was self-protection. An armour. Sarkari was a hired gun. But without money, he'd have been dead a long time ago. He had to pay informers, cops, minor goons. Money was clout. If he needed a new weapon, he'd have to acquire it from the Russian mafia operating out of Goa. Or the Israelis. In the old days, guns would be smuggled in from Dubai or Pakistan.

The players were different now. More sophisticated. And much greedier. Sarkari also needed a big hit at this point in his career. If he pulled this one off, he'd regain a bit of his old reputation. But he knew if he botched the job, his body would be thrown into some nullah and there wouldn't be a single mourner at his funeral. That is, if someone bothered to claim his body from the morgue in the first place. What was left for Amrita to figure out was the hefty five-crore bounty she had grandly offered Sarkari. Where on earth would she get the money from?

Amrita's mind was in overdrive as she headed to meet Babuji. It certainly hadn't been her charms that had made Sarkari agree. Sarkari was too tired and unwell to bother about women. She was just another rundi. All women were rundis – the Maroushka business would have taught him that. It just depended on who did the negotiations, that's all. He had taken Amrita slightly seriously as she had come via Bunty. Plus the money she had offered was substantial enough. But she knew what had been the real lure – the job itself. It would be the most high-profile killing of the year, why, of the last few years. Sarkari would, if it all worked out, be back in the game. That was Sarkari's real kick, Amrita concluded. And now it was time for her to break the news to Babuji. There was no going back. This was the first time Amrita had allowed herself to take an independent decision. An outrageously audacious and dangerous decision. She was ready.

CHAPTER 49

Late that night MK returned to the safe house when Sethji was asleep. As Amrita opened the door for him, he grabbed her wordlessly and kissed her deeply, not allowing her to move or greet him. With his mouth sealing hers, he began to undress her, right there, next to the door, a few feet away from Sethji's bedroom door. He could tell from the alarmed expression in Amrita's eyes that she was nervous Sethji would hear them. But Amrita found her arms and hands pinioned against the wall by MK, as he moved his mouth lower, to cover her throat, and then further till his tongue touched the tip of her erect nipple, through her thin cotton choli. Briefly, he looked up and whispered, 'Still no bra! You haven't changed.'

Amrita tried to wiggle out of his grip, but he stopped her with a sharp and sudden movement, as his right hand grasped her slender neck and he pressed his strong thumb forcefully against her windpipe, nearly choking her. Amrita was afraid she would cough and the sound would alert Sethji. Her body was tense, as MK ripped off her sari, which fell in an untidy heap around her feet. He undid the drawstring of her sari petticoat and in the same motion pulled down her lacy, skin-coloured thong. Amrita was shivering. There she was, near-naked near the entrance, clad in just a choli, her breasts nearly bursting out of her diaphanous blouse.

Why hadn't MK removed her last shred of modesty – the skimpy choli? Amrita remembered with a start. That had always been a turn-on for him. She smiled at the memory, as MK kneeled before her and buried his face between her parted thighs. No other man had ever been allowed that special privilege. It was reserved for MK. Just as Amrita would not take any man into her mouth. Sethji was a few feet away from this scene of passionate lovemaking, unaware that his daughter-in-law was about to surrender every fibre of her being to a man who was as dangerous as an ally as he was as an enemy. By then, Amrita was beyond caring. What was it about this man that made her give up control so easily?

She collapsed to the floor and said, 'Take me, MK . . . take me . . . I want to die . . . like I used to.' MK unzipped his jeans, but kept them on, as he entered Amrita with familiarity. There wasn't a single missed rhythm, just perfect synchronicity as he thrust powerfully into her, and she clung to him. 'Beg, jaan, beg. I want to hear those words again,' he commanded. Amrita moaned softly, and whispered, 'I beg you . . . I beg you . . . I beg you . . . fuck me, MK, fuck me hard.' Within minutes, MK had found his release and withdrawn. Amrita stayed limply on the floor, her body in a foetal position.

Later, as she lay in his arms after having made love a second time, Amrita felt the kind of release she hadn't felt in a long time. She tried to imagine what it would be like to be his wife. Waiting up for him to come back home from work and having dinner together. Make love in their own bedroom. To have his children. Then she reminded herself, what did she actually know about his life? He had never spoken about his wife. In their first encounter after years, he had left her frustrated and in the dark about the identity of the little girl who had phoned him in the hotel suite that tumultuous night of the accident. While they had been engaged in passionate lovemaking, at that. That was testament enough of his devotion and dependability. MK had always been a shadowy, mysterious and impetuous man, even when they were college students – those were the very qualities she liked about him. He didn't ask questions, was not possessive about her. He hadn't once asked about her husband. MK was as supremely selfish as Amrita. Why was she even thinking about a future with such a person?

It wasn't just MK's physicality. Yes, MK was an attractive man – a very attractive man. Yes, MK was a skilled lover. MK knew women . . . read them well. But MK was still a low-down bastard whose adept manipulative powers were pretty obvious to Amrita. But the moment he touched her, Amrita's defences, her good sense, her principles, instantly vanished. She stared at MK as he stroked her thighs lightly, played with her hair, kissed her earlobes, her toes, the soles of her feet. At that moment, he was the most tender lover she had known. His entire being seemed focused on making her feel cherished and precious.

'Jaan,' he said to her softly, interrupting her thoughts. 'There is some bad news . . . about Suraj.' Amrita began to tremble in shock as she heard him. 'I'd always known Suraj would come to a violent end but now that it has come, I feel so unprepared. What shall I tell Babuji? Suraj was his sun, moon and all the stars in the firmament.' MK said, 'You don't have to tell him yet. Wait for him to get better. Come on, get up . . . get dressed . . . let me leave now.'

As the two walked out into the living room, they saw Sethji waiting for them. 'Babuji!' exclaimed Amrita. 'I wanted to see this lover of yours, Amrita,' snarled the old man. 'Isn't it time you introduced us? Surely MK Saab would like to discuss Arun Mehta with me?' Amrita, shamed and scorned, stuttered, 'I don't know what you are talking about.' Sethji raised his hand to silence her with an impatient gesture. 'MK, shall we talk?'

Sethji had never bothered with useless social formalities, thought Amrita wryly. Straight to the point and blunt as a butter knife when it came to such things. He would always advise his sons to go into something with their homework done, eyes wide open and brain on red alert. 'Only chootiyas get caught on the wrong foot because they are not fully prepared. When you cut a deal – any deal – be it with a rundi or a businessman, be prepared to accept the downside.' But his sons had never learned these invaluable lessons.

Noticing Amrita's eyes well up with tears, he asked, 'What's happened? Is there bad news?' Amrita said almost in a whisper, 'Babuji, I was going to wait to tell you, but there is no use keeping this terrible news from you now. It's Suraj. Car crash. He had managed to escape . . . but the killers caught up with him. Bhau's orders. It was instant. Suraj didn't suffer. No other details so far.'

Sethji turned pale and gripped his chair tightly. Amrita went over to him and held his hand as he shook with grief. 'My beautiful, brilliant boy. Mera beta,' he groaned to himself. 'He didn't deserve such a fate. This is the worst, most dreaded moment in any father's life. To lose a son is to lose a part of your self, your soul, your seed, your future. I will never forgive those who did this to me. Never. And I will make sure that harami Bhau burns in hell for this and so do those sons of his.' Amrita watched the old man rage to himself, unable to say a thing herself. What sort of words could possibly comfort a father grieving for a dead son?

After a while, controlling himself, Sethji said, 'Bhau may not know where we are at present, but we are still in their hands. At their mercy. Bhau will also kill Srichand. I know it. This is what he wants to convey to us. We don't have much time. The highways contract will be announced any day now.' Sethji mused to himself, scratching his groin as he did when he was deep in thought. 'The most important thing is to use our dimaag. No sudden or obvious move. For that, Amrita, your old aashique will be required. We cannot do anything by ourselves in this strange city.' And Sethji turned to confront the man who had robbed him of the one person he couldn't live without – Amrita.

MK had kept himself in the background as father-in-law and daughter-in-law talked. He marvelled at Sethji. So this is why the old man was such a legend. His mind was already ticking, minutes after receiving the devastating news about his beloved son's ghastly death in a distant land. Not one thought expressed about his favourite son's last rites. No questions asked about the recovery of his body. All Sethji was thinking about was his own skin. How to save it. And revenge, of course.

MK was not surprised. This was Sethji. The ultimate survivor. Here he was, a grief-stricken father but already he was planning moves on the chessboard. Plotting the downfall of his enemies – his son's killers. What a man! Sethji too was looking at MK and wondering. Amrita was obviously enamoured of him. That man had to be something! Was he as infatuated? MK appeared tough and competent, but was he reliable? Would Amrita's good-looking lover help or betray them? Could he take such a gamble with this unknown but obviously well-connected man?

Their only bridge was Amrita. Both men wanted her. But at this point, both men also needed each other. 'If you want a favour from me, MK, I need one from you. Get Srichand out and bring him to me. And then we'll talk. I want my son back – bas!' ordered Sethji. 'Impossible,' MK replied. 'Aadesh has increased the security around him. It will be difficult even for me.' Sethji was silent. Then he commanded, 'Just do it. Here is the offer – I will get you Arun Mehta. You get me Srichand.'

'No wait, I have a plan,' said Amrita interrupting the two men. 'But for that to work, someone has to die.'

CHAPTER 50

'Where the hell have you been, Sethji?' demanded Arun Mehta, when he heard Sethji's voice on the phone. 'Jethia called making threats. All of Delhi is talking about your disappearance. Luckily no one has made an official police complaint, so the story hasn't got to the press yet. I told your secretary Santosh to tell the party and the government that you had gone to Tirupati with your family for a private pilgrimage to give thanks for your victory.'

'Arun, you always liked a good joke,' laughed Sethji. Sethji was famous for his irritation with temples and rituals, preferring pujas at home. But lately such high-profile visits had become mandatory. It was de rigueur for politicians hungry for recognition to make a trip to Tirupati and ensure the press covered the visit extensively. 'I am fine. There have been difficulties, some maamuli health issues. And I couldn't call earlier, but I am perfectly well now. Forget my health bulletin – I need something from you.' It was Arun's turn to chuckle. 'That goes without saying, Sethji. Or else would you waste money on a phone call? Our contract is theek thaak? There have been rumours floating around.'

'Arunji, trust me. Don't worry about the contract. It is in your pocket. The official announcement will take place shortly. I am working hard to ensure there are no last-minute problems. I hear the Home Minister is croaking and asking faltu questions, recalling files and all that. My men will handle him. My call was for something else – I need you to make an urgent trip to Mumbai. Bahut confidential. I will tell you when we meet here. But if we want our matter to proceed smoothly, a few things have to be arranged first. No time waste. My suggestion is that you make some bahana, and come . . . but don't tell your people where you are going. I want you to meet someone in Mumbai. You might find him very useful.'

***

MK and Arun Mehta met in an obscure flat in Andheri (East), located in a narrow, shady lane. Both had arrived in taxis. Both had come alone. 'Is this place safe?' asked Arun. 'Yes, I had it rented just yesterday,' said MK. 'No one will have had the time to wire it.' The two men talked for an hour, each sizing the other up.

'What do you want from me?' Arun finally asked MK, who took his time to respond. 'A hundred million USD in a specified bank account. Plus, I want to represent your European businesses. I know you are expanding rapidly in Europe . . . East Europe, in particular. And you might need someone like me to look after your interests in international markets. My forte is arranging complicated marriages – acquisitions and mergers.'

Arun was pacing around restlessly, smoking one cigarette after another. MK noted with some pleasure that Mehta was anything but a cool customer – Mehta made his discomfort a bit too obvious. Rivals and adversaries could easily read the signs and gain advantage over such a man. MK was secretly delighted – it would be a piece of cake representing Arun in Europe. All MK had to do was flatter the man's vanity.

After taking Arun through a maze, designed to confuse him, MK moved quickly to seal the deal. Arun was surprisingly compliant. He didn't ask too many questions and seemed eager to close the deal. Arun's restlessness was another trait MK would exploit . . . but all that would come later. For now, they needed just one thing – a quick and safe exit route for MK and his family. Arun was his ticket.

Arun was deep in thought as he continued to pace across the grimy floor. MK was handing him a platter full of riches. Not only crucial information about Jaiprakash but it sounded like MK was willing to defect, shift loyalties and, most important, share information. Information was wealth. Information had more value these days than any blue-chip investment. Let fools call it insider trading. This was the main game all over the world. Arun realized he would not have the luxury of time to mull over his conversation with MK.

Sethji had spelled it out during their phone call. It would be the fastest decision Arun was being forced to make. And without expert advice from his legal team at that. Arun made a few quick calculations. Aadesh, Yashwant and Bhau without Jaiprakash were weakened adversaries. A weakened Bhau meant Jaiprakash's hold over Mumbai would be weakened too. It was MK who had the brains. It was MK who was recognized as a strategist par excellence. He was also the only person who knew Aadesh's and Bhau's every move, every deal, every secret.

'I think we can do business,' said Arun, extending his hand. MK grinned. 'I had zero apprehensions on that score.' To lighten the tense atmosphere, Arun asked casually, 'So how's

Sethji? All good? And the lovely Amrita?' MK's expression remained distant and impersonal as he replied, 'Yes. All good. They are in my care.' Arun nodded knowingly and raised his eyebrows. 'In that case, I'm sure everything's on course. Great to know Sethji is back in the game.' MK responded with a slow smile, 'When did Sethji ever quit?' Both men laughed, and Arun walked out into Mumbai's crush, to hail a cab.

MK took his time to clear out of the dingy suburban apartment. MK had his own thinking to do. He decided to pre-empt Aadesh's call by hitting his own cell phone first. Aadesh's voice betrayed tension and anxiety as he asked, 'On track?' MK laughed. 'As always, boss!' Aadesh hesitated before continuing the conversation. His words were stilted and vague: 'Have you found the right person? Is he trustworthy? Or should we rethink the plan and wait a little?'

MK was pleased to note Aadesh's wobbly tone. He answered smoothly, 'I am on top of it, boss. Sab kuch under control hai. Our movie will be a superhit. Kya climax hoga! You don't have to worry. Go ahead with your personal plan. Leave the rest to me.' MK could hear Aadesh sighing audibly. For once, Aadesh's characteristic cockiness was missing as he signed off with a weak and rather idiotic 'Achcha . . . good luck, buddy!' Almost as if he was wishing MK before a particularly tough law paper during their college exams.

CHAPTER 51

It was the day of the premiere. For the first time Amrita felt diffident about their chances at succeeding in this risky endeavour. She suddenly thought of her mother and an earlier life. Could the two of them have ever imagined she'd be in such a peculiar predicament some day? Here she was plotting the murder of one of the most powerful, most influential, most well-connected and certainly the most guarded men in India. A man who through his business associates controlled an illegal, clandestine empire of a billion-plus dollars, who had thousands working for him.

He travelled in a convoy of bulletproof cars, with well-armed bodyguards provided by the government, besides his own team of security personnel riding alongside on motorcycles. To get him required either superior brainpower or awesome firepower. Amrita was shaking and shivering as she repeated her daily prayers, her throat as dry as her lips. The last time she had felt this nervous was when she was a little girl running a very high fever that the family doctor just could not diagnose.

The fever had disappeared as mysteriously as it had appeared, but the memory of those long nights, shivering under a pile of quilts, still kept Amrita awake sometimes. She wrapped an extra shawl around her slim shoulders and continued praying. Her mind was blank. Yes, it was a panic attack, Amrita told herself as she held on to an armchair. She couldn't afford to panic, not today of all days. Amrita's teeth were chattering as she tried to focus on the mantras she knew so well, but which were merging in a jumble as she chanted them mechanically. Was it a divine sign? A bad omen?

Should she contact Sarkari and tell him the hit was off? Amrita's mind was all over the place. Sethji and she had eaten very little at breakfast. She had not slept at all the previous night. There were just a few hours left to go for the premiere . . . and here she was, as unprepared as a schoolgirl swotting for an entrance exam. This was one test Amrita couldn't afford to either bunk or fail. The results would be out in just a few hours. The sound of a clock ticking from its place on the bedside table was so loud Amrita picked it up and impatiently buried it under a pile of pillows. Tick-tock. Tick-tock. Tick-tock. The sound didn't stop . . .

***

Bhau told Yashwant he was feeling more under the weather than usual that morning. 'I don't feel like dressing up, meeting all those showy people at the premiere tonight. It's best I stay home and take it easy for a week.' Yashwant wouldn't hear of it. 'Baba . . . without you by my side, there will be no shaan, no glory. I am clear, "No Baba. No premiere". That's it. I want you there. It's our biggest production . . . and how can the show go on without its megastar? No, no, Baba. We'll call doctor saab to check you thoroughly before we leave. He can accompany you in the new car I ordered just to bring you in style to the premiere. It's a Bentley, Baba, a Bentley!

You'll be very proud of me when you sit in it like a badshah.'

Bhau coughed into the towel and asked, 'Why not take Aadesh in my place? It will look good, too. Our partywallas will be happy to see the brothers together after so many months. It will send out a positive signal. We must stay united for the elections.' Yashwant's face crumbled. 'I did request Aadesh but he said he had to visit Chiplun urgently for a party meeting. Aadesh has launched a free ambulance service there. He told me it was not possible for him to attend a film premiere and ditch an ambulance project. Aadesh is right, Baba. Besides, this film is a part of our dream as well, yours and mine – it is our most ambitious venture to date. If this movie clicks, investors will flock to us.'

Bhau's tired eyes registered zero enthusiasm. 'I'll make the decision later,' he said, waving Yashwant off. 'I have to look after my health first . . . everything else, later.' Yashwant nodded, unable to conceal his disappointment. 'Your health and long life are all that matter, Baba. I can only pray that you'll feel strong enough to join me tonight. I need you, Baba. And don't worry about your clothes. I have kept a new silk dhoti-kurta-angavastram ready for you in your room. In your favourite colour – saffron. Jai Bhawani. Jai Jagdamba.' Bhau shrugged philosophically. Yashwant had left him with no choice.

***

Sethji too had been restless the whole day. Mumbling to himself, talking to Leelaji. They switched on the TV to watch the coverage of the premiere on a popular entertainment channel. Amrita recognized Shaazia, the most successful item girl in Bollywood and the current object of the nation's lust, the one whose scorching cabaret had shocked and delighted audiences as she gyrated provocatively to 'De do, de do, na . . . mujhe de do'. Amrita spotted MK. There he was – looking as sharp and self-contained as he always did! Next to him stood Yashwant, holding Shaazia by her slim waist, as he smiled at her every throwaway line to the cameras. 'How can anybody refuse an invitation from Yashwantji? He's my chweetie-pie and I am so looking forward to doing his next film,' she cooed. Yashwant threw back his head and laughed. 'Shaazia is our banner's lucky mascot! I can't think of launching a movie without her.' Shaazia leaned her head against his chest and sighed deeply.

Amrita couldn't take her eyes off the screen, not even when Sethji bellowed for a glass of water, adding harshly, 'Are you deaf, woman?' No, Amrita wasn't deaf. Just dead, numb. Her heart beating so fast that she was sure Sethji could hear it sitting next to her. She watched the top stars of Bollywood arriving at the venue in the latest luxury cars and being temporarily blinded by countless popping flashbulbs. Through it all, MK stood near a heavily decorated entrance under exotic arches made out of off-season orchids, his eyes ever alert to spot the next VIP, his arms almost permanently extended to hug prominent guests. Right next to him stood his petite wife, Tabassum, dressed demurely in an outfit that covered her tiny frame from top to toe, leaving just her pretty face for the invitees to gaze upon in admiration.

It was a face so innocent, trusting and open that Amrita could only stare wistfully at her. Tabassum looked alarmingly young and virginal after bearing two kids. Both children were present at the venue, with their flashily dolled-up nannies in tow. Even as Amrita tried to calm her nerves, she wondered looking at them if MK would ever leave his beautiful wife and gorgeous children for her. Of course, Amrita knew the answer. But like countless foolish women the world over who fell for married men, she continued to hang on to some insane hope. They made such a picture-perfect family, MK, his begum, their bachchey. Amrita's head was reeling, as the anchor babbled on about so-and-so's gown and someone else's hairstyle. If she heard the words 'And who are you wearing tonight? You are looking gorgeous!' again, she'd throw something at the TV set.

Suddenly, her eyes were drawn to some commotion on the small screen as all the camera crews present at the event rushed to cover the grand entrance of someone who was about to emerge from a stately Bentley. She saw MK hurriedly excusing himself from a small group of newbie movie stars as he quickened his step to greet the new arrivals. It was Bhau and Yashwant. 'Jai Jagdamba. Jai Bhawani,' said Bhau, raising his right hand, as MK dived for his feet to show respect. It was at that precise moment that a gunshot was heard and Bhau slumped lifelessly to the ground.

A pool of dark, viscous blood could be seen clearly forming around his head. Bhau's best-kept secret lay exposed that dramatic night, when his toupee came unstuck and lay by the side of his bloodied bald pate, like a wet rat. Amrita heard shrieks and screams as guests ran for cover, the women tripping over ridiculously high heels with the unmistakable red soles, men rushing past them roughly, not bothering to look back at those who had fallen down. Utter chaos! Total pandemonium! Police sirens. Police whistles. Screams. Children howling. 'Ambulance! Ambulance . . . bhai . . . ambulance bulao.'

An old bystander was trying in vain to control people from running helter-skelter, shouting, 'Keep calm! Keep calm!' Madness. Was it for real . . . or a part of the film's publicity? Could it be a stunt? TRPs ke vaastey? Anything was possible these days.

The horrific development was so sudden and so surreal that it made it hard for people to believe it had actually happened. Bhau had been assassinated! Bhau! The man whose raspy voice alone was enough to freeze Mumbai. And someone had had the audacity to kill this feared, revered, reviled and worshipped politico like a stray dog in full public view. 'Kuttey ki maut,' an anchor was repeating, as total mayhem followed. The city of Mumbai . . . innocent people, would be at risk now that Bhau had been finished off with 'one goli', as a bystander kept repeating. Mumbai would burn. Mumbai would shut down.

Mumbai's streets would witness violence the likes of which could not have been imagined. Streets of bloodied, butchered bodies would remind people there once was one Bhau and one Bhau alone. By attacking him, his enemies had attacked India's most valuable metropolis, shredded its fabric, displayed its weakness, exposed its rotted gut. Mumbai's heart would be ripped open, its insides would spill out. Bhau was dead. It was war.

Bhau's supporters moved quickly. Very quickly. Within minutes, armed gangs had swarmed across the length and breadth of Mumbai torching, stabbing, plundering, looting at random. Bhau would have been proud of his 'boys' had he been alive. Bhau was still lying on the street . . . the area hastily cordoned off, the red carpet area, which minutes ago had been milling with Mumbai's most glamorous, suddenly deserted and empty. Only the TVwallas stayed on, the way vultures stay on after a bloody carnage, waiting to gouge out choice pieces from defenceless cadavers. One of the anchors shouted, 'This is breaking news, yaar. Keep rolling, man, this is big, get as close to Bhau's body as possible, push, push your way forward. We can try for an exclusive.'

CHAPTER 52

Ten minutes after Bhau was shot, fifteen armed men, who had been flown in from Delhi, broke into a small hotel in an alley behind the Mumbai international airport. They rushed to the third floor where Srichand was being held captive. The corridor outside his room was full of guards on their cell phones, trying to discover exactly what had happened during the premiere. Bhau's assassination had sent shock waves among them, exactly as MK had anticipated, and they were entirely unprepared for the intruders who quickly overpowered them before entering Srichand's room. They didn't have to break the door – it was already open. There in the huge, ugly bed lay Srichand, with a hint of a smile on his face and a single bullet hole through his forehead. Next to him was the naked, lissome body of a woman, also shot dead. But through her heart.

A sea of saffron merged with the orange flames of a city on fire as Bhau's supporters swore to destroy his enemies and bring down the state government for its failure to protect their iconic leader. Amrita had remained glued in front of the TV, numbly watching the violent scenes being played out live. The images seemed eerily familiar, and she wasn't sure whether it was a movie channel she'd switched on instead of the news. Everything looked staged. Mumbai resembled a lavish Bollywood set. Even the cars and buses that were being set on fire by incensed party workers could have been props, and the men, junior artists from an action film.

Hundreds of rioters carrying lathis, trishuls, even drawn swords were running towards a structure in the middle of a broad avenue. It was an old, abandoned mosque. How had these goons gathered there so swiftly, she wondered. And how come they were armed? Were these flash mobs or did men in Mumbai generally walk around with stout lathis and trishuls?

Amrita walked into Sethji's room and saw him sitting up in bed and watching the same images, his eyes narrowed to take it all in. The lights in the room were dim and gloomy. The images on the small screen seemed a bit too bright, the kind that would have been lauded by critics and won awards for art direction had they been part of a film. Who was the art director of this production?

Sethji looked up briefly at Amrita, shook his head in disbelief and said, 'Shabaash.' Amrita didn't flinch. Not a muscle moved in her face. She said nothing. Both of them remained stony and silent for a few minutes.

'The car is here. Are you ready?' Amrita asked Sethji. 'Haan. Paise hain?' 'Haan. Hain.' MK had thrown bundles of thousand-rupee notes on the bed before leaving, saying, 'Keep the money . . . you'll need it.' Amrita had stared long and hard at the man who had loved her . . . screwed her . . . used her . . . betrayed her. She felt no hatred for MK. Just a deep sense of regret and longing. It needn't have been this way. What a sad end to a saga, Amrita concluded, checking her tears, even as her constricted throat stopped a single word from escaping. What was left to say, in any case? Amrita stuffed the notes into her handbag, looked around the tiny apartment, kept the TV and lights on, before assisting Sethji off the bed. He was limping and in pain. But that didn't stop him from pushing towards the door, displaying his characteristic impatience. 'Come on, woman. Hurry. Before the police barricade the roads to the airport. We are going home. Hum Dilli ja rahey hain . . .'

The two managed to flee a devastated Mumbai, arriving in Delhi on a late-night flight. Sethji had been calm throughout the drive to Mumbai airport, patiently lying to the questions at all the high-security checkpoints known as 'nakabandis'. ('I am a sick old man', 'I had come for treatment to Mumbai. Mumbai hospitals are the best! What doctors!', 'This is my bahu. She looks after me well. I'm a small trader from Delhi. We have a small shop in Paharganj', 'Bhai saab, let us go or we'll miss our flight. My heart is weak. We are ordinary people, bhai saab. Hamara kya lena dena hai with this lafda. Please, we beg of you, let us go quickly before my heart stops again.') His strategy had worked. And they'd made it to the airport safely, leaving a burning city behind them.

CHAPTER 53

On the flight, Sethji asked Amrita when Srichand would join them in Delhi. The arrangement had been that MK would coordinate with Sethji's men and get Srichand out. Amrita took a deep breath. MK had called her with the news but she had decided to keep it from Sethji until they were safely out of Mumbai. He was much too frail, physically and emotionally, and Amrita didn't have the words to comfort him. Finally, she took a deep breath and said slowly, 'They finished off Srichand, Babuji. It happened just after Bhau was . . . was . . . declared dead. By the time our men broke into the hotel and gheraoed everyone, one of Bhau's guards had already slipped into Srichand's room and killed him. One shot, Babuji. Just one shot. It was quick.' Sethji stared wordlessly at his daughter-in-law. His expression was thoughtful, distant. As if he was trying to figure out a puzzle.

'Who told you?' he asked after a couple of minutes. 'MK,' Amrita answered. 'Jhoothi! Liar! Kutti! You have become a vidhwa but your cunt is still waiting for that haramzaada's cock – that kutta who killed your husband. He promised me Srichand but instead he killed my beloved son. My heir, his mother's firstborn. I curse you, you wretch. I knew from the moment you walked into our home as a bahu that you'd bring bad luck to our family. Destroy us all. Why don't you kill me also? I am the only one left. Take everything! It's all yours now. What is my life worth without my sons?'

Amrita let out a long sigh and held Sethji's hand tightly. 'Babuji, you know it was a terrible, unfortunate mistake. MK tried his best and he saved us too. We wouldn't be on this flight without him. I know you are deeply, deeply wounded. I know you are in pain . . . in sorrow, but so am I. Maybe I never loved Srichand as I should have, but whose fault is that? You know I have tried to be as good a bahu to your family as I am capable of. To the very best of my ability. Do you doubt me? I can give up my life for you. Test me, Babuji. Just test me! But never lose trust in your bahu. Would I be here without you? It is our karma that we have to bear with one tragedy after another.' Sethji's breathing had changed. Amrita was surprised to see tears streaming from his eyes. Tears Sethji didn't bother to hide or wipe. Amrita let him weep. She wished she could have wept, too. But her tears had dried up a long time ago.

Amrita wished she had loved Srichand even a little. Or showed him more respect perhaps, faked what she did not feel. But from the very beginning, from her wedding night itself, Amrita had resigned herself to a life devoid of passion or love. Looking back now that he was gone, she felt she could have demonstrated some genuine affection . . . even a little. Unfortunately, Srichand had done nothing to earn it. It was a pity. That's how he'd lived and died – ignorant of an emotion called a wife's love. Amrita thought of the last time she had seen him. What a pathetic way to close life's innings. Drugged out and in the arms of an indifferent whore.

***

Sethji had become quiet. He had avoided any big display of emotion at the news of Suraj's ghastly murder, and after his outburst he was back in control. This reaction did not surprise Amrita. Sethji was an expert at numbing himself when needed. She knew his breakdown would come without warning, perhaps the next day, next week or even a decade later, when Sethji was ready to confront the truth. For now, he was impassive and stoic, pretending to take the twin tragedies in his stride as an inescapable 'part of dhanda'. Amrita had not fooled herself for a minute. She had been extremely affected by both deaths. Whatever she felt about the two brothers, they were all the family she had. But her thoughts were not on Suraj and Srichand. Both men were dead. She had been preparing herself for that eventuality from the day she entered Shanti Kutir. Her first and only concern was for her own survival. Hers and Sethji's. Yes, his too. Staying alive. Amrita pulled herself together. There was no time to lose now. Every tension-filled minute counted. It was time to start thinking about the future. A future with Sethji.

CHAPTER 54

Predictably, the Mumbai police had failed to crack Bhau's assassination. Taklya, a deranged shooter belonging to a small-time gang, was picked up and charged. Everybody laughed at the brazenness of it all. Taklya! What a comical scapegoat. Couldn't the cops find a more convincing one? Nobody believed his story that he'd been paid to kill Bhau by Arif Bhai, his mafia boss who lived in Jakarta. It was over a property dispute with Bhau, claimed Taklya. A dispute over an old mansion on Nepean Sea Road, one of Mumbai's toniest areas. Taklya's boss was to partner Bhau and his sons, to redevelop the property after tearing it down. There was big money at stake – 1000 crore, according to real-estate agents. But Bhau had dared to double-cross Arif Bhai, after using the don's goons to terrorize the ageing owners of Laxmi Garden into vacating the place and signing it over to Bhau. Taklya said he was paid a paltry ten lakh by Arif Bhai to kill Bhau. Even the police chief found it difficult to keep a straight face while recounting Taklya's story at a press conference. Sarkari had treated himself to an extra malpua that night.

* * *

Immediately after the killing, MK had gathered his wife and children and headed into a waiting car with packed suitcases. A private plane, arranged by Arun, was waiting to take them to Brussels, where MK would take over Arun Mehta's European businesses. But the car had made a brief detour before it went on to the airport. Asking his family to wait in the car, MK entered Mumbai's most exclusive five-star hotel, a small distance from the international airport. He managed to slip into the Honeymoon Suite, using his contacts with the boys in housekeeping.

'Is the bridegroom nervous?' Aadesh was startled to hear MK's voice in the lavish suite that had been festooned with dozens of fragrant garlands strung out of sweet-smelling chameli blossoms. There were rose petals strewn all over the deep pile carpet. And the suite was softly lit by dozens of discreetly placed aroma candles. A magnum of champagne rested in a crystal ice bucket by the side of the gigantic bed that was covered with delicate petals gently pulled off flowers without crushing them. They were Shoaib's favourites – the highly fragrant sontakke, also called Chinese lilies by Mumbai's flower merchants.

Aadesh whirled around to face the barrel of a gun. Instinctively, he reached for his own snub-nosed pistol, but realized he had not carried it with him for his night of love with Shoaib. MK ordered him to sit down on a divan covered with purple velvet (it was the hotel's royal suite, dominated by the colour purple, walls included). Aadesh did as directed, and tried to distract MK by saying, 'What's happening, MK my friend? Why this hostility? Hasn't our job been done? We should be celebrating. Come, come, have a glass of champagne with me.'

MK shut him up, bringing the gun closer to his head. 'I am here to settle hisaab kitaab, saaley madarchod. I am not here to disturb your honeymoon with that gandu-actor. Let us settle this quickly. So now, listen to me carefully, your job has been done. But not as you imagined.

'It is Bhau Saab who got killed – not your brother. Big difference. Fight it out with your brother and I wish you the best of luck. As for me, I am moving overseas to begin a new life. But if a single hair on either my family's or my head is ever touched, I will ensure that you are finished. Do you understand? Leave me alone. And I promise to leave you alone too. Don't try funny tricks with me, Aadesh. If you have your connections, I also have mine. I won't spare you.'

Aadesh showed no signs of nervousness as he continued to stare expressionlessly at MK. He tried to lunge towards a serrated fruit knife placed near a gilt-edged porcelain platter with four ruby-red pomegranates arranged on it. Seconds later, Aadesh was on the floor, writhing in pain, screaming, 'Haramzaadey, what the fuck are you doing? Have you gone mad? The carpet is getting spoilt. Killing me won't solve your problems. My men won't let you get away. How far can you run?' MK watched coldly as a patch of blood spread over the carpet. He'd aimed for Aadesh's leg, but got him in the right arm instead, as Aadesh went for the fruit knife.

'Then keep still, you behenchod. If you keep talking and I keep getting angry, your penis will go, then how will you fuck the chikna? All your life you have waited for this moment, bloody gandu. Admit it, saaley. You lied about everything all your life, including the desires of your cock. Now you are still playing your games! I am going to leave now, but stay on the ground. Don't move, don't call security and don't call your men. And remember one thing. Today I could have finished you but I haven't. But I won't be as scrupulous next time, Aadesh. So don't fuck with me.' The barrel of MK's gun was on Aadesh's groin. He slammed it into Aadesh's thigh saying, 'This one is for my daughter,' and walked out, leaving a groaning Aadesh grovelling in his own blood.

* * *

Later, sitting in his plush offices in Brussels, MK would give an exclusive interview to a news channel, claiming that he was 'shocked and deeply saddened' by the 'dastardly attack' on a revered icon of Maharashtra and sent his deepest condolences to Yashwant and Aadesh, who were like his brothers. 'It only exposes the weakness in our system.' The riots that followed, targeting a certain community, also highlighted the growing intolerance in the country and a complete disregard for the legal system. He said he feared for his family's safety in such an environment and added he had come back to India with high hopes after acquiring a great education. But he was a disillusioned man after this assassination. He was forced to leave a country he loved and make a fresh start abroad. Arun smirked while watching MK and said to himself, 'I've hired the right man. Touché, MK.'

* * *

As for Yashwant and Aadesh – just as Sethji had predicted – they were too obsessed fighting each other to seriously pursue MK, especially after Yashwant discovered that Aadesh had intended to have him killed. It was no secret that the brothers would split the party without Bhau to keep them together. Their wives had already indicated as much by holding two separate public condolence meetings for Bhau on the same day. It was feared the brothers would declare open war and Yashwant would win it, wresting control of the party from Aadesh, a man who was moping around like a sick puppy, and who had in any case been unpopular with Bhau's cohorts.

It was obvious from the heavy-duty attendance at Yashwant's shraddhanjali for Bhau as to which brother was seen as the true inheritor of Bhau's legacy. Almost the entire state cabinet had turned up to pay their last respects to Bhau at the large, heavily guarded Dadar auditorium, close to the cremation ground on the edge of Dadar Chowpatty where Bhau's last rites had been performed in the presence of several national leaders. Yashwant had been unofficially anointed as the next chief of the tattered party while his supporters kept up a steady chant of 'Bhau Saab amar rahein. Yashwant Saab, zindabad.'

But the truth was Bhau's party died with him – a fact that Sethji had gambled on. Under the protection of Arun Mehta, MK never needed to fear revenge from Bhau's sons. The highways contract tender was announced the next day with no hitches. Jethia was presented with a fait accompli and could do nothing more than gnash his teeth and plot his next move to destroy Arun. Only Amrita and Sethji were adrift, with no obvious gains and no immediate plans. They had survived . . . but at an enormous cost.

They'd have to plunge into consolidating the party, regrouping immediately, scrounging around for money to fight the next local election. Their candidates stood a good chance of winning, but not without handy cash to pass around even with Arun's generosity. Amrita began to plan for a life in Shanti Kutir without Suraj and Srichand. A more austere life. Suraj's fancy cars would have to go. And she'd have to reorganize the kothi's staff, sack some of them, scale back wasteful kitchen expenses. Chop, chop, chop monthly budgets. But it was all pretty doable. Managing Sethji was going to be her biggest challenge. Amrita shrugged. She'd manage. She always did.

CHAPTER 55

'Are you safe? All well?' MK's voice was low and loving. Amrita was quiet for a few seconds. 'I'm surprised it matters to you. But yes, we are both fine. We got to Delhi safely and are back home. And you are in Brussels with the family?' Amrita's voice was polite, cold, impersonal.

MK sighed. 'You are upset with me. I wish we could have said a real goodbye, jaan.' Amrita didn't say anything in reply. Her mind was on the image of the picture-perfect family at the premiere. How ironic, when she was finally free to be with MK, he wasn't available. But why kid herself? MK had never ever been available. Nor had he made any such promise. That had been a pattern in their relationship ever since it began. His appearances and disappearances were never to be talked about – that was the unspoken pact they had made.

It was her foolishness that had kept her hopes alive, despite knowing the score with a man who was incapable of emotional investments. His portfolio was reserved for investments of a different kind. 'What next, MK? I'm tired of running, tired of this life, tired of looking after Babuji.' MK measured his words carefully. 'Let's hope things work out. We can still see each other, jaan. Let's meet in Europe. I'll be travelling to Geneva frequently. How about a dirty weekend in the Alps? I'll buzz you when I'm in Delhi next.

I hate leaving you. I have always hated leaving you. But it's best you don't try and contact me in any way now that I have moved to Brussels. It's too dangerous, jaan, with the Arun Mehta–Sethji connection. Dangerous for you, too. Nor should we probe or ask each other too many questions. You are free to conduct your own life. I respect you too much to intrude. Inquisitiveness, possessiveness, jealousy, all those are for ordinary people – not people like you and me. We belong to nobody. We belong to ourselves. Which is why we get along. You are the female me, and I the male you, but your breasts are better! And I love my cock!'

Amrita found herself pleading pathetically, 'Don't leave me hanging like this, MK. We are perfect for each other. Leave your family. Leave your wife. I will move to Brussels to be with you.' Amrita uttered these words and felt instantly diminished and humiliated. She had prepared herself to hear words of farewell and knew she was not going to get her way, even as she pleaded. Woodenly, she half-listened to MK utter his half-truths. In the background she could hear the squeals of children. 'These things are not in our control, Amrita. You know I won't leave my family. I can't! My children mean everything to me. But that doesn't mean we have to end anything. You are the only woman I have ever loved. You know that, don't you? We are made for each other, but things are complicated.'

'MK,' Amrita laughed bitterly, 'the truth is, we were cowards back then and maybe we still are just that – miserable, sad cowards. But we could have done things differently. Our lives didn't have to be this, this . . . shitty.'

MK sighed deeply. 'Amrita, we both chose. Okay? Now let's make the best of those choices. I have a life. You have a life. And then, there is the other life, the beautiful one we can share together. We don't have to lose what we have . . . have always had . . . can continue to have.' Amrita lashed out at the one man she had felt something close to love for. 'Stop this bullshit, MK. It's bullshit. That's what it is. Your life, my life, total bullshit! Look at me, pathetic and desperate. Hiding and sneaking around corners. Why? This was not the deal I was promised. I am the loser. I am the sucker. There's nothing in it for me, nothing at all! There never has been. Why should I settle for such a one-sided arrangement? You, with your double life. Your sweet wife, your lovely kids. The great facade of domestic bliss. And me? With nothing! I feel used . . . used by Babuji, used by every single person, and that includes you, MK.'

Without a husband, a lover, family, her life was in limbo. She was on her own. But she also knew, deep in her heart, for the first time in her life, that she was life's mistress. There was no man to pander to, no man to please, no man to wait for. She was finally on top of life itself. It would all be well. She didn't need MK. Maybe she had never needed him or any other man.

CHAPTER 56

Back home, Amrita and Sethji slipped into their old patterns. Sethji had his regular visits by Himmatram and Bholanath. Amrita had Phoolrani ready to give her a foot massage, a head massage, no matter what the hour. Sethji went to the Party HQ every day, and began to plan the unveiling of the tutorial scheme in UP. Amrita ran the house as efficiently as always. The only difference was the absence of Suraj and Srichand. Two large framed pictures of the sons were kept in the hall next to their mother's portrait, and garlanded each day. Sadly but not surprisingly, it was just Rocky 1 and Rocky 2 who missed the men.

Amrita had taken to wearing shapeless salwar kameezes, which Sethji repeatedly told her he hated. Finally, she snapped, 'Babuji, I don't dress to please you.' Sethji chuckled. 'Achcha? But you used to, or have you forgotten?' Amrita sighed tiredly. 'Please also remember we are supposed to be in mourning and I am a widow now.' Sethji started guffawing. 'Don't say such things, bahu. You make me laugh. Playing a chaste pativrata and now a vidhwa does not suit you at all. I have lost everything, everyone. My wife, now my children. God is testing me. Am I pretending? Crying? Beating my chest? No! You know why? Because I am an honest man. Honest and honourable. I will not waste my time crying uselessly. I will do something much better. Watch how I vindicate the death of my beloved sons, while you shed crocodile tears and wear shabby clothes. Remember, bahuraaniji, now it's just you and me. It's better if we acknowledge a few bitter truths at this stage – no lafda later. If you want to leave me, and make your own life with a new man, do it now – right now. But if you decide to stay, it is strictly on my terms. I shall protect you, provide for you to the best of my ability. Till my dying day. That much I can promise. You can have whatever you want.

'My money is your money. My kothi, your kothi. Whatever I possess, I will leave to you. Who else do I have? Oh, in case you are wondering where my money is? Forget it. I'll never tell you that! But all I will say is that it is in a safe place. Even the boys didn't know where I'd kept it. But if you want to leave me, go now. Goodbye. Ram-Ram. Think that I am dead. If that is your decision, also know this – there is no returning, no turning back, no taking a chakkar with someone else and then coming home, weeping and saying, "sorry, sorry". You will also be dead to me. Bolo, manzoor hai?'

Amrita stared expressionlessly at her father-in-law. She was silent, as her mind raced. She spoke up after a few minutes, her voice controlled and calm. 'What exactly do you want from me, Babuji?' Sethji chuckled. 'A lot! So take your time and answer carefully.' Amrita shook her head impatiently. 'There is really nothing to think. I want clear responses to my direct questions, Babuji. What do you mean by a "lot"?' Sethji's tone was serious and firm when he looked his daughter-in-law in the eye and said quietly, 'Your body. Bas. As and when I require it.' Amrita grimaced. Her revulsion was evident as she gulped and sat down abruptly.

Sethji was watching her closely and she could tell he was

trying to read her mind. He came towards her and placed his hands on her shoulders. Amrita squirmed and tried to move out of his clumsy embrace. Sethji said, 'Do you really think I don't know how much I repulse you? How you hate my touch, my presence? I have always known it from the very beginning. I gave you no choice then, and forced you to submit. You were young and scared. You didn't know how to refuse your own father-in-law. Who could you turn to? Your useless husband? Or your scheming mother? Neither of them cared. Suraj? He would have promptly raped you himself. And then thrown you into the nearest dustbin. But the truth is you did not completely object to my attention, either. You used your body to gain control over me. More importantly, you played your game very well. As if you were doing me the world's biggest favour by letting me fuck you. Bakwas!

'You are a dhongi, Amritaji! You pretend very well. I know you, Amrita. Maybe I know you better than you know yourself – your confused and conceited self. I know not just every inch of your body, but every fold of your cunning brain, as well. Every thought that passes through your mind, every desire, every worry. I know you, Amrita. I know you. Unlike most other women, your brain functions like a man's – it is capable of hard, unemotional decisions. It is ruthless when required. Arun had said to me once that you – not my sons – were my biggest asset, and I, even after knowing everything you have done in Mumbai, I still believe him. So . . . listen carefully to what I am saying . . . I'm spelling it out so that there is no confusion in the future. For the exclusive use of your body, I am offering you my protection not just as a father-in-law but also as a mentor. Come, join the party officially. Stand for elections. You will win, Amritaji! Meri guarantee!

'I am prepared to teach you everything I know about this game called politics. And from what I know of you, you will probably learn from my old tricks and play them against me. But I'm willing to take that risk. Because you are a smart woman. And because I need you in every way. As a woman in my bistar, as my partner, adviser, confidante, supporter. Sab kuch. I will leave you to think about all that I have said. This is a new beginning. For you . . . for me . . . for us. Why waste time fighting with each other when we can spend it better on ourselves and on building the party? Our understanding has always been good. It can only get better. But let me not say anything more . . . let Maaji tell you. Listen to Maaji and Maaji alone . . . believe me for once when I say this – I understand you, I always have . . . I'll look after you. I shall wait in the adjoining room while you talk to Maaji directly. Once you get your answer, call me. If she tells you my plan is not good, I'll hand over a gun to you and you can shoot me dead. But if she blesses me . . . blesses us . . . then don't look back for a single minute.' With those words, Sethji shuffled out, yelling for Himmatram.

Amrita considered his direct proposition without allowing herself the luxury of any emotion. She remembered her mother's words to her before she was married. 'As women, our bodies are our sole wealth. A woman who understands the value of her body and trades it wisely is the one who succeeds. If she uses that knowledge shrewdly, she can even control the world. Such is the power we possess.' At the time, Amrita had been puzzled, upset and enraged. What an ugly, awful 'truth' for a mother to be sharing with a young, inexperienced daughter! Amrita had withdrawn completely after that conversation, preferring to spend her spare time lying on a hard cot in the small outer room of their home, staring glumly at mynahs chattering noisily on the branches of the neem tree in the courtyard.

But today she would have answered her mother differently. She would have said, women do have another choice. A woman did not have to look at her body as a way of controlling men. Amrita wished her mother was alive to see her now. It was time to take charge of her life. Be realistic. Assess all the options. After all, which man had stood by her? Srichand? MK? No, the only constant in her life had been this indomitable, impossible father-in-law of hers. Yes, he had his own selfish motives. But ironically he was also the only man who had recognized her potential, encouraged her, pushed her, given her the opportunity to make something of herself, on her own terms, using her brains and not just her body.

She experienced a wave of unexpected tenderness for Sethji sweeping over her. It surprised Amrita. How could she be feeling this way for this awful man who had used her, abused her for so many years? A man who did not understand anything finer in life and was aroused by a thali filled with gooey, sticky sweetmeats which he ate greedily, noisily, sloppily? And yet, Amrita reasoned, he was the only man she could count on. Paradoxical, but true. She guessed he felt the same way about her as well. They were two of a kind, she concluded. They were just too similar. Too ziddi. That was perhaps why they had stuck together. Were still together.

* * *

She heard the bells in the prayer room ringing. The evening aarti had just begun. The heady fragrance of sandalwood incense wafted up through an open window. Amrita inhaled deeply. Home! Amrita shivered. Delhi would be foggy and chilly. Amrita smiled. Gajar ka halwa with roasted almond flakes, adrak-chai in the courtyard. A slightly frayed but wonderfully warm shahtoosh to cover her shoulders. Slanted, late-afternoon golden light. Gigantic dahlias nodding their heads in neatly tended flower beds. The dogs! The maids! Servants, maalis and drivers! Phoolrani's energizing maalish with warm til oil. Her old room, all to herself.

Diwali was round the corner and Shanti Kutir, her home – hers and Sethji's – needed a fresh coat of whitewash before the first diya could be lit. Amrita hugged herself and smiled. Maybe, for the very first time, there would be 'shanti' inside Shanti Kutir. Maaji would be pleased. It was going to be a long and lovely winter. There was so much to do before the searingly hot summer heat got to her and Sethji. Amrita would deal with it when she had to. For now, she wanted to savour this delicate moment. Her life was all hers now in a way that it had never been. And Delhi was waiting for her – ready to nestle in the palm of her hand.

Acknowledgements

Sethji crawled inside my head over a decade ago, and refused to go away. I took that as a sign, and started writing the novel. Once again, it was Sethji who decided he wasn't ready for an airing. Like any wily politician. He wanted to time his entry perfectly. He remained inside my head – a very vibrant, even persistent presence at that. Which was extraordinarily annoying since there were other books to write and many columns to file. That didn't bother Sethji. He waited. 'Timing is everything in politics, Madamji,' he taunted, as I got down to narrating his story a year ago.

Well . . . here he is. Loathsome or lovable – you decide.

When I handed him over to Chiki Sarkar, my editor, I was slightly worried. It was a little like handing over a particularly difficult child to an unsuspecting caretaker. I needn't have fretted. The day Chiki phoned from Delhi to confess coyly that she had had a risqué dream about Sethji, we both knew Sethji was going to have the last laugh now that he was under both our skins. Creepy, but true. This was my first book with Chiki. It didn't get off to a great start. Chiki talked logic to me. And I protested! Logic? In politics? Several stand-offs later, one fine day, Chiki and I found ourselves on the same page – that slimy Sethji had done it again! Sent us both separate messages! I relented and gave in to 'more' logic. Chiki accepted the surrealistic jumps. We had our book.

Thank you Team Penguin – my extended family, really. It's been a twenty-five-year-old association and we've had the best fun together! John Makinson, I owe you a drink . . . maybe several! As for you, dear Hemali, I am determined to make you kick up your heels and dance at the book launch. We have had such great times through fourteen book launches, and countless crazy evenings.

A small confession: I would have loved to thank the late Sitaram Kesri, God bless his soul, since he intrigued me sufficiently to go forth and create Sethji. But now that the novel is written, I wish Sethji would leave me alone.

Mumbai   Shobhaa Dé
May 2012

More bestsellers from
SHOBHAA DÉ

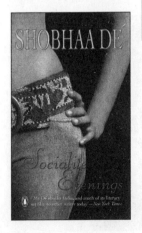

More bestsellers from
SHOBHAA DÉ